MISSING BEFORE DAYLIGHT

BOOKS BY CAROLYN ARNOLD

Justified

Sacrifice

Found Innocent

Just Cause

Deadly Impulse

In the Line of Duty

Power Struggle

Shades of Justice

What We Bury

Girl on the Run

Her Dark Grave

Murder at the Lake

Life Sentence

SARA AND SEAN COZY MYSTERY SERIES

Bowled Over Americano

Wedding Bells Brew Murder

MATTHEW CONNOR ADVENTURE SERIES

City of Gold

The Secret of the Lost Pharaoh

The Legend of Gasparilla and His Treasure

STANDALONE

Assassination of a Dignitary

Pearls of Deception

Midlife Psychic

CAROLYN ARNOLD

MISSING BEFORE DAYLIGHT

bookouture

Published by Bookouture in 2024

An imprint of Storyfire Ltd.
Carmelite House
50 Victoria Embankment
London EC4Y 0DZ

www.bookouture.com

ISBN: 978-1-83790-934-6
eBook ISBN: 978-1-83790-933-9

In loving memory of Ken Martin

PROLOGUE

DECEMBER 18TH

Fill N Go Gas Station, Woodbridge, Virginia

Leah adjusted her reindeer antlers in the domed mirror that was nested in the far corner of the store. Her boss wouldn't approve of her show of holiday spirit, but what he didn't know wouldn't hurt him. He put on this persona of Scrooge, all *bah humbug*, but she sensed a deep sadness in him. It only motivated her to spread seasonal cheer with more gusto, especially just a week before Christmas Day. Hence the antlers, but the Christmas decorations didn't stop there.

She'd brought in a small pre-lit tree, and out of her own money, had also picked up baubles and ornaments from the dollar store and thoughtfully set about placing them. The icon of the holiday took up residence next to the till. Garland draped the front of the counter in two big swoops, and a red bow was fixed in the middle. No mistletoe in sight, not wanting to send out the wrong message for those who came in the store.

Those who did venture out at this hour usually filled their tanks and paid at the pumps. That suited her fine too. It gave her more time to read and daydream about her future. Or she should say, *intended*, for deliberate manifesting.

Working here certainly wasn't her endgame. It was just a stepping stone to help make her grand plans a reality. People told her, at only eighteen years old, she had it together more than some adults twice her age. Leah took that as a compliment, even if her decision to become a vet came easily to her. It really was a no-brainer given that she had loved animals all her life, with an especially soft spot for cats and dogs. Clocking hours here would help pay for her schooling. Although her parents never said it, she knew they couldn't afford college. Each dollar her father earned went straight towards putting food on the table and a roof over their heads.

If she kept her goal clear in mind, it made the long, tedious night shifts bearable. With school out for the Christmas holidays, she had requested extra shifts too. It meant more time away from her family, but it was a small sacrifice. She was only adamant that she be off Christmas Eve and Christmas Day. Those days were sacred to her and spending them with her loved ones made them perfect. To make this year even more special, her great-grandmother would be celebrating her one hundredth birthday. Nothing would keep Leah from missing that epic milestone.

The door dinged, and a man in a heavy coat stumbled in.

Leah set her novel aside, popped up from the stool she'd been sitting on, and grinned widely. "Merry Christmas." Her enthusiasm was met with a grumbled response, but she wasn't about to let his bad mood sap her joy. Who knew what he was going through in his life.

The man headed for the refrigerated drinks.

"Is there anything I can help you find?" she asked him.

He ignored her, opened a door, and plucked out a bottle of water, holding it up at her as he walked to the counter to pay.

Not exactly the talkative type. Got it. She scanned the barcode and told him his total.

He fished out a handful of change and set each coin onto the plastic topper that covered the lotto tickets instead of into her waiting palm.

She hadn't finished collecting them when the door dinged again as he left.

Nothing personal, she reminded herself as she often did when she didn't feel seen. This time of year wasn't everyone's favorite like it was hers. To her, there was a vibration in the air, a warm tingling sensation that was nothing short of magical and possibly otherworldly, and she did her best to "sprinkle that shit" everywhere. She smiled, recalling seeing that meme online.

A look outside showed no one in the lot, no one at the pumps, no one driving by. She dropped back onto the stool and picked up her book again. It was a light cozy mystery about a talking cat who was solving a murder with its owner, making it a good choice for working the night shift solo. Nothing too dark to stir her imagination into a frenzy, even if there wasn't much time left on the clock.

In just over an hour, she'd be tucking into her bed, though she'd need to face her mother first. Her father was harmless. He'd be settled at the kitchen table with the day's newspaper—in print, believe it or not—with her mother nattering away about what needed his attention around the house that day despite his full-time job. She'd only pause long enough to point out to Leah, yet again, that it wasn't safe *or right* for girls her age to work night shifts at a gas station. Leah would counter with the argument of equality, why was it okay for men and not for women? Their discussion would end with her mother throwing her hands in the air and walking away while mumbling something incoherent. It was the same shtick that followed every night shift.

A ding alerted Leah that a vehicle had just rolled over the line outside. She looked up to see a gleaming silver Mercedes sedan at pump four. Leah could own a car like that one day. *In my wildest dreams, maybe.* But if she had that much money to throw around, she'd put it to better use. She'd open no-kill animal shelters to give dogs and cats a second chance at an ever-after home.

A brunette got out, who had to be nearly six feet tall. She was dressed impeccably for this time of the morning in a thigh-length burnt orange peacoat and crisp black slacks.

She is a businesswoman or politician on her way to Washington, less than an hour's drive away. There she holds a position of importance in some fancy office building and manages staff with an authoritative yet gentle hand.

Leah smiled at the woman's story she'd written in her mind as she watched her fill the tank of her luxury car.

Another vehicle came in. This one a boxy, white Ford van.

Rush hour at the Fill N Go, she thought and chuckled to herself.

Leah shifted on her stool, not about to get up unless someone came inside. She liked to afford people the decency of rising to her feet for them, intending for it to make them feel special and seen.

The van parked at the back of the lot next to Leah's old Nissan Versa.

Leah set aside her book, prepared to stand, as she expected the door would open in a few seconds, but it didn't. The person in the van must have been held up in some way. Fishing for money in their console perhaps. Leah had been there.

The woman finished filling the tank of her Mercedes, settling the huge bill with electronic payment at the pump. Instead of getting into her car, though, she came into the store.

The woman was attractive, of fair complexion with delicate features, but there was a hard edge in her eyes. They told of a dark past and unhealed hurts. Being able to read people was a natural gift and one her great-grandmother had pointed out. Leah would wager this woman had been through some trying things in life.

Leah shoved all her observations aside, popped up from her stool, smiled broadly, and offered a cheery "Merry Christmas!"

"Merry Christmas." The woman smiled, a fleeting expression that barely graced her lips, and walked to the gum and snack aisle.

The door dinged again, and a man wearing a balaclava entered.

A knot twisted in Leah's gut, and her heartbeat kicked up speed. The temperature had dipped, but not enough to necessitate the face covering for a casual outing.

Leah coached herself to relax and think logically. *He has a sensitivity to the cold. He's already unwell and doesn't want to make himself any worse.*

She squared her shoulders and greeted him, but he didn't bother looking her way. There was no way he hadn't heard her.

Maybe he didn't respond because he doesn't want me to hear his voice?

If that was the case, he was most certainly up to no good. She swallowed, even though her mouth was dry. Goosebumps trickled paths down her arms.

He strolled down the aisle one over from the woman. She seemed to be debating which gum or mints to buy, conflicting with Leah's impression she was the type to know exactly what she wanted.

The man didn't appear to browse, but he rounded the far end of the aisle and headed toward the woman.

Leah watched through the mirrored dome. She saw him pull something from a pocket, his hand gripped around it. *Is that a—?* Leah's stomach tossed.

The man had a gun and was edging closer to the woman.

Leah opened her mouth to call out a warning, but no sound left her lips.

The woman stiffened, and her movements slowed. She must have sensed something off about him or seen his weapon.

Leah looked at the panic button. She just had to press it and the police would come, but it was out of arm's reach. Her legs weren't responding. They were quaking and heavy as if the pull of gravity had increased and tugged her feet into the earth. She stood there, powerless, terrified. Helpless.

The woman acted quickly, striking the man across his chest with an outstretched arm and an elbow to his chin.

The attack must have caught him off guard as he flew backward into the shelving. Bags of chips rained to the floor as if spilling from a smashed piñata.

The man quickly regained his balance, his gun pointed at the woman again.

Leah could hardly breathe. *This isn't happening!* Finally, her legs cooperated, and she lunged for the button.

The woman cried out, "Get down!"

Leah was too slow to respond to her warning. There was a sharp bang followed by an intense burning as a bullet cut through her flesh and burrowed into her chest.

Time slowed to a near stop.

The man continued to face her, his gun still raised.

The woman's face was etched in a mask of sheer agony.

Leah staggered, her hand to the wound. She lifted her palm. It was crimson. It was just a few precious inches to the panic button. She reached out, her fingers grasping at air.

Another thunderous boom.

The impact of a second round pushed her back, and she stumbled to stay upright. Her insides were on fire.

Blood bubbled up her throat and down her chin.

Her legs gave way beneath her. She reached out to stop her

fall, but her fingertips simply brushed against the plastic fir, and she collapsed to the floor.

The small Christmas tree crashed beside her, and Leah saw her reflection in a red bauble.

A sudden warmth overcame her, and the pain receded. Tears wet her cheeks, and she knew. *This is how I die.*

ONE

Amanda had no preconceived notions this week was going to be an easy one. With Christmas around the corner, more people were depressed, suicidal, and homicidal. The latter was what impacted her life the most. The phone call she'd received at five fifteen this morning did nothing to boost her outlook.

It had been Scott Malone, her sergeant with the Prince William County Police Department. There was a shooting at a local gas station, leaving one dead on scene.

"She's only eighteen."

It was one hell of a way to start a Monday morning and had her springing from bed with a quick nudge to her boyfriend, Logan, who was lying beside her. She gave him a kiss and let him know she had to leave. She'd also peeked into her eight-year-old daughter's room. An ache bloomed in her chest that she wouldn't be able to greet Zoe when she woke up.

Amanda hated it more when children were victims. An eighteen-year-old, equally tragic. Her life would have just been getting interesting for her and those around her. Where would her path take her? Would she meet somebody nice and get married? Her mother may have anticipated grandbabies in the future.

All of that was eradicated with two bullets.

She was still processing the tragedy as she and her partner, Detective Trent Stenson, were en route to the Fill N Go gas station. After Malone's call, they had met at Central Station, their home base in Woodbridge, signed out a department car, and hit the road.

Ahead, strobing lights on police cruisers lit the early dawn, a collective beacon to mark the scene of a nightmare from a few streets back.

Trent pulled into the lot.

Aside from law enforcement, there was an older Nissan Versa parked near the back of the lot and a hybrid at the pumps. No sign of anyone from the Office of the Chief Medical Examiner or the crime lab yet. Both were stationed out of Manassas, about a half hour from Woodbridge, and would be on their way. Same applied to Sergeant Malone, who told her he'd meet them on scene.

A scrawny woman wearing an oversized knitted hat in a rainbow of colors and olive-green puffer jacket leaned against the hybrid, arms crossed, as she spoke to Officer Wyatt. She kept adjusting her posture, the positioning of her legs, crossing one ankle over the other, then in reverse. Only her arms hung motionless at her sides. Wyatt seemed to be writing down everything she said.

Amanda and Trent left the car. A damp chill cut the air. It smelled of snow. Amanda burrowed into her jacket, wishing she'd brought her heavier one, but she'd have to make do with what she had for now.

Officer Cochran stood at the door for the store. Traci was a good cop, and an even better human being, from what Amanda knew of her. She had a warm, empathetic heart. That quality would either take her far in her career or tear her life apart.

They exchanged greetings as Amanda and Trent put booties over their shoes, and Traci got the door.

"She's behind the counter," she told them.

Amanda dipped her head and thanked the officer. Inside, perfumes and colognes mingled with the metallic smell of blood. The tangible density of death was thick and heady, all consuming, almost suffocating. The unseen accompanied the visible such as the high-velocity blood spatter on the wall and counter.

Her legs were leaden as she walked to the end of the counter. Macabre images layered, one upon the other in her mind, conjured up from previous murder scenes. Her life as a career cop gave her a catalog to pull from. It would be healthier if she could simply ignore them. After all, why put herself through the torture of dwelling on what had been? How one violent act wiped out all dreams and ambitions. But this was where she took over with the sacred duty of finding these souls justice and providing their loved ones with closure.

Sadly, this one was a child, barely a legal adult.

Amanda caught her first glimpse of the girl.

Ginger hair. A few shades lighter than Amanda's.

Time suspended while the tether between this life and, possibly, the next stretched taut. She debated the existence of an afterlife, but to accept that nothing came after death felt so incredibly empty and meaningless. When her husband and six-year-old daughter died nearly eight and a half years ago, she was given a front-row seat to death that rivaled any she'd encountered while working in Homicide. It was an all-immersive hell that stole her breath and capsized her desire to carry on. Seared and kissed by its flames, broken, and nearly destroyed, she eventually emerged from the deep pit. The darkness gave way to a pinprick of light. She dragged herself toward it, and the journey led her to discover her strength and taught her resilience. While the heartbroken widow would always remain a part of her, she had learned to survive despite this. Even flourishing alongside her.

Amanda took another step.

The young woman was on her back, head angled to the left, her arms at her sides, palms facing up. One was stained red, probably from touching her wound. An instinctual, yet ineffective, response.

Her mouth was gaped open, blood on her chin, and her green eyes were staring blankly.

Amanda followed the girl's sightline. Across from her, a tabletop Christmas tree lay tipped over, its white lights flashing. Generic and inexpensive baubles and ornaments were scattered on the floor.

Her gaze back on the girl, she took in the reindeer antlers on her head, and the melancholy of the scene hit Amanda. *Hard.* No one should lose someone this close to Christmas.

"You all right?" Trent put a hand on her shoulder.

She nodded. Next month marked three years for them as partners, and he knew her well, how cases with younger people affected her, touching close to home.

The victim wore a red, long-sleeved shirt with a paw-shaped pin attached near the collar. It read, *Dogs are for life.*

The door chimed and the soles of dress shoes, dampened by plastic booties, slapped the linoleum floor. It was Malone, and he got right down to business.

"Name's Leah Bernard. Eighteen. A Berta Russo found the deceased at five AM when she came inside to pay for her gas. There were no calls to nine-one-one prior to that, so presumably no one heard or saw a thing. Of course, we'll get officers out canvassing. But that's all we currently have."

Again, Amanda took in the young woman. The whimsical touch of the antlers had Leah looking younger than eighteen. Maybe fifteen or sixteen even. "Then pretty much nothing."

"She didn't push the panic button?" Trent pointed to a small red domed light under the counter.

"She must have run out of time." A cold summation of her reality. The totality of it.

Malone picked up and said, "The owner of the gas station is on his way over. He didn't handle the news well and said that he gave Leah night shifts against his better judgment."

Typically, the next of kin were the first notified, but they needed to watch the security footage. It was assumed that was the reason Malone had called the man. "Is he insisting on a warrant?"

Malone shook his head, getting the underlying reference. "He's agreed to be fully cooperative. Whatever we need. He's prepared to bring up the video the minute he gets here."

"That's good at least," Trent said.

Malone frowned. "The poor girl was due off at six. A man by the name of Marty Evans was scheduled to relieve her then."

That was less than twenty minutes from now. "Was she still living at home with her parents?" Amanda scraped out, her thoughts painting the scenario of anxious parents awaiting their daughter's return home, only to be left in limbo.

"Yeah."

Her poor parents. They'd soon find out Leah would never walk through their front door again. Amanda pushed the heartbreaking thought aside and turned her attention to the scene.

The till drawer was shut, and the display of lottery tickets appeared untampered with. The only thing that appeared out of place was some broken shelving and busted bags of chips. It could indicate an altercation, but there was nothing to suggest a robbery had taken place.

"What happened here?" It was a slip, the words tumbling from her lips of their own accord. They sat out there, rhetorical and dangling, roping in the great cosmic existential question of why. The energy in the room intensified.

Malone eventually broke the spell with, "I think that's your job to figure out." He smiled, as if to soften the blow and rubbed his beard. It was always short and neatly groomed, but the mannerism was one he sometimes employed when trying to tamp down intense emotions, be they grief or anger.

"It doesn't look like a robbery," Trent said. "Personally motivated?"

The suggestion raised her hackles, the sheer coldness of the possibility, even if the scene supported the theory. In fact, the most immediate path would be digging into the girl's life to see if they could unearth the shooter. Even if the surveillance video revealed something else, one thing was certain: the hearts of Leah Bernard's parents were about to break.

TWO

Amanda typically preferred to be armed with more answers before serving notification to loved ones. Something that might support offering assurance or an explanation of some sort. At this point Leah Bernard's death had no meaning. It hadn't been a robbery and might not have been Leah in the wrong place at the wrong time. They'd be going to the Bernards with so few pieces of the puzzle, but the goal was to reach them before they started to fret when their daughter didn't arrive home. That was one small kindness they could extend.

After hearing Amanda's plan, Malone said he'd stay around and wait for the owner of the gas station, though he stepped out of the store. As he was walking out, crime scene investigators Emma Blair and Isabelle Donnelly were coming in. They held tightly to their collection cases, grim expressions on their faces. They must have heard it had been a young woman to lose her life.

"She's behind the counter," Amanda told them, her words taking her back to Officer Cochran saying that to her and Trent. What felt like hours ago had only been a handful of minutes.

Wyatt intercepted her and Trent on the way to the car and filled them in on Berta. "She lives in Maryland and has a clean record. Far as I see it, she's not who we're looking for. We have her info if you wanted to follow up later on."

Amanda shook her head, picking up on his implied question. "She stays for now. The owner's coming so we can review the security footage. After that, we'll revisit this conversation."

"I'll go tell her the good news." Sarcasm alive and well and, with that, he spun to leave.

Amanda wasn't going to feel guilty about her decision. Until they knew what they were dealing with, they couldn't afford to release her. "Oh, Officer Wyatt," she called out, and he turned back to her. "Should a Marty Evans show up, keep him around too."

"And who is Mr. Evans?"

"An employee here who is due to start at six."

Wyatt looked at his watch. "Past that now by a few minutes, but I'll keep an eye out for him. Or should I send a car around to his house? Just in case he's involved with what happened."

"Give it a few more minutes, and if he's a no-show, send a car and call me," Amanda said.

Wyatt dipped his head and resumed his path back to the woman.

"Maybe we should hang around," Trent said. "Wait until he shows up?"

"No. I want to get to those parents sooner than later. Besides, who knows when he'll show up." *Or if he will.* That sour thought fired through uninvited.

"Let's buckle up then."

She appreciated the double meaning that was both literal and figurative. They needed to prepare themselves for the emotional ride ahead of them.

The van from the Office of the Chief Medical Examiner

was pulling into the lot while Trent was driving out. Hans Rideout, the medical examiner, was behind the wheel, and his assistant, Liam Baker, was in the passenger seat. Baker waved, and Rideout dipped his head, his expression somber.

Following them was a Chevy sedan, a perplexed-looking man in the driver's seat. He leaned forward, his chest practically pressed against the steering column.

"How much do you want to bet that's Evans?" Trent said.

"Actually, Trent, stop the car, please." She couldn't forgive herself if she didn't talk to the man and he was involved in what happened to Leah. Her parents would need to wait a few minutes longer.

Trent reversed to clear the hood from the road, and Amanda got out.

She tapped on the Chevy's driver-side window. The man lowered it, and she held up her badge. "Detective Steele, Prince William County PD. Can I ask your name, sir?"

"Marty Evans." He licked his lips and sounded parched as if he'd walked through the Sahara Desert and was in desperate need of water.

"Your identification, Mr. Evans." She clipped her badge back on her waist and held out a palm.

He jammed a hand into the front pocket of his jeans and gave her his driver's license. Name was Marty Evans, Woodbridge address, age forty-one. She gave him his ID back. "What's your business here, Mr. Evans?" She wanted to hear it from him.

"I work here. I was due to start about five minutes ago. What's going on?"

"There was a murder here this morning. Would you know anything about that?"

A rough swallow had his Adam's apple bulging. "Murder?"

"Are you normally late getting to work?" She couldn't

ignore the possibility he may be responsible for Leah's murder. He could have killed her earlier, left, and returned.

"Sometimes. Who was killed?"

"I won't say until the next of kin has been notified. Why were you late this morning?"

Marty massaged the bridge of his nose. "I kept hitting snooze on my alarm. That's all."

"Can anyone verify that?"

"Whoa. Hold up. Am I a suspect here?"

"I don't want you leaving until we've had the chance for a proper talk. Am I understood?"

"Yes, ma'am."

She pivoted toward the department car.

"Excuse me, ah, ma'am. *Detective?*" The latter tagged on a little louder.

Amanda returned to Marty. "Yes?"

"When do you think we'll have that 'proper talk'?"

"Are you in a hurry, Mr. Evans?"

His posture shrank, and he shook his head.

"It will take the time it takes. That's all you need to know, but the officers here will watch over you. If you need water or anything, just let them know."

Marty nodded, and Amanda made a stop to inform Officer Wyatt that Marty Evans had arrived and what little conversation they'd had.

"Not a problem," Wyatt said. "I'll keep an eye on him, make sure he doesn't go anywhere."

"Thank you. Also, the owner should be arriving shortly. I'm not sure if I mentioned that in so many words."

"You didn't, but good to know." Wyatt offered her a solemn smile, which she returned.

Back in the department car, she filled Trent in on Marty Evans.

Trent was laughing as he merged onto the street.

"What?"

"'A *proper* talk'? It almost doesn't even sound like you."

She shook her head but was unable to deny the accusation. It wasn't entirely in keeping with her character but seeing that young woman on the floor had rattled her. And the thought of informing her parents that she wouldn't be coming home had the grieving mother inside of her rising for air.

THREE

Walter and Margo Bernard struck Amanda as a kind and gentle couple. In their early forties, Margo had Leah when she was twenty-three. Seeing their friendly faces at the door, even at six twenty in the morning, made what she and Trent had to tell them more difficult. Their bungalow was in a middle-income neighborhood only a few minutes from the gas station.

The couple took her and Trent to a comfortable but dated living room. An artificial Christmas tree was set up in the corner, and mistletoe dangled in the doorway. A rather comprehensive Christmas Village, placed on top of cotton batting, took up a table at the far end of the room. Leah came by her love for the holiday honestly enough.

The couple sat on a couch while she and Trent dropped into chairs. The Bernards watched them, leery expressions tugging at the corners of their mouths and eyebrows, and their eyes were watery. Amanda speculated their sixth sense was already telling them something had happened to Leah.

"Mr. and Mrs. Bernard," Amanda began, "we regret to inform you that your daughter—"

Margo gasped a sob, her maternal intuition kicking in.

After a few beats, Amanda tried again. "Leah was shot this morning, and I'm sorry to say that she is dead."

Walter wrapped an arm around his wife, who appeared shell-shocked, frozen in time. Mouth slack, eyes wide, tears falling down her cheeks and dripping from her chin. The sight tugged on Amanda's heart as she knew that searing pain all too well.

"What happened?" Walter's voice was husky, and he cleared his throat. "A robbery?"

"We're still in need of answers." She saw that as more effective than dismissing it altogether. Amanda briefly caught Trent's eye, and his mouth twitched, a subtle tell that he was also struggling with this notification. For her, it wasn't just because of Leah's age, but the fact they had so little to offer the Bernards.

"How can you not know that much?" Margo blinked, and her lashes refreshed with a load of plump tears. "Why aren't you telling us the truth?"

"We are, ma'am," Trent stepped in, relieving Amanda of some burden.

"I don't understand." Margo rolled the hem of her shirt in her hands and looked at her husband. The eye contact contained request for asylum and explanation.

"I don't either," Walter said. "How can you *not* know? What else could it be?"

She couldn't blame them for wanting an explanation, but she couldn't manifest one from thin air either. "As I said, there is a lot we need to find out."

"Surely, you must have something to tell us." Walter swallowed roughly. "A reason. *Why?*" The strangled single-word question sounded like it had scraped from his throat, inflicting damage on its way out.

Amanda stiffened, barricading herself behind a wall she erected. For the sake of justice, she couldn't absorb the

Bernards' grief, no matter how much she empathized with them. There was no answer to that universal question that could ever satisfy. It was only acceptance and cold surrender that made life bearable in the shadow of death. "Unfortunately, we rarely have all the answers at the beginning of an investigation."

"It doesn't sound like you have any," Margo snapped.

Her husband squeezed her tighter to him.

"Detective Stenson and I just wanted to inform you as soon as possible, knowing that you would be expecting Leah shortly."

"Though it turns out we'd have had reason to worry," Margo whispered. Her bottom lip quivered as did her chin, and a fresh stream of tears fell.

"At least we're not left wondering, Margo." The man reached across himself to take his wife's hand and squeezed. "It's better than not knowing." Walter looked at Amanda and Trent. "Thank you for that consideration."

Amanda simply nodded. Now she considered that leaving them to stew might have been the friendlier option. After all, hope existed in uncertainty, but it was too late to extend that mercy. "We do have a few questions you might be able to help us with."

Walter's body stiffened, and Margo retracted her hand from his and leaned against him, still secured under her husband's arm.

"Did Leah usually work the Sunday night shift at the Fill N Go?" If it was routine, it was possible the killer targeted her, counting on her to be alone. Though that net would capture everyone from those in Leah's world to regular customers.

Margo shook her head. "Just last week and last night."

Walter spoke. "Since she got off for Christmas break from school, she asked for extra shifts."

"I told her over and over again how dangerous it was for a young woman to work alone at that time of night. She wouldn't listen." Margo's facial expression pinched in on itself, making Amanda think that grief and anger were facing off in an internal battle. "Was she...?" She met Amanda's gaze in a moment of woman-to-woman telepathy, and Amanda was quite sure what Margo wanted to know.

"There's nothing leading us to believe that Leah was sexually assaulted," Amanda said with some confidence.

"But you don't know for sure?" Margo's blue eyes were electric.

"I'm sorry, but we don't," Amanda said softly. The shooter could have raped her, dressed her, then killed her, though the likelihood was slim.

Margo nodded, a few more tears falling in silence.

"How long had Leah worked at the gas station?" Trent had a tablet with him, and it was on, the screen of the notepad app open and awaiting his entries.

"She's been there for about six months now," Walter said.

"Did she regularly work nights?" She'd asked specifically about Sundays a moment ago and wanted to clarify. The owner of Fill N Go could tell them, but the more answers they had sooner than later, the better.

Walter shook his head. "She covered a few Saturdays because she could sleep in the next day."

"If she'd only listened to me. And why now of all times? It's Christmas, Walter. We're supposed to be together as a family." Margo's cheeks flushed red as she looked at her husband, her lips pursed together in a tight line.

It felt like husband and wife had retreated into their own world and she and Trent were trespassing. Amanda sensed the impact of the loss was sinking in. They would never celebrate another Christmas with their daughter. The first one without Kevin and Lindsey had been brutal, and they had died six months prior to the holiday.

After giving the couple a few moments, Amanda said, "We

won't be much longer, but was Leah seeing anyone or did she have any ex-boyfriends who weren't thrilled about breaking up?" It was just one scenario to explore.

"You think that someone targeted our sweet girl?" Margo winced from the brash nature of her own question.

"I'm just trying to cover all possibilities, Mrs. Bernard," Amanda said levelly.

Margo looked at Walter to field this one. "Our daughter is one of the most gentle, loving spirits I've ever known, and I'm not just saying that because she's our girl. She was making the world a better place. 'Leave it better than you found it' she'd often say." Walter paused, a rogue tear spilling out, which he palmed away. "She was saving for veterinary college. She absolutely loved animals. Dogs especially."

Amanda picked up on the slips from present tense to past and understood the full transition to the latter would take time.

Trent looked up from his tablet. "She was wearing a pin that said 'Dogs are for life.'"

"Leah wore that one a lot, more so around Christmas," Walter said. "It broke her heart when people gifted puppies and they wound up being dropped off at a shelter. She talked a lot about opening a slew of no-kill shelters across the US. She was a big dreamer."

When the victim had been someone as kind and impactful as Leah Bernard, the loss belonged to everyone. "Your daughter sounds like she was an incredible human being." If the murder was personal, it was hard to imagine motive at this stage.

"She is— *Was*." Margo hiccupped a sob and folded into herself.

Amanda allowed Margo a few more seconds to calm down, then circled back to her initial question. "It's not easy to think of someone wanting to harm your daughter, but if anyone comes to mind, please tell us. Maybe a current boyfriend, or an ex?"

"If she had one, she never told us. She could be very private about her personal affairs though." Walter prattled this off as if he were speaking of a stranger. Logic was stepping up to butt against sorrow, resulting in a cool detachment.

"Mrs. Bernard?" Amanda prompted, and the woman shook her head. "What about close friends that Leah had? She might have told them about her love life."

"Her closest pals were Janie, Tammi, and Charlene," Margo said. "All nice girls too. They're going to be devastated."

"We'll need their last names, if you have those." Trent looked at Margo eagerly, but it was Walter who gave them the surnames. "Thank you," Trent told him as he tapped them into his tablet.

Amanda stood, Trent following her lead, and she handed Walter her business card. "We are very sorry for your loss."

Margo wiped her cheeks and sniffled. "Oh, and this is going to break Great-Gamma's heart. What are we going to do?" She looked at her husband, the skin beneath her eyes already dark and puffy.

"We have to tell her." Walter's chin trembled, and he told Amanda and Trent, "My grandmother's turning a hundred this Friday. Leah was excited about a big bash we're throwing her." He swallowed roughly. "I suppose that will be canceled."

The hits kept coming for the Bernard family, but this was just the beginning. There would be endless reasons to grieve and other occasions when Leah's absence would be especially felt or plans that would never come to fruition. "Again, our sincerest condolences. We can send someone from Victim Services to be with you and help you navigate this time."

Victim Services was a branch of the PWCPD with qualified counselors to assist victims of crime and their families.

"We'd appreciate that." The acceptance came from Walter, and it moved Amanda. Men stereotypically tried to project strength even to their own detriment.

Outside, Amanda and Trent loaded into the car. The clock

on the dash told her that it was nearing 7 AM. She was so drained that it might as well have been seven *at night*.

"And this is just Monday." Amanda sighed and glanced over at Trent as he put the vehicle into gear.

"It's going to be one hell of a week, that's all I've gotta say." He got them on the road toward the gas station.

FOUR

On the way back to Fill N Go, Amanda placed a call to Victim Services requesting that they pay the Bernards a visit.

A new car was in the gas station's lot and likely belonged to the owner. Marty Evans was slumped in his sedan until he saw her and straightened his posture. A sure sign he was eager to have their talk and get clearance to leave. She didn't let on that she noticed him and beelined for Rideout and Liam, who were loading the body into their van.

Liam closed the back doors, sealing Leah Bernard inside. Her next stop would be the Office of the Chief Medical Examiner in Manassas, more specifically, a slab in the morgue for dissection. A sad but necessary reality. While her cause of death seemed to clearly be the result of gunshot wounds, the slugs or bullet fragments inside her would need to be retrieved. They'd be pieced together, and the lands and grooves examined. These were caused from the rifling in the barrel of the gun and provided a fingerprint of sorts that would only match the specific gun used.

Hans Rideout was shaking his head and looking at the back of the van. "This is all such a shame and so meaningless. You can be assured we're going to take care of her." His solemn tone made it seem as if he were making this vow to Leah herself.

Regardless, Amanda said, "I have no doubt." Her history of working with the medical examiner had earned him her respect. Not only was he serious about his work, but he also had morgue humor down pat, which he dispensed when tension was at its highest. "What was the time of death?" she asked when no one spoke.

"I'd preliminarily estimate within the last three hours."

Amanda pulled her phone and woke the screen. 7:05 *AM*. "She was found at five, so between four and five."

"That was an easy one to narrow down," Rideout said. "But as I said, *preliminarily*. I'll be able to confirm for certain once I've spent more time with her."

"We're supposed to have security footage to watch too, so that should give us an exact time," Trent said.

"Text me with that if you get so lucky. I can tell you that from a look at her wounds, she was shot from a distance between six to eight feet."

Amanda and Trent glanced at each other. If Leah had been targeted, that margin would be smaller. Though he or she may have stood at the door, fired, and left. "Can you tell from which direction?"

"CSIs Blair and Donnelly found two nine mil bullet casings in the snack and gum aisle. A nine mil is consistent with the victim's injuries."

"Huh. That's interesting." That revelation pivoted her earlier thinking. If the shooter had gone to the gas station intending to kill Leah, why mill about the store? Did they get cold feet and delay? If so, she circled back to why they had fired from a distance once they decided to go ahead with their plan. If this was a revenge killing, wouldn't that person want to look Leah in the eye when they pulled the trigger?

"You look taken aback by that," Rideout said, "but I'm sure

the CSIs can tell you more." He turned to Liam and asked, "When is the autopsy?"

Liam handled Rideout's schedule, organizing it in an electronic calendar on a tablet he carted around with him. "Ten this morning," Liam told him without needing to consult the device.

Rideout gestured toward his assistant while looking at Amanda. "There you go. Should we expect you to drop by?"

"Too early to know where we'll be with the investigation by that point," Amanda started. "But keep us posted on any urgent finds. As for the slugs or bullet fragments—" She stopped talking at the appearance of a smile on the ME's face. She arched her eyebrows.

"I know the job, Detective Steele. I've been doing this for a very long time."

"Suppose you have." She smiled in return at the ME's enclosed, yet gentle, reprimand. He didn't need to be micromanaged. Rideout would know that whatever existed of the round would need to be forwarded to the lab for ballistics testing immediately. It must have been the lack of answers for the Bernards weighing on her. A false assumption that if she ushered others along, she'd somehow regain control.

Rideout and Liam loaded into their van and pulled onto the road, while she and Trent watched them leave.

Trent then turned to her. "If Leah was targeted, it's strange the shooter was so far away from her."

"I thought the same. And if they were going to fire from a distance, why not do it next to the door and run off right after?"

"There are definitely aspects we're missing."

"Doesn't that go without saying."

"Detective Steele?" Wyatt ambled over. "I pulled the background on Marty Evans. He was scheduled to work from six until three today. His background is clean, as is the owner's. His name is Porter Landry. He's arrived."

The new car in the lot.

"Should I let Evans go?"

Amanda considered. They might have questions for him after watching the video and speaking with the owner of the gas station. They still had the woman who'd found Leah hanging around. "Just have him stay for a bit longer."

Wyatt nodded and pivoted to leave.

"Hold up a second," Trent called out.

"Yessss?" Wyatt dragged out.

"Where's Porter Landry right now?" he asked.

"Inside with Malone." Wyatt resumed walking in the direction of Marty's sedan.

Amanda and Trent put booties over their shoes and entered the store.

Yellow evidence markers dotted the floor in front of the counter. Blair's and Donnelly's collection cases were there, their lids yawning open waiting to be filled. From the looks of it, there were a few pieces in plastic bags already. One contained a cell phone, and another a blood-spattered novel. There were also the bullet casings Rideout had mentioned.

"You two appear to be off to a good start," Trent said.

"Oh, yeah. Lots of foot traffic in here, which means a forensic goldmine," Blair responded.

"Can't say I'm surprised. It's a busy place," Amanda said.

Donnelly straightened from her haunches in the next aisle, holding something in her gloved hands. Whatever she had found she'd pulled from under the end of the shelving unit.

"Rideout told us you figure the gunfire came from down the snack aisle," Amanda started, "that you found nine mil casings there?"

"That's right." Blair walked about two thirds down the gum aisle and spun, holding her hands out as if wielding a gun. The camera she had strapped around her neck was left to rest against her chest. "Just about here."

Amanda turned away, just the visual of seeing the fatal

shooting somewhat re-enacted sending a firebolt through her. How was she going to handle watching it play out on video? She addressed Donnelly, who was now putting her find into a plastic bag. "What do you have there?"

Donnelly walked over to them, holding up a silver heart and a tangle of fine silver chain. "It's a locket. I'm trying to get it open." It finally complied. "Ah, here we go." She extended it for Amanda and Trent to see.

Staring back at them was the picture of a striking woman with an oval-shaped face and black hair dusting her cheekbones. There was something vaguely familiar about her, and a look at the outside of the locket had Amanda thinking she'd seen it before. Was her mind trying to generate a lead from thin air, or was this their first clue on the path to finding a cold-blooded killer?

FIVE

Before Amanda and Trent joined Malone and the owner of the gas station in the office, Blair and Donnelly assured her that they'd process the locket to see what they could get from it.

Porter Landry was mostly bald except for a few long wisps of hair sprouting from the crown of his head. He was seated at a desk with three monitors, and the keyboard tray was pulled out. Live video played out on the screens. These covered inside the store, the parking lot, and the carwash bay. Porter swiveled his chair when Amanda and Trent graced the doorway, and Malone turned to look at them too.

"These are the detectives I was telling you about, Mr. Landry," Malone said. "Detectives Steele and Stenson." As he said their names, he gestured to them each in turn. He added, "This is Porter Landry, the owner of the Fill N Go."

His complexion was pale, but his cheeks were flushed, and his eyes had a wide, wet look of shock to them. "Hi," he said.

"Mr. Landry has agreed to show us any footage we wish to see. No warrant required." Malone repeated what he'd already relayed before.

Being a cop taught her that generosity and humanity weren't guarantees. Not everyone cared about other people. Sad but true. "Your cooperation is greatly appreciated, Mr. Landry."

"It's the least I can do. I just can't believe this has happened." He swallowed roughly, and his gaze drifted past her and Trent to someplace behind them.

"You know, this might all be a bit hard for you to watch," Amanda said. "If you want to tell us where to find the files and how to work the program, we can take care of it."

"Actually, I would prefer that." He gave them a quick run-through, which seemed straightforward, and excused himself.

Malone stepped out with Porter to ask an officer to escort him from the store. He also told them to keep Porter on scene as Amanda and Trent may have questions for him.

Trent assumed control over the video and hit play after Malone returned.

The interior camera was positioned behind the counter to capture the faces of customers, and potential criminals, which made sense. They saw the back of Leah Bernard's head. Her ginger hair and reindeer headband gave her away. She was reading a paperback, but it didn't stop her from reaching out periodically and adjusting trinkets on the small tree.

Leah set her book down and fussed with her headband. It appeared as if she were watching her reflection in the domed security mirror located on the other side of the store.

The chime on the door jangled. A man came in, and Amanda's heart rate kicked up anticipating he was the shooter, but he just bought a bottle of water and left.

When the door opened again, the timestamp read 4:40 AM, and Amanda's breath froze in her chest at the sight of someone the three in this room knew well.

Katherine Graves had served as interim Homicide sergeant when Malone was convalescing from surgery to remove a malignant brain tumor a year and a half ago. More recently, she retired from law enforcement and put on an apron at her aunt's local diner. Katherine being here this early was understandable as Hannah's Diner did a healthy business starting first thing in the morning.

The three of them shared a brief glance.

Back on the video, Leah got off her stool and greeted Katherine with a cheerful, "Merry Christmas!"

Katherine offered a brief smile and reciprocated the seasonal greeting before going down the snack and gum aisle.

Goosebumps rose on the back of Amanda's neck and trailed down her arms. Surely, her being there was nothing more than a coincidence. She could have been long gone before the shooter arrived.

But there was that silver chain and the familiar heart locket with a picture inside... A bad premonition tore through Amanda, making her nauseous. Had it looked familiar because it was Katherine's and Amanda had seen it around her neck before? If so, what was it doing on the floor of the gas station? Though the clasp could have failed, and it simply fell off.

Another customer came into the store, and Katherine glanced over her shoulder toward the door. It was a man of solid build wearing a balaclava.

"It's not cold enough for one of those," Malone said.

Amanda prepared herself for what was coming. This guy had to be the shooter. The time of day and the face covering had *Bad News* written all over it.

In the snack aisle, Katherine appeared stalled by indecision over gum and mint options, but that wasn't in Katherine's personality. She'd have come inside the store knowing exactly what she'd wanted. Amanda would guess this man had Katherine's cop instincts at high alert, and she was calculating her next move.

The man ambled down another aisle but circled around the

back, stopping next to Katherine. He put a hand into his coat pocket and pulled out a gun, inching ever closer to Katherine.

"He's going for her," Malone said.

In an attack that was lightning quick, Katherine struck out with an arm and knocked him off balance. He fell against the shelving but bounced upright quickly as if his legs were rubber and his feet were anchored to the floor.

He raised his weapon on her. There wasn't a word that passed between them, but Katherine yelled for Leah to get down.

During this time, Leah had been creeping along the counter, presumably to the panic button Trent had pointed out when they'd first arrived on scene.

The man fired and, within a blink, the girl had been shot.

She didn't make a sound and put a hand to her chest. She pulled it back, and her palm was full of blood.

Another blast from the shooter's gun, and Leah's arms were flailing out in an endeavor to stop her from falling. To no avail. She collapsed, her body out of the camera's sightline, the small tree crashing after her.

The timestamp showed 4:45 AM.

They had their time of death.

Trent stopped the video. The three of them held a reverent silence for the life lost and shock at what else they had just seen. Katherine had been here and involved in an altercation with the shooter.

Just a few more seconds to catch their breath.

When Amanda rediscovered her voice, she said, "Can you zoom in on the gun? Maybe we can tell what make and model it is."

"One second." Trent managed to satisfy her request and groaned. "A Glock 19, one of the bestselling guns out there."

"Tracking the shooter down by gun type alone will be impossible. Please, resume playing, Trent."

The video continued, and the man in the balaclava grabbed Katherine's arm and rushed her out of the store. She stared right into the camera. Considering the situation, her facial expression was one of calm. *Almost as if this doesn't surprise her.*

Trent stopped the video, the frame freezing at 4:47 AM.

Malone flailed his arms in the air. "What is going on? Who is this guy, and what does he want with Katherine?"

And why is she so calm about it? Amanda kept the question to herself, dismissing it as adrenaline and cop training kicking in.

"Switch over to outside," Malone told Trent. "Let's see where this guy takes her."

"You got it," Trent said. "Let's cross our fingers for a license plate."

"That's if he didn't take Katherine in her own Mercedes," Amanda pointed out. "It's not in the lot. I would have noticed it."

"We'll get a BOLO started," Malone said.

A Be-on-the-Lookout would alert all cops to keep an eye out for Katherine's car.

"Come on, Stenson, what's taking so long?" Malone tapped a foot, tugged on his beard.

Trent was working the mouse quickly, but Amanda understood Malone's rush for answers. They were all plagued with the same frenzied urgency. Katherine was taken by an armed assailant hours ago. They were already behind their trail.

"Here we go," Trent announced as a video started playing on screen.

Katherine and the man emerged from the store a minute or so later, and he ushered her past her car to the back of the lot where there was a white Ford cargo van. The plates were dark, possibly blacked out.

Another figure, smaller than the first and also in a balaclava, got out of the passenger side and hustled toward the shooter and

Katherine. This person flicked something that held a tiny glow from their hand onto the pavement.

"A cigarette butt," Amanda said. "We'll need the CSIs to collect that."

They continued to watch a brief interaction between the three of them. The shooter tossed something to their partner that they had taken from Katherine.

The smaller figure hustled toward Katherine's Mercedes, which was parked at pump four, and got inside. The item passed over must have been the key fob. That presented other possible dangers. There wouldn't just be one key on the loop. There would be ones for Katherine's house and the diner. Possibly one for her aunt's place. May Byrd, the owner of Hannah's Diner, also a long-time friend of Amanda's.

Amanda's heart pounded, and she tried to slow her breathing. It would have been too easy to give in to the fear, empathy, sadness, righteous anger that was coursing through her. But she had to stay focused. Not doing so wouldn't help resolve this in the least.

The Mercedes left through the north exit at a controlled speed, wisely doing so to limit drawing attention. Did that indicate a career criminal or just someone smart?

In the background, the shooter was coaxing Katherine into the van. He gave her one more shove and shut the doors. Before loading into the driver's seat, the shooter slammed something to the concrete and stomped on it with his foot.

A little light crept into Amanda's soul. Another piece of tangible evidence that might bring them answers and get them to Katherine before it was too late.

Trent let the video play out until the van used the north exit too and headed east, same direction as the car.

The time stamp showed 4:50 AM.

"Son of a..." Malone spun, a hand on the top of his head. "Did we just see what I think we did?"

The sergeant didn't require an answer. What they had just watched was self-explanatory.

Katherine Graves had been abducted, and poor Leah Bernard had lost her life as nothing more than collateral damage.

SIX

Katherine jostled with every bump in the road, every uneven patch the tires ran over. She was left unrestrained in the back, a mistake on the part of her captor. As soon as the back doors were flung open, she was going to launch herself at him. Unless he had a gun on her, which was probable.

That poor sweet girl at the counter didn't stand a chance. Katherine didn't think she'd ever be able to erase her look of sheer terror and shock when she was shot the first time. She clearly recalled the sadness that dulled her eyes and shadowed her expression when the second bullet struck her. She had known she was going to die. Regrets over adventures she'd never have flashed across her face, more tangible than science could ever explain. It wasn't even a concept Katherine would normally entertain.

Katherine gasped as the recollection pierced her soul, and she grieved the young woman she never knew. She'd clearly been a gentle soul with her cheery greeting and holiday-themed headband. She didn't deserve to go out like she had. That was for sure.

But Katherine's thoughts were also on what the man had

planned for her. It couldn't be good. To start, he hadn't hesitated to kill a young woman to get to her.

And while being a cop most of her adult life meant she'd learned to stay calm under pressure, right now, threads of her sanity were barely hanging on. She was freaking out.

Being a cop left one with a slew of enemies, and she had her fair share. She'd even received threats before. Maybe she should have taken them more seriously. Just like she'd dismissed the sensation of being watched recently as paranoia.

Her mind served up a slideshow of suspects, but it did her little good. Until she understood what he wanted, she'd be left guessing at motive and his endgame.

And where is he taking me?

It felt like they'd been driving for a long time, but with her nattering mind, the passage of time wasn't reliable. There were no windows back here, making it a black cube and robbing her of situational awareness. She didn't know if five minutes had passed or an hour. This didn't help calm her mind any. Instead, it had her conjuring up an isolated area so remote that no one would hear her screams for help. She trembled thinking that if he'd wanted to kill her, she'd already be dead. His plans for her must be even worse. The possibilities of torture and sexual assault paraded through her mind. Or a violent death by drowning, being burned alive, or suffocated. Another option was a drawn-out death from neglect, thirst, or starvation. She could be stuffed in a box and left to wait until the oxygen ran out!

Shivers tore through her, and tears rushed down her cheeks.

Will this be how I go out?

She hated how her mind was working against her. If she was going to survive long enough to escape, she needed to get it together.

Think, Kat, think!

A few deep breaths had panic subsiding just enough to afford her some objectivity. The entire scenario at the gas station spoke to an orchestrated attack. Two accomplices working together. The shooter had been calm when he shot that girl, and it had her speculating whether he had killed someone before today.

Katherine pinched her eyes shut. *Focus, focus, focus. Who would want me dead?*

But her thoughts were going wild, making it hard to pluck out any one person. Maybe she needed to consider another possibility. After all, some aspects testified to a professional criminal while other elements did not.

One, they struck in a public place with cameras. Why not target her at home? This was obviously not random. They must have followed her from home, but she hadn't noticed a tail.

Two, they had left a body behind for the police to find.

And speaking of *they*, there were two of them. The second one's size told her it was likely a woman, possibly the man's girl-friend. It was all the uncertainty that attacked Katherine's sanity, threatening to topple her reasoning. And she needed her head, to keep her wits about her. Continuing to paint hypotheti-cals would drive her crazy. She had to focus on what she knew, even if it was little.

The pair had abducted her and were willing to kill to get to her.

If she could muster some patience, she'd discover who they were and what they wanted soon enough. As her anxiety about herself eased some, her concerns shifted elsewhere.

Poor Aunt May!

She'd be expecting her at the diner. When she found out what happened, how would she handle the news? Who would be telling her? Katherine wished it was Amanda. They had butted heads when she'd first transferred to the Prince William County PD, but she had quickly grown to respect the detective. Her partner, Trent Stenson, too.

Yes, she needed them on this. Neither of them would stop until...

Katherine's thought froze there. *Until what?* Her death? Her rescue? One thing was certain, her captor was capable of murder.

Again, her mind tortured her with why her. If putting her in the ground was their intention, her body would be back at the gas station with that young woman.

The van started to slow, and an uneven terrain rocked the chassis side to side.

Katherine strained to listen. Nothing. She had been carted to someplace isolated. *This isn't good at all!*

The car stopped, and he got out of the front. Sometime later, tires crunched, and she heard a car's engine that sounded much like her Mercedes. Next, a woman said, "We pulled it off."

"Don't get too cocky, or you'll jinx the whole thing. And what took you so long? You left before me."

"I... I had to—"

There was the sound of flesh striking flesh.

The woman yelped.

"You better not screw everything up."

What was *everything*? Shivers tore through Katherine again. This confirmed they had more planned for her than just murder. The seemingly unstable dynamics between her abductors didn't help her nerves. Unpredictable equaled extremely volatile and dangerous.

Footsteps crunched over stones and twigs and headed toward the rear of the van.

Katherine was holding her breath as the rear doors were opened.

Their faces were covered, and he was holding a gun on her. So much for fighting back. That would have to wait.

Who are these people, and what do they want with me?

SEVEN

7:30 AM, MONDAY

Missing for 2 hours, 40 minutes

The clock had started, even if time seemed to lag. But they were already nearly three hours behind. And every second that passed diminished their chances of finding Katherine alive. Emotionally, Amanda was numb. Physically, she moved slower for a few moments. Her legs had weakened and her eyes became unblinking. But once the initial shock had worn off, everything swung into full action.

They replayed the video and followed the shooter out of the store again. On a second viewing, they noted his height was five eleven using the security tape next to the door as a guide. But Trent had spotted something else. When the shooter reached out to throw the door open, the sleeve of his winter coat rode up his arm a few inches, exposing some flesh between it and the cuff of his glove. Zooming in, they were looking at a tattoo on his left wrist. They couldn't distinguish what it was depicting, but detectives in the Digital Forensics Unit could possibly enhance the video. A copy of it would be sent to them. They might even be able to make out the obscured license plate or other distinguishing features on either the shooter or his partner.

A lot of things happened at once. The BOLO was issued for Katherine's Mercedes, and a request was made to track its current whereabouts through its GPS. Since stolen vehicles were sometimes used in the commission of a crime, Malone was getting two other detectives in the Homicide department to look into any white Ford vans that were reported stolen. If that didn't pan out, they'd check for registrations within Prince William County and pull backgrounds on those people to see if any led to possible suspects. In the case all that failed, local vehicle rental companies would be contacted to inquire about Ford vans that may have been recently rented out. A request would also be made for CCTV footage from intersections east of the gas station. They might help determine if the shooter continued in that direction. If they were lucky, maybe one or both let their guard down and removed their balaclava.

CSI Blair collected a cigarette butt from the area that the accomplice had flicked one, and pieces of a smartphone were also in that area. It would presumably be Katherine's to cut off their ability to track her, but that still needed to be confirmed. Regardless, there was a trace being done on her number, just in case it wasn't hers.

Trent had also texted Rideout with Leah's time of death.

All these pieces clicked together seamlessly as if this was something the team experienced every day.

The woman who had found Leah was released, but they showed Porter Landry and Marty Evans a picture of the man's left wrist. The tattoo was out of focus, but it still might jog their memories. They added they suspected the shooter was five eleven of solid build. Neither were able to confirm they'd seen him before. It had been a reach, but a necessary one, and they were sent home.

Arrangements were made for an officer to update the

Bernards on the situation while Amanda and Trent took care of something else.

Trent was driving them to Hannah's Diner, and with every turn that took them closer, Amanda braced herself for the conversation that was to come. May Byrd was a dear friend and had been a part of Amanda's life since she was young. Assuming Katherine was next planning to go to the diner, May would be worried sick about where she was.

The lot was full of vehicles, and people were bustling in and out of the diner. May had established a strong customer base with her stellar coffee, but the diner's recent success could be attributed to Katherine's advertising efforts.

The increased business meant May had to take on more staff. Until recently, it was her and a full-time cook who stepped up as a server when needed. Now, in addition to Katherine, there were five part-time servers and two cooks. It looked like Hattie Knox was working the counter with May today. She was the newest employee, in her late fifties, and had taken an early retirement from her career in finance only to find life had gotten tedious. This and a desire to get out among people had her applying for the job.

Trent parked and turned to Amanda. "Do you want me to handle this?"

"No, I'll be fine." She was lying to him, to herself, but whatever got her through the next half hour or so. Informing May that her niece had been taken wasn't going to be easy.

Inside, they sidestepped a line that went from the door to the counter. As they did so, a possible motive behind Katherine's abduction hit. It may be far-fetched, and it was just one of many theories, but the diner's financial growth could have caught the eye of someone who thought they could hold Katherine in exchange for ransom.

May handed the customer at the front two to-go cups and a paper bag. Her motions were robotic and slow, in contrast to her usual flair. Normally she was quick to smile and part with terms of endearment. She barely mumbled a thank-you to the man. Her gray hair was frizzy around her face and her cheeks were flushed, obviously haggard. The next customer stepped up, but May met Amanda's eye.

"Just stepping away for a bit, Hattie," May told her help.

The woman seemed to kick things into high gear in May's wake.

May rounded the counter quickly, but slowed her steps as she approached Amanda. "Don't tell me that something happened to her. Is she... *is she* alive?" May's chin quivered. She must have been unsuccessful in reaching Katherine, and it had planted the worst-case scenario in her mind. Sadly, those imaginings weren't far from the truth.

"Let's take a seat." Amanda spoke slowly, calmly, doing her best to evenly space her words, wanting to exude strength. She didn't want to shock her. Putting an arm around May, she guided her to an available booth, knowing in just a few seconds she would deliver news that would break her heart.

EIGHT

May dropped heavily on the bench as if her legs had given out beneath her.

Amanda sat across from her and moved along to make room for Trent. "There is a situation," she said.

May's mouth opened, then shut. Her eyes filled with tears.

"Katherine was abducted this morning from the Fill N Go in Woodbridge." The nightmare rolled off Amanda's tongue in a torrent with a power all its own. It wielded the strength to destroy, but she had to redeem the situation for May's sake. "She's alive," Amanda quickly added. *At least she was three hours ago, but why bring that up?*

"Abducted," May muttered. "I just knew something bad had happened for her not to be here, to not answer her phone. I was going to give it another half an hour and call you. But why? Who would do this?"

"We're going to figure that out." Amanda's words indicated confidence and bordered close to a promise.

"Where will you start? Do you have any clue where she might be, where they've taken her? What they want from her?"

"A lot of questions still need answers." Amanda wanted to

cover more ground before she shared possible theories for motive, including the one of ransom. "A man and an accomplice were working together. We're confident the accomplice is a woman. Would you have any idea who might do this?"

"Not a clue," May shot out, her chin trembling and tears spilling onto her cheeks.

Amanda thought back to how Katherine had seemed aware of her abductor from the moment he walked through the door. Katherine's pre-emptive attack also struck Amanda as prepared. Was her action the result of a trained cop who read the room and detected danger? Or had she anticipated trouble coming her way? It was possible Amanda was reading too much into what she saw. Still, she asked, "Has Katherine been any different lately? Acting mysterious or anxious? Maybe even coming across like she was afraid of someone or something?"

"I never noticed any of that, but I've always gotten the sense she's holding back from me."

"Any idea what that might be?" Trent asked.

May shook her head. "I didn't press her on it. You must keep in mind we just came back into each other's lives fairly recently, and the reunion wasn't without its emotional baggage. It's been a year and a half, which might sound like a long time, but deep hurts need time to heal."

"I can imagine," Amanda empathized. There would be a lot to process. May could harbor bitterness from the fallout with her sister, Katherine's mother, but some of that may get projected onto her niece. And Katherine might be holding on to the fear of being abandoned or rejected by her aunt. After all, it had been May who left their lives all those years ago. "But you both seem to be working through everything just fine. Whenever I see the two of you together, you're always smiling or laughing."

May sniffled. "Her returning to me was a real gift. She makes me happy, Mandy."

"I bet she does." Amanda reached out and squeezed May's hand. The woman was doing a pretty good job of holding herself together except for a few tears earlier, but her twitching lips and wavering voice revealed she was a hair's breadth away from really breaking down. It hurt to see May suffering like this. "We will get her back for you." The clearcut promise tumbled out, hitting Amanda's ears with the weight of a locomotive.

"I know you'll do all you can, Mandy, but nothing is guaranteed in this life, as you know."

Amanda nodded, that widow and mother who lost her child turning over within her. "Do you have a hunch about what she might have been withholding?"

"No. I get the sense you think whatever it is resulted in her being taken."

"We can't ignore the possibility." The light dulled in May's eyes, and Amanda rushed out, "None of this is your fault." She suspected May was assuming the burden because she hadn't pushed and pried.

"I know, but it doesn't really make me feel better. Sometimes when we'd get talking, her eyes would take on a darkness."

"What were you discussing when this happened?" Trent asked.

"Usually it was when we talked about her life in New York. I surmised it had to do with her work there as a cop."

May's words presented a valid avenue to pursue. They might be looking at someone Katherine had a hand in putting away. Could fear of retaliation be what shadowed her expression? While her stint with the PWCPD had been brief, and as a sergeant, it was still possible she'd upset someone locally. But given what May had just said, it sounded as if Katherine was triggered when talking about her old life. "Did she speak much of her time with the New York City Police Department?"

"Some, yes. But she'd become guarded about it too."

Again, this struck Amanda. Something about Katherine's time with the NYPD still haunted her.

May continued. "She liked the excitement and chaos of the big city, of being needed and in demand. But as I said, there was a change in her when we'd discuss it too much. She never told me why she'd left, and I was never bold enough to bring it up. Something else I should have pushed on, but I assumed it had to do with grief over losing her mother."

Amanda had been given a glimpse at Katherine's past because of a newspaper article published last June in the local paper, *Prince William Times*. What she didn't gather from there, Katherine ended up divulging. The short of it was her stepfather had killed her mother after years of abuse. He was put away for the crime, but it was a small price to pay in recompense. Katherine had been quite upset that her past was made public, but was it due to her privacy being violated, or did she have a larger concern? Was it linked to whatever caused her eyes to go dark when on the topic of her time with the NYPD? "Did she leave soon after her mother's murder?" Amanda asked.

"Within the year. The trial happened quickly and ended just as fast."

If Katherine feared for her well-being in NYC, with her mother gone she might not have had anyone else keeping her there. Amanda was about to inquire about Katherine's friends and lovers when Trent spoke.

"Ms. Byrd—" he began.

"Oh, please, child, just call me May." She pressed her lips in a tight smile.

"May, did Katherine ever mention any specific cases she worked on when she was in New York?" Trent asked.

The older woman shook her head. "I didn't figure she wanted to get into any of them with me."

"What about friends she had there?" If they could get

names, Katherine may have confided in them about particularly troublesome investigations.

"She's mentioned the name Tasha Bauer, though I suppose her given name would be Natasha. My Kat isn't a highly sociable person. She's focused, ambitious. Heck, she's turned my diner into the most popular place to stop for coffee in the entire state. Or at least it feels that way." A small, tight smile. "She's more work than play."

"I think she has a hard time letting people in," Amanda offered.

"Oh, yeah." The jovial expression caved in on itself as May's face pinched with a blend of guilt and sadness. "I spoke you up often, Mandy, said that you have a lot in common with both being cops, but she'd smile and say you were nice but leave it there. Why, I don't know. She doesn't have friends her own age here in the area, but she joins me sometimes for book club."

A group that viewed reading as fourth on a list of importance, following wine, cheese, and gossip. "Was she close with any of the members?"

"Nah. Most of them are my age."

May's age was something she kept from most people, but Amanda knew she was sixty-one. Katherine was forty-seven, but relatively speaking the generational gap wasn't humungous.

"I think it's sad she doesn't have any friends in the area. When I get on her, she just says how great it is we're in each other's lives again. She's caught up in the fact I'm her closest living blood relative. She has my daughter, Hannah, too of course. Kat's cousin, but her mother's murder really hit her hard."

Hannah was May's only daughter, and the diner's namesake. She was a successful defense attorney who lived in Washington, DC. But Amanda could understand why the death of Katherine's mother would have deeply wounded her. The hardest part of the job was delivering the news to loved ones.

And once the killer was arrested and put away, her involvement ended. For those left to grieve the victims, their story was just getting started. When murder was the manner of death, there must be a lot of rage. Was that what prevented Katherine from putting down personal roots? She'd been in Prince William County for a year and a half. Or was it something more menacing? Was she keeping people at a distance to protect them or herself?

NINE

Amanda gave more thought to Katherine's isolated and insular existence. She'd made a conscious choice to stick to herself. The closest thing she did to building a life here was getting involved with the diner. Was it because she wanted the freedom to run, or even needed it? But surely, she needed to have a semblance of a social life. Did she keep in regular contact with her friends in NYC and that was enough for her? "Do you know how close Katherine and Natasha were?"

"Close, for sure. They met at university and despite Kat's move here, they still talk."

"And what does Natasha do for work?" Trent asked.

"She's an assistant district attorney in New York."

That was a promising connection. It was feasible the two would have worked cases together. Natasha might know of one that weighed heavily on Katherine. Though Amanda found it hard to accept that Katherine would make herself vulnerable by confiding her emotions to others. Best friend or not. "You wouldn't happen to have a number for Natasha, would you?"

"I don't. I encouraged Kat to invite her down, but I think Tasha's life is quite busy."

As an assistant district attorney in one of the largest cities in the United States, Amanda could believe that. While this Natasha might be a good place to start for insight into Katherine's personal life, there was also another. "May, would you happen to have a key to her place? It could help to have a look around."

"I do." With that May hoisted herself up from the booth, and she moved slowly as if every joint in her body were stiff. Maybe she rarely sat still because it was hard to get going again.

"I can get it for you, if you tell me where to find it," Trent offered.

"That would be nice of you. My purse is on the hook in the kitchen. It's the blue one."

"Be back in a sec." Trent left, and Amanda's phone started ringing.

Malone's name was on the screen. "I need to get this."

May bobbed her head, her eyes glazed over.

Amanda patted May's hand as she slipped out of the booth and answered her phone.

She stepped outside. The cool air nipped at her nose. She rounded the building to shelter herself from the wind.

"The cell phone in the lot did belong to Graves," Malone said, getting right to the point. "Obviously making tracking it pointless. Her call history has been requested, and I've asked that be rushed along."

"And the tracker on her car?" Amanda could barely breathe as she asked this question. She just wanted the nightmare to be over for Katherine. Being able to provide closure for the Bernard family by apprehending their daughter's killer would also be a bonus.

"Nowhere yet, but you'll know the second I do. I've got the entire department on this. Graves is one of our own, far as I'm concerned."

"Agreed." Amanda hadn't taken much to Katherine when

she'd first arrived at the PWCPD but had come to like and respect her. She informed Malone they were with May and would be heading to Katherine's house soon.

"I want you to take a uniform as backup. Just in case."

"All right. Speaking of uniforms, I think we should get officers to sit on May, to make sure she's safe, and just in case it's the shooter's motive in all this, get a tap on her cell phone and home line should there be a ransom demand." She hadn't even had a chance to talk with Trent about this theory.

"You think all this was for money?"

Amanda peeked around the corner to all the activity in the diner's parking lot. It showed no signs of slowing down. "Business is good. It's better we're prepared than not. From just looking at the diner, the people who took Katherine might believe May can pay up."

"I'll get an officer to escort May home and get the rest taken care of too."

"Thank you." The call ended with the promise to keep each other apprised of any new findings. Amanda tightened her grip on her phone, a realization sinking in. If Katherine kept mostly to herself because she feared she'd put people in danger, that meant May might not be safe.

Amanda returned to the diner, and Trent was holding May's purse out to her, the strap hooked over one of his fingers.

"I never go into a lady's purse, if it can be helped," he said.

May glanced at Amanda and smiled. Back to Trent, she said, "Aren't you something special?"

A touch of color splashed Trent's cheeks, and he handed off her purse. May rummaged through it and came out with a key ring. She worked one off the loop and gave it to Trent. "This is for her front door. You'll also need to disarm her security system. The passcode is *Ninja*."

Amanda was curious of the reason behind "Ninja." Was it a pet name? But she let the thought go as there were more pressing matters. She sat down again. "I haven't spoken with Trent about this yet, but one possibility is Katherine's abductor may be interested in money."

"You mean like a ransom?"

"Exactly like that." Amanda sensed Trent's inquiring gaze on her, but she'd explain herself in the car and why she'd gone ahead of him in this regard. "An officer is on their way to escort you home and stay with you."

"Do you think I'm in danger?"

"I never said that, but it's better to err on the side of caution. Other officers will be coming to your house to set up a tap on your phone line, and they will stand by in case a ransom demand does come in."

"I have money, but I'm not what you'd call rolling in it."

Amanda didn't want to point out the obvious success of the diner as that might make May feel worse somehow. "We're just being proactive. It might not happen. Trent and I need to leave now, but is there anyone you would like me to call for you? Hannah or a friend who could come be with you?"

"Hannah's in Mexico. My girl never takes a holiday and the one time she does, something like this happens. I'll let her know what's happened, but I'll call Dee to come over."

If Amanda was Hannah, she'd want to know about her cousin. She'd likely catch an immediate flight home to be with her mother too. But at least May wasn't without friends in town. "That's a good idea." Deena Roberts was May's closest and longest friend and fellow member of her book club. Amanda gave May a hug and offered words of encouragement.

"Just find my Kat. Please."

May's words were still ringing in Amanda's ears as she got into the car with Trent. "Why does it feel like we just set off a bomb and walked away?"

"In a way we did."

"I would have talked to you about the ransom theory, but it

didn't work out that way. Then Malone called, and I floated the theory past him. I thought it best to get on it sooner than later."

"I think it's a solid theory. If the shooter wanted Katherine dead, she would have been shot on scene. That alone tells me there's some other endgame here." With that, he hit the gas and set them in the direction of Katherine's house. Down the street, he asked, "What did Malone call to tell you?"

She filled him in, and summed up with, "He didn't have a whole lot."

"I'd say." Trent took a right-hand turn and added, "It's not a surprise it was Katherine's phone in the lot. Her abductors were smart to leave that behind. Are we looking at professionals?"

"Some aspects have me leaning that way. The gloves, tinted plate covers, the partnership, but other factors not so much. Why kill an innocent girl? Why would the shooter leave the bullet casings behind? We need to dig into Katherine's life, focus on her past in New York and the cases she worked there."

"In complete agreement," Trent said. "There's some reason Katherine would go dark when talking about her time with the NYPD."

"Yep. I suspect it factors in to why Katherine distances herself from people. It could be to protect them or herself," she said, sharing her earlier thinking.

"We need to reach out to Natasha and Katherine's former boss at the NYPD and see if they can point us in anyone's direction. Someone she put away perhaps," Trent said. "But if we're looking at someone from New York City, how did they know where to find her?"

"That's the easy part. Remember that article from last year?"

He looked over at her, and his eyes widened. "Right. I remember that, but it only would have gotten them as far as Prince William County. It's not huge but it's not small either. So how exactly did they track her down?"

TEN

Amanda had to leave a voicemail for Katherine's former boss, Lieutenant Warren Catherwood of the NYPD 63rd Precinct. She stressed that it was a life-and-death matter relating to Katherine Graves. She also called the District Attorney's office for the ADA, only to get their voicemail system. Instead of trying to navigate through, she'd call back. It was 8 AM, but they opened at nine.

Trent pulled into Katherine's driveway, and the officer who had followed parked on the street out front.

This was Amanda's first time here. It wasn't like her relationship with Katherine ever extended outside the department when they worked together at the PWCPD.

The house was a two-story and held a substantial footprint. It was also in a neighborhood that primarily catered to those in a higher tax bracket, typically higher than any honest cop could expect to see.

Trent let out a whistle. "She drives a Mercedes and lives here. Are we sure she's one of the good guys?"

"I'm sure. Perhaps she made good money in New York, or she might have inherited after her mother died." She was thinking more along the lines of an insurance policy, but it could have also been financial investments that were passed along.

"If so, not worth the price of admission to upper class. Katherine's abductors wouldn't need to see the diner to antici-pate a payday though. This place alone screams money. They could force Katherine to withdraw money herself and, in exchange, she keeps her life."

"Good point." She made a quick call to Malone and requested that they gain access to Katherine's finances and get someone to watch them for recent transfers or withdrawals. He assured her he'd get on this as soon as possible.

Stepping inside, Katherine's pungent lily of the valley fragrance hung in the air. It conjured all the smells from that morning at the gas station. With this context, Amanda realized she had detected the scent there. Something as simple as spritzing oneself with perfume was so ordinary. The day would have started off that way for Katherine before it took its drastic turn.

Trent punched the code into the security system, and it beeped. "We're in. Ninja, ninja," he prattled off with a smile, and she shook her head despite appreciating the insertion of joviality.

Amanda wiped her shoes on the front mat, resisting the urge to take them off. She had expected to feel like she was tres-passing or invading Katherine's space, but she didn't. Maybe it was because they had a purpose being here.

The home was clean, the wood floors and tiled entry gleaming with the sunlight that was streaming through huge windows. There was an expansive sitting room to the left, and to the right was a dining room, the kitchen behind that. Stair-cases, one leading up, the other down, were across from the door, and sat in the middle of a wide hallway that ran to the back of the house.

They did a sweep of the main level, and everything looked like it was in order. There were no signs the place had been ransacked. They returned to the entry.

"Something to help direct our steps would be nice," Amanda said.

"Well, we haven't got to her home office yet. We might find a clue there?" Trent's suggestion wasn't delivered with much confidence given the arch of a question.

"I'd guess we'd find that upstairs." Amanda led the way.

A bathroom was straight ahead at the top of the landing. To the left were two doors, and to the right double doors stood open inviting entry into a massive primary suite. It was tempting to go there first, if only to snoop and see how the other half lived. Amanda refused her impulse.

She entered the first door on the left and found a sizable office with sparse furnishings. But the bare minimum, combining function and comfort amid zero clutter, seemed to be the theme for the house. Everything served a purpose.

This space housed a stately desk with a credenza, a plush leather chair, a laser printer, a waste basket, and a recycling bin. A tropical tree too, which seemed the only indulgence toward a visible personal touch in the home.

Trent was going through cabinets in the credenza, and she went for the desk drawers. They both wore gloves as a precaution. The shooter or his accomplice could have been in Katherine's home. She and Trent were certainly due for a change in their luck.

Amanda opened a long drawer in the middle of the desk and took out her find. "We've got a laptop." It was a newer model than the relic Amanda had, but that wasn't saying much. She placed it on the desk and hit the power button. It came to life, and a passcode screen came up. She typed *Ninja*. No luck.

Trent stood next to her. "You tried Ninja?"

"You know it. We'll need to get it to Digital Forensics

ASAP. They'll be able to get into this thing." Normally she dealt with Detective Jacob Briggs, but he often worked the night shift. They didn't have the luxury of waiting for him.

"I'll hand it over to the uniform out front with instructions to get it over to Digital." Trent left with the laptop.

She turned her attention back to the desk and another drawer. This one was locked, and that made her want in even more. A quick look around, and her gaze landed on a container of paper clips. Guess it was time to find out if she possessed an inner James Bond. Unfolding a clip, she pushed the tip into the keyhole and wriggled it in there. Just when she was about to give up, success. She opened the drawer and gasped. *What the...?*

"Officer Brandt is taking the laptop right over," Trent said, returning and speaking from the office doorway. "Another uniform is taking his place here."

She didn't say anything but pointed to the haul she'd removed from the drawer to the top of the desk.

"Whoa. You hit a jackpot while I was gone."

"Not sure about that, but we'll figure out what it all means." She took in the extent of her find, which was a stack of cash, a passport, a key ring with a single key, and an old cell phone. There was the possibility these clandestine items had nothing to do with Katherine's abduction, but even if there was a glimmer of possibility they did, she and Trent needed to follow this lead wherever it took them.

Trent picked up the cell phone, a clunky blue Nokia. "I haven't seen one like this in years."

"That's because it probably dates back to the early 2000s." She turned it on, having her suspicions it would power to life and it did. "That confirms it for me."

"Confirms what?"

"If this was just an old phone kicking around, the battery would be long dead, but it's not. It shows three quarters full."

"It's a burner."

"Safe bet." Often older or base models were used for this purpose. They predated GPS tracking.

"So why does a former homicide sergeant have a burner phone, cash, a passport, and a mysterious key in her desk drawer?"

"More to the point, *locked* in a desk drawer."

ELEVEN

Amanda and Trent tried a variety of passwords to unlock the phone but didn't have any luck. Digital Forensics would need to deal with it. At least Trent was able to reach Officer Brandt by phone. He returned for the Nokia and would drop off both it and the laptop together and stress the urgency.

Amanda was trying to come to terms with what she had found, and what it might mean. Had Katherine been a dirty cop? She flipped through the passport. It was issued six months ago, in Katherine's name, and didn't have any stamps. With her working full-time at the diner, getting away would be impossible. The drawer could have just been a safe place to keep it.

"You doing all right there? You look deep in thought. Something you want to share?" Trent's voice pulled her from her thoughts.

She held up the passport. "She never left the country, but I wish I knew what Katherine is caught up in."

"I'm with you there. Her little treasure trove makes me think she's wrapped up in something she shouldn't be. I mean, who has that much money sitting around? How much would you say is there?"

Amanda fanned the half-inch stack of fifties. "Just a guess? Five K."

"As I said, a lot of money to be sitting around."

Amanda was cautioning herself not to jump to conclusions, but it wasn't easy to refrain. "Let's extend her the benefit of the doubt." Saying this twisted in her gut. What they'd stumbled on could be the reason for that morning's events, also what Katherine was hiding from May. Amanda reached back into the drawer for a manila envelope that was at the bottom.

Trent moved in close so they were elbow to elbow. "What have you got?"

She looked at him and raised her eyebrows. "Impatient much?"

"Just a bit. Whatever is coming out of that drawer has my interest."

She slipped her hand inside and withdrew four white, letter-size envelopes.

"Dear God, it's like those Russian nesting dolls."

"Not quite." Amanda laughed at Trent's obvious eagerness.

None of the envelopes were postmarked, but each had Katherine's name typewritten front and center. Based on the uneven distribution of ink, Amanda would surmise the stationery had been loaded into an actual typewriter.

She opened them one by one, pulling out a single tri-folded piece of paper from each. She read them as she went along. "'You ruined my life. I will ruin yours.' 'You owe me. I'm coming to collect.' 'You lie. I will expose the truth and bring you to your knees.' 'You will hurt. I will get you alone one day.'"

This discovery was punctuated by a few moments of stunned silence.

Trent was the first to speak. "These weren't mailed but hand delivered. That means this person has been to her house."

"Not necessarily, and since we don't know when she

received them, it's really hard to know where they were dropped off."

"Well, you're not denying the shooter from this morning knew where she lived."

"I'm not, but it doesn't mean he's the sender of these threats either."

"But he could be."

This debate could go on all day, but Amanda was literally saved by the bell. The ringing doorbell was followed by a knock and a call out of, "Yoo-hoo." The voice was that of a woman. Whoever she was, she'd let herself inside.

Amanda abandoned the threats and led the way from the office.

A mature woman was standing in the entry tucking some of her gray hair behind her ears. Her face was pale, but she had the most piercing blue eyes Amanda had ever seen.

"Excuse me, ma'am," Amanda said to her. "We're Detectives Steele and Stenson. And you are?"

The woman stepped back and rubbed at her arms, but she pushed out her chin. "Nancy Orr. Why are you in Kat's home?"

Amanda relaxed at the woman abbreviating Katherine's name as it indicated a friendship, but she couldn't let her guard down. "We could ask you the same."

Nancy pushed her gaze over to Trent, lingered some before returning to look at Amanda. "I live next door, and I want to know what's going on."

Amanda could give the woman credit for her honesty. "Are you friends with Katherine?"

"I suppose you could say that. Sometimes we sit out back and pass time in the evenings. Say, is she all right?"

A span of silence. Trent must share her quandary about this question, appreciating it was a technicality nightmare. They had no way of knowing her current welfare.

"Would you be kind enough to talk to us for a moment?"

Amanda gestured toward the front sitting room, and Nancy complied, though her movements were slow and hesitant.

She sat on a white fabric couch, and Amanda and Trent each dropped onto matching chairs. *Only people without kids dare buy white fabric.*

The older woman's chin quivered as she darted her eyes back and forth between them. "Something's wrong, isn't it?"

"There is a developing situation involving Katherine." Amanda opted to drop the surname, abandoning the formality she would normally use at such a time. She also did her best to squeeze out the most menacing threat from her mind. *You will hurt. I will get you alone one day.*

"What does that mean? A *situation*? Is she alive?"

Amanda debated how to respond as she had before when May asked. She decided to stick to that path. "She is."

Nancy let out a gust of breath and laid a hand on her chest. "Thank God for that, but what's the *situation*?" Her brow creased, and her eyes narrowed.

"It pertains to an active investigation, so we're not at liberty to disclose much at this time. You might be able to help us though. Help Katherine." Amanda was quick to add that last bit as Nancy's body language had closed off with crossed arms and a hardened facial expression. At Amanda's appeal, the woman's posture relaxed.

"If I can. Though without knowing what's going on that might be tough."

"We appreciate your cooperation. Have you lived next door for long?" Amanda asked this to lay the groundwork for her next question.

"Twenty years. Gerry and I bought intending to stay here until the day we died. He beat me to it."

It turned out Amanda's question had teed things up beautifully. As a long-time resident in the neighborhood, Nancy would know if any new people had been loitering around. It was logical the shooter and his accomplice would have done some recon before that morning. "Have you seen anyone you didn't know near Katherine's house? Possibly lingering or watching her?"

Nancy's eyes widened and glazed over. "Don't think so."

Amanda didn't take that to be an absolute, but if they knew where Katherine lived, why had they picked the gas station as ground zero? Did they want her abduction to be public, or did it somehow feel less risky than striking in a residential neighborhood?

"Do you know any of Katherine's friends?" Trent asked.

The older woman shook her head. "I don't think she got out much. Or brought anyone around. I'd bug her about getting herself a boyfriend. I told her that she's too young and pretty to be alone. I've had my romance. Lost my Gerry ten years ago and don't expect to find another catch like 'im again. But Kat has her entire life ahead of her." Nancy's eyes watered.

Amanda wished she could disclose more to the woman, to ease her anxiety, but it couldn't be helped.

"No one at all came by?" Trent asked, skeptical.

"Nope, well, just her aunt. Love that lady. Oh, and Dee, nice lady too."

Amanda smiled at mention of May's best friend but said, "It's quite easy to love May." It seemed pointless that Katherine had such a huge and beautiful house but didn't share it with anyone. Did it have anything to do with the hidden cache? "When did you last see Katherine?"

"Last night. We had some wine on my back deck."

Trent had his tablet out and was pecking away adding Nancy's comments. "What time was this?"

"Around seven. We bundled up, and I have a heater that knocks off some of the chill. I just love being outside."

That didn't sound like Amanda's idea of a relaxing evening. "When you saw her last night, how did Katherine seem to you?"

"Like her normal self."

Hearing this took Amanda's thoughts back to the video from the gas station. Katherine didn't strike her as being cautious or paranoid. She didn't peek over her shoulder while pumping gas or walking into the store. She'd only glanced at the door when the man in the balaclava entered. And yet she had threats against her squirreled away in a drawer. Surely, she gave them some credit regardless of when she'd received them.

"You said 'normal,' does that mean anxious or withdrawn in any way?" Trent must be drawing from what May told them, that she had the impression her niece was hiding something from her.

"Kat has always been a private person, but she opened up to me about her mother and aunt's estrangement and then her reuniting with May. Such a heart-touching story. Tragic she lost her mother, of course, but at least she's home now."

Amanda stood, convinced they'd gotten all they could out of Nancy. "Thank you for talking with us, Ms. Orr," she said and handed her a business card. "Call me if you remember anything or anyone hanging around. Whatever might help our investigation."

Nancy took the card without looking at it. She kept eye contact with Amanda. "You never told me what the *situation* was, so how will I know what might help or not?"

Amanda considered, longing to give the woman something while not upsetting her too much. "Katherine Graves is currently missing, and we're trying to find her."

The woman tapped Amanda's card against the palm of her other hand and worried her bottom lip. She sniffled and nodded. "Thank you for telling me that much."

Amanda simply dipped her head in response, and Nancy saw herself out. Trent shut the door and secured it behind her.

"She seems to really care about Katherine," he stated.

"She does. Unlikely friends, the two of them." She'd

responded to Trent, keeping the narrative thread, but her mind was wandering. It was revisiting her thoughts about Katherine. Did she know her fate or not? Surely if she was involved with something shady, she had to expect it could catch up with her. "I think Katherine's habit of keeping people at a distance was to protect them."

"I think it's entirely possible, especially considering those threats we found. Regardless of when she received them, she saw fit to hold on to them."

"I thought the same. But why didn't Katherine show any signs of being leery at Fill N Go this morning?"

"She did when the guy in the balaclava showed up."

"Uh-huh, but not before that. It didn't look like she was living in fear, I guess is my point. Was it just the fact he was wearing a balaclava or did she recognize something about him?" The latter thought just hit her.

"Not being a mind reader, I can't say." He added a smile to lessen the sarcasm of his words. "But while I hate to say *this*, was she involved in something that got her into this trouble? She's got a nice house, luxury car, high-end furniture."

"Furniture?"

"Yep. The furniture in the front sitting room is designer. That set would easily cost mid to high five figures."

"And you know that how?"

"Wendy has expensive taste. She dragged me around furniture shopping one day and insisted on hitting stores far outside of her tax bracket."

Wendy was his younger sister. "Okay, let's assume Katherine wasn't involved with anything shady and she came by her money honestly. It might have been an inheritance like we mentioned before. Where does that leave us? The threats aren't entirely helpful as they are rather vague."

"Well, we considered we might be looking at someone she

put away. And the burner and cash might suggest she was prepared to move if it came to that."

Amanda nodded, her mind on the threats. "One of those letters called her a liar, another said 'you owe me.' Is this about money or more metaphorical?"

"Whatever the case, someone wants to cause her harm, and for some reason Katherine was hiding it."

Amanda had nothing to say to that.

TWELVE

They had put a sack on her head and yanked her out of the van. The fabric wasn't cinched around her neck and followed the contours of her face allowing her to see her feet.

Katherine strained to hear anything that might afford her a clue as to where they had taken her. All that returned to her ears was birdsong. She inhaled deeply, trying to distinguish smells. Nothing much past the cool, brisk air that threatened snow. Wherever they were, it was remote and far from civilization.

Her captors worked together, the man on her left and the woman on her right, and wrangled her in the direction they wanted. She tugged, but both had a firm grip. The woman's slight build was deceiving, but she was definitely the subservient one of the two. The man was muscular and strong, an observation she'd made at the gas station, but he was shorter than her six feet by at least an inch or two.

Looking down, she was walking on gravel, flattened brown grass, and then a concrete path. "Where are we?" she asked but didn't expect an answer.

"Don't you worry about that," the man said.

As if that alone would stop her. She was God-knows-where with people who wanted God-knows-what with her. They had killed a young woman who couldn't have been twenty years old. The needless loss of life stung, but more so, it pissed her off. "Why are you doing this? What do you want?"

"Shut up," the man said.

Obedience wasn't her strong suit. Some might call that a weakness, but she viewed it as a strength. Independent thinking was an asset by any measure. "You won't get away with this."

"I said *shut up*."

The fact the man spoke again confirmed he was the dominant in this partnership. This dynamic might be something Katherine could exploit once she figured out how.

Next, squeaky hinges and a clanging noise hit her ears. A steel door? They were unlikely about to enter a house. Maybe a shed, shop, or garage? Even so, it still told her absolutely nothing definitive about her location.

They pushed her forward, and she crossed an expansive threshold. Their footsteps followed, then the metal door clanged shut and a deadbolt thunked into place.

Only the man held her arm now. The floor beneath her feet was linoleum. *An abandoned medical clinic or school?*

They stopped and directed her into a room. It was brighter in here as light seeped through her head covering. Again, she asked, "Where are we?"

"I told you. Not your concern," he hissed close to her ear and shoved her forward again.

She stumbled and fell into a hard, plastic chair. Its metal legs scraped along the floor as her weight had the chair shifting.

The woman stepped in front of her. She held Katherine in place, a hand gripped on each of her shoulders. While Katherine knew she towered over her and outweighed her, making a move now would be foolish. The smell of stale beer told her he was nearby, and he'd be armed.

The soles of his shoes then slapped the floor and came up to Katherine's side. His shins were in view as he tied her wrists to the arms of the chair so tightly her fingers tingled. At least her legs were still free. Did she dare make a move?

On impulse, she rose and spun, using the legs of the chair as a weapon, and was able to sideswipe the woman.

She crumpled to the floor with a yelp.

Katherine's heart was pounding, unsure where the man had gone. She couldn't see his feet or hear him. *Where did he go?*

Something hard met her skull, and all strength left her body. As everything became dark, she remembered one of the threats she'd received.

You will hurt. I will get you alone one day.

THIRTEEN

Amanda was doing her best to remain objective about what she found in that desk drawer, but it wasn't easy. It still might not factor into that day's events or condemn Katherine as a criminal. "I'm going to let Malone know what we've found." She announced her intention to Trent and made the call on speaker. Malone answered before the second ring.

"Tell me what you've got."

She filled him in on the neighbor, but he fell silent after she told him what she found in the desk drawer.

"You found threats? We need those processed immediately."

"I'm not sure that would do much good," she said. "We don't know how long she's had them or how often they'd been handled. If there ever were prints left by the sender, they may long be compromised."

Malone huffed. "Why didn't she reach out to any of us? We would have helped her."

Pride and deniability were the two reasons that occurred to her, but she remained quiet.

"Those other things don't look good for her either. How much cash, do you figure?"

"Close to five K," Trent said.

Malone whistled.

"Yeah, it's a lot for her to have lying around," Amanda agreed.

"We need to figure out what she was caught up in ASAP."

"We're doing what we can, boss," she told him. "As I told you, Trent and I spoke to one of the neighbors, but it might be a good idea to have uniforms talk to more of them. Someone could have seen a stranger lurking around."

"Do you think these people latched on to her at her house?"

"It's most likely," Trent said. "She would have gone from here to the gas station this morning."

"And how did they find her home?"

It was a question that Amanda and Trent had considered already. "Anyone's best guess. One option is they found her at the diner and followed her home."

"And all this raises the question, why didn't her abductors take her from her bed?"

"We don't have an answer for you." As she admitted to that, an idea hit which she'd pursue when she got off the phone. "No updates from you?"

"Nope." Malone hung up.

Amanda looked at Trent, and he raised his eyebrows. "He's just a little frazzled," she said, defending Malone.

"I am too."

"Me three, but I have an idea." She brought up the web browser on her phone. "We talked before about how the shooter knew where to find Katherine."

"That article from a while back, but it would only get them to the county."

"Uh-huh, but I just remembered that Katherine set up a

website for the diner. She could have mentioned herself. Then they tagged on to her from there."

"Worth looking into."

The site loaded on her screen, and Amanda selected the "About Us" page. "Here it is."

Trent leaned in. "Unless I'm not seeing it, there's nothing about Katherine."

"No, there isn't." All that Katherine had included was information on May Byrd, the founder. Amanda quickly skimmed the write-up, and there wasn't even mention of May's daughter, Hannah. "I have another idea. With the diner getting some serious business these days, that means attention, possibly online reviews. One of them might have mentioned Katherine specifically."

Amanda googled Katherine's name, and goosebumps rose when there were hits related to Hannah's Diner. Some were standard online reviews, but there were a few blog posts. She clicked on the first one. "Here's a review that mentions Katherine." She scanned the article and read a tidbit out loud. "'Katherine Graves, niece of the founding entrepreneur, brings a breath of fresh air to a well-loved Dumfries establishment.'"

"Guess we could conclude if someone had their mind set on finding her, it wouldn't have been difficult."

"Still, though." Her thoughts were like wisps of fog, escaping her grasp and not fully taking shape. There was something telling in all this, but to hell if she knew what. "Was it someone local from a case she oversaw while with the PWCPD or did her abductor follow her from New York?"

"I'm not sold on it being someone from the county. She was the sergeant behind the scenes. We're the ones testifying in court and building the cases."

"She put her stamp of approval on all of them, but I see your point. There's also what May told us about Katherine's reaction to talking about the NYPD sometimes." She took a few breaths, appreciating they had already covered this ground.

"Though there was at least one person who did have an issue with Katherine while she was interim sarge. You know who's coming to mind?" He met her gaze and seemed to be trying to keep a straight face but was failing badly.

"This has nothing to do with Logan." A year and a half ago when Katherine first came to the PWCPD, she was set on charging Logan with the murder of his estranged wife for a quick close and to impress the higher-ups. Amanda had been his ultimate savior, realizing all the evidence against him was too convenient. Thankfully, she eventually got through to Katherine and was able to cuff the real killer.

Trent laughed and held up his hands. "Hey, you're the one who said his name, not me."

He was trying to laugh this off, but she sensed an under-lying resentment toward Logan. Trent's attraction to her was no secret. He'd kissed her before, and she had kissed him back. While that had been some time ago and prior to Logan, a charged energy buzzed between them. But as long as they were partners, a romantic relationship was off the table. Their feelings for each other put them at enough risk. All this aside though, she was adamant about Logan's innocence. He didn't have a tattoo and would never shoot a teenage girl. "I'm with your earlier opinion. We're not looking at someone from the county. This goes back to Katherine's time with the NYPD, whether it was while she was a sergeant or before she advanced rank. It's time we find out what hornets' nests she stirred up there."

FOURTEEN

Amanda still hadn't heard from the NYPD lieutenant. It was concerning that her message, stressing a life-and-death matter, hadn't prompted a call back. "I'll follow up with Katherine's former boss, but we also have Natasha Bauer, Katherine's friend and assistant district attorney. Katherine might have confided in her about something that will help us. To start, she might know who sent those threats." It was past nine thirty now, so the office would be open.

"And I hate to say it, but we need to keep our minds open too. We don't know if her abduction relates to a previous investigation," Trent said.

"I realize we could just be spinning. Meanwhile, Katherine is God knows where. Being tortured? Already murdered?" She paced in a circle, a hand to her forehead. She was gulping air and doing her best to swallow fear and anger before they took complete hold of her. There was so much anger. "We're talking about a fellow cop, Trent. We need to do all we can to get her home safely." *Once an officer, always an officer.*

"No one's arguing." He reached out, his fingertips barely grazing her forearm, but it stopped her from pacing.

She regarded him, her eyes blazing.

"The best thing we can do is keep a level head and take one step at a time." He smiled at her.

Amanda appreciated his positivity, but her thoughts turned dark. While Katherine wasn't currently a cop, the career had a way of branding a person for life. There was inherent danger that came with that. And when one was active in law enforcement, every shift was unpredictable. The people they encountered were at their lowest and things could take a hostile, and fatal, turn in a hot second. Coming home safe and sound was like the roll of the dice. None of this vulnerability was eased by the masses who drummed up violence against law enforcement and rallied for it to be defunded. It was like that old saying about throwing the baby out with the bath water. Yes, there were corrupt cops, but they were the minority not the standard. And while aware this hatred was out there, this was Amanda's first time facing off with it. While the motivation behind Katherine's abduction was currently unknown, it was a crime against her sister in blue. It struck as a personal affront, like this perp had assaulted blood.

Really, the next second, the next breath, was never a guarantee for anyone. But this job stacked the odds against a person. Life was fragile, and the next moment couldn't be taken for granted. For all she knew, this day could be her or Trent's last.

Amanda looked down, prompted by the warmth seeping from Trent's fingertips. His hand was still on her arm, and it washed away her ability to think clearly. Letting herself go on impulse, dipping into flow, she stepped forward and put her mouth on Trent's.

He stiffened, and she feared he was going to push her away. Just when she was certain he would, he pulled her closer and deepened the kiss.

Afterward, they parted in unison. Moved back a few feet.

Her heart was pounding, and she could hardly catch her breath. "I shouldn't have done that. I'm sorry." *Even if I'm not...*

"No, don't apologize." He shook his head. "This is on me too. Well, obviously. I should have just..." He left the rest unsaid and met her gaze.

Her heart ached at his seemingly instant regret. "I say we just forget this happened." Such a ridiculous, futile, stupid, and impossible notion. They had tried that before.

"What does this mean, Amanda? Why did you do that?"

"I don't know."

"You know."

Silence fell between them like a lead weight, dragging them both down into their respective thoughts.

She took a shuddering breath. "I got caught up thinking how this job makes us so vulnerable, and there's so much uncertainty."

"So you kissed me because you were feeling your mortality?" His words came as a slap to her face.

The back of her neck tightened, and her cheeks heated. She squared her shoulders. "As you said, you're to blame too."

"*Pft.* Unbelievable." He pivoted and swept out the front door.

Her stupid mouth had opened, words tumbled out, and she'd managed to make things worse. She stood there, cursing her stupidity and impulsiveness. There was no justification for what she had done. After a few beats, she went upstairs to retrieve the threats, cash, and passport. Once she was armed with those, she reengaged the security system and locked up.

Through the car window, she saw Trent slapping his palms against the steering wheel, not the exaggerated movements of a temperamental person in a rage, but someone who was battling frustration. This was all her fault. All because she'd acted on a damn impulse. Her life was usually so well structured, every decision premeditated. Just this once she'd left the rails and look where it had gotten her. Sadly, the immediate consequences would bloom into awkwardness and regret. Trent was her partner. He had her back, and she had his. He understood her better than she did herself sometimes and even he was put at a loss by her actions. But no wonder. She hadn't played according to script.

Amanda glanced back at the house, wanting to put off the conversation that needed to happen. Also the genuine apology she owed him. It wasn't a secret how Trent felt about her, about her relationship with Logan, and she'd just toyed with his heart.

Nancy Orr stepped onto her front stoop and waved a solemn goodbye. Amanda dipped her head in response, loaded into the passenger seat, and did up her belt.

Trent had the car running, and heat was seeping from the vents, but he didn't pull out of the driveway. He wasn't looking at her either.

She pinched her eyes shut. "I can't apologize enough. What I did was uncalled for and unprofessional."

"Jeez, Mandy. *Unprofessional?* Is that what you're going to hurl at me?" He looked over her, the pain in his eyes transforming them into a cold deep blue.

"I just mean that we're partners. On the job," she was quick to add.

"Right. I see you how you saw fit to emphasize that point."

She opened her mouth, but words failed her.

"Were you thinking at all? You're with Logan. Whatever our feelings, they need to be left unexplored. And that's fine, I get it. I even started accepting it." He smacked the wheel again and shook his head.

She wanted to reach out to soothe him but resisted the urge to make physical contact. It would only make things worse. "It will never happen again."

"No. It won't." He started to drive, and she couldn't get herself to ask where he was taking them.

Her heart was beating in an uneven rhythm, and a headache was moving in. The tension in the car was suffocating. She'd done this to them, all because she let her thoughts carry her away, sweeping her into a frenzy of fear and uncertainty about the future. She'd leaned on Trent, when she should have turned to Logan, and that wasn't fair. In fact, she'd have hurt two men she cared about once she came clean to Logan. But what was she going to tell him? Did she want to break things off and talk with Trent about pursuing whatever sparks existed between them? An ache burned in her chest, because if she were being honest with herself, her feelings for Trent were the real deal.

FIFTEEN

Not knowing where Trent was taking them compounded the tension in the car. Was he taking them to Manassas for Leah Bernard's autopsy? If so, they'd be at least thirty minutes late. It was 10 AM and due to start now. Regardless of their destination, Amanda could hardly wait to get there. Being confined to a vehicle, and so close to him, was intense. The air pulsed with an electrical current of conflicting emotions. Regret and excitement clashed as did anger and happiness. For her, she was also confused about what this meant for her relationship with Logan. If she loved him as much as she thought, then she wouldn't be kissing her partner.

Amanda tried to focus on the road, and soon recognized the route they were on. A few minutes later, Trent pulled into a spot at Central and turned the car off. She reached for the door, but he didn't move. It had her hesitating and looking over at him.

"I'm seeing someone," he said, his voice low. When she hadn't responded for a few seconds, he glanced over.

"Well, that's good." She pressed on a smile, but it was weak and had faltered before it fully formed.

"I shouldn't have kissed you and vice versa."

"I think we've covered that." She hated being so full of guilt and just wanted it to go away, along with the memory of what had happened. Forgetting and moving forward would have to work for her.

"You're right. We're beating a dead horse." He gave her a glimmer of a smirk, but it faded quickly. "But what if..."

She could piece together what he seemed daring enough to consider. That they pursue whatever *this* was and see where it took them. But that would involve a lot of upheaval when a relationship between them might not even work out. This wasn't just about them either. Other people were involved, and Zoe loved Logan. Amanda shook her head, tears beaded in her eyes.

"Yeah, what I thought."

She cleared her throat. "I'll let you decide what happens from here, from a professional standpoint. I understand if you want to report this and request a new partner."

"Just when I think you know me better than anyone, you spew that shit?" He got out of the car and left her behind, trembling.

She was such an idiot. This just proved the intelligence of thinking things through *before* acting. Amanda took some time before leaving the car. It wasn't until several minutes later that she caught up with Trent in his cubicle.

She stood tall and latched on to the job to see her through this. If she put her concentration on the investigation, she wouldn't have the bandwidth to keep overthinking her blunder. "Natasha Bauer should be in the office now. I'll call her."

"Hold up. I'm already one step ahead of you." He pointed to his monitor, where he had the directory listing for the district attorney's office.

There was no need to say anything. Her partner was back, and so was she. At least for all intents and purposes.

He called the number on speaker, and a curt receptionist

answered with a stilted greeting.

Trent told her who they were and that they needed to speak with Natasha Bauer.

"ADA Bauer is unavailable, but I can take a message."

"Is there any way you could give us her cell phone number?" Trent asked, beating Amanda to that question.

A slight pause, then, "You expect me to accept you are who you say you are?"

"Call the PWCPD. Have them put you through to my desk if that's what you need to do," Trent volleyed back, thinking quick.

"It wouldn't make a difference. I'm not at liberty to give out her mobile, but I can leave a message for her to call you back."

Trent parted with his number, full name, and badge number and added that it was regarding a very urgent, life-and-death matter.

"I'll pass this along." The receptionist hung up without a goodbye.

"Wasn't she a ray of sunshine?" Amanda said, trying to insert some levity, though she realized how badly she was failing at that endeavor.

"In her defense, she probably has to screen a lot of whack-a-dos."

"True enough. I just hate sitting around though. There must be something we can do." She was racking her brain to think of what that *something* might be. All they could do was already in motion, leaving them in limbo. They still didn't have Katherine's call history or the location of her Mercedes.

"Glad you're here." Malone sidled up to the opening of Trent's cubicle, a piece of paper in hand. "GPS on Graves's Mercedes came back and shows it being at Captain Ron's Beach Marina in Lorton since six-oh-five."

And just when she feared she'd be left twiddling her thumbs. "Let's hit the road."

SIXTEEN

Lorton was just a ten-minute drive from Central. Amanda was keeping her expectations grounded about Katherine's Mercedes aiding the investigation. But she had expected to spot the car when Trent pulled into the lot for the marina. "Am I just failing to see it?" She squinted in the morning sun.

"If you are, so am I."

Malone in his sergeant's SUV and two officers in police cruisers accompanied them to the marina. Everyone parked and gathered for an impromptu meeting.

Malone's cheeks were a bright red like he was about to lose his temper. Trent was quiet, the angles of his face hardened. She couldn't be sure if it was disappointment or if he was stewing over what they had done. She had to release it.

The Occoquan River was mere feet away. The boat slips were empty as all the vessels would have been winterized for the season. "I'm not sure how deep the water is right off the boat ramp, but would the Mercedes send off its GPS location if it was submerged?"

"Don't know about that, but this could just be the last area it gave off a signal," Trent said. "One possibility is the accomplice or the shooter disabled the GPS system."

Amanda mulled over the options. If they ditched the Mercedes in the river, it suggested the shooter and his accomplice convened here and left in the van. If they disabled the GPS, that provided more uncertainty for the investigation, though they must realize the car could still be flagged from the active BOLO. She said, "It wouldn't hurt to get divers out to take a look around."

"We'll stick a pin in that for a bit." Malone walked over to the water's edge and looked down.

Amanda stepped up next to him, and all she saw was black ink and her reflection.

"If they dumped it, we can kiss goodbye to forensic trace," Malone said, scratching at his beard, his forehead wrinkled into deep furrows. "And divers take a beat or two to arrange."

His hesitance to move on this told her he wanted more to support ordering a dive team. Amanda looked around, striving for some grand epiphany. Then she paced and thought.

Given the time of year, the marina was pretty much abandoned. That made it an excellent choice for a clandestine rendezvous point but for what purpose? It seemed they'd planned the abduction, so it stood to reason they had an endpoint in mind. Why not just drive straight there with him in the van and the woman in the Mercedes?

Her earlier thought returned. *The boat slips are empty...* She turned her attention to the large billboard on the side of a huge warehouse where boats were stored for the winter. She smiled and pointed at the sign. "They promise their customers twenty-four-hour surveillance."

"Well that's a good start." Trent sounded pleased but didn't look at her.

"Let me call the number." Malone pulled his phone out and walked a few feet away.

Amanda turned to Trent. "We did discuss that we're possibly dealing with professionals. It might better support them having the capability of disabling GPS. That's assuming they did."

"But why come here at all? Were they obtuse to the ad on the side of the warehouse, to the fact there are cameras? It would have made more sense for them to stop on a country road."

She wasn't close-minded to the possibility of the Mercedes being in the river either, but said, "I don't have all the answers, but they'd know we'd be a while behind them. We need to watch the video, to start. Building on what you said, I'm not sure they are too intimidated by cameras. They did take her from Fill N Go. They'd have to know they'd have them there."

"The duo isn't exactly camera shy, though they hid their faces. They must have known there could have been other casualties, but that didn't stop them from going ahead."

"Whoever they are, they are highly organized, highly motivated. They even had foresight to put tinted plate covers on the van."

"They seem willing to do whatever necessary. Thugs for hire?"

"That would be a nightmare and make tracking down whoever it is even harder. I don't think we'd be far off the mark to assume these people have criminal records though. His prints could be in the system and be why he wore gloves. But did he think of that when loading his bullets?"

"If not, he might have left prints on the casings. That would be unprofessional, but so was leaving them at the scene. They're not an elite kidnapping crew, whoever they are."

She'd fire a quick message to Blair, but she had confidence the CSI would be processing the casings for prints.

"I think this guy possibly killed before too," Trent said. "He didn't seem to hesitate to pull that trigger."

Amanda's mind flashed to what she'd seen on that video, and Trent was on the mark with his comment. The shooter had raised the gun and fired without hesitation. He also had good aim.

Malone returned to them. "Good news. Two cameras cover the lot, and the manager's coming in now. Should be here in less than ten."

"Good news," she said, half-distracted, trying to resurrect that glimpse of an epiphany. Just before his return, a thought was edging in. Now it was gone.

"Really? You sound like I ran over your dog."

"Don't mean to. Trent and I were just talking everything through. The shooter and his partner seemed to have planned everything out, starting with the tinted plate covers on the van." Amanda told him their speculation about the shooting and the background of the perps, or perpetrators of a crime.

"And they aren't shy taking her from a public place," Malone said thoughtfully. "Brazen."

Trent was nodding. "Or driven. That makes it more likely it's someone Graves had a hand in putting away. If we pursue that angle, we can release the idea of a hired third party."

"A gun for hire," Malone said as if chewing on it. "I'd keep the theory in play. They did take Katherine alive. It could be to deliver her to someone."

Amanda still didn't want to give too much thought to that. "I have a message in with Katherine's former lieutenant at the NYPD, and Trent left one for her best friend back in New York." With that, the earlier slippery epiphany came into focus. "It doesn't have to be someone Katherine wronged directly. It could be someone *in*directly affected."

"Jeez. Doesn't that open a barrel of monkeys," Malone said. "Where could we possibly start?"

This was yet another question she didn't have an answer

for. She leaned back on one fact. "There haven't been any ransom demands yet."

Malone shook his head. "Still lots of time for that. We're hardly into the first twenty-four hours. And this might not be about money at all."

"Which leads us to ask again, what is it about?" Trent interjected, his rhetorical comment serving as a break in the conversation.

"Any progress on Katherine's hidden stash?" Malone asked. "Ideally, any clue where that key belongs?"

She refused to say she didn't know again. Even she had her self-esteem. Thankfully, though, she had an idea. "Most luxury makes have apps that allow owners to see the status of their vehicle at any given time. Obviously if the GPS system was tampered with this won't help us moving forward, but it should include some travel history." Amanda knew this because her brother, Kyle, loved motor vehicles and made his livelihood running a garage. He also insisted on sharing his knowledge.

"All right, I already have a contact at Mercedes Corporate," Malone began. "I'll reach out and ask about that app and if it will give us what we're after."

"Sounds great. Thanks, boss," Amanda said.

A red Chevrolet sedan pulled into the lot, a balding man behind the wheel.

"Here we go." Malone swiped his arm through the air to get them moving toward the marina building.

The man got out of his car but didn't venture far.

"Mr. Orchid?" Malone asked.

The man ran a hand over his head. "That's me. You, ah, can call me Edward."

"Sergeant Malone, and Detectives Steele, and Stenson." He gestured to them, in turn, as he introduced them.

"You wanted to see the video?" Edward waved awkwardly

toward the building as if he were a wounded bird flapping a wing.

"That we do."

The group of them walked to the structure, including the uniformed officers. Malone backstepped to talk to them. Amanda looked over her shoulder to see them both retreat to their cruisers. One left, the other got in his vehicle but stayed put.

Malone rejoined them as Trent's phone rang. Amanda hung back with him as he took the call.

"Detective Stenson," he answered.

Her impulse was to get close to him to see if she could hear his caller, but given their recent *slip*, it was best she kept her distance.

"You tried everything?... Uh-huh... okay. Thanks." He pocketed his phone. "That was a detective from Digital Forensics. They couldn't get anything from the burner. No call history. Nada."

"It could have been brand-new and never used."

"*Or* Katherine intentionally deleted her history as she went along."

Amanda didn't like the sound of that. It was mysterious enough that she had one to begin with, but if she took efforts to keep it clear, she really didn't want to risk anyone getting their hands on the phone.

What are you hiding, Katherine?

SEVENTEEN

The marina office was cluttered with paper. It was spread across the desk and fanned over a sizeable bulletin board. The room smelled heavily of motor oil and wood, and it was doubtful the space had ever seen the business end of a duster or vacuum. But the computer was state of the art, something Edward proudly told them. He said the same applied to the security system.

"The video is HD quality," Edward added as he sat behind a desk.

"Please just bring up six AM today," Malone said.

Edward brought up the footage from the camera that covered the rear of the warehouse and offered a glimpse of the river in the back. They watched it play for several minutes, but nothing was happening.

"Could we try the other camera, please," Amanda requested.

This footage covered more of the parking lot and afforded a better sightline of the water. They were quickly rewarded with Katherine's Mercedes coming into view. The driver was still wearing the balaclava they had been at the gas station. It had turned out to be too much to expect they had gotten careless and removed it.

On the screen, the Mercedes was parked next to the water. Their theories had been the car was run into the river or the GPS was disabled.

The driver remained in the car and was leaning toward the dash, doing something.

"I think she's disabling the GPS," Trent said. "In plain view of the camera, no less."

A few minutes later, the woman put new license plates on the vehicle and left the lot in the Mercedes.

"Does she think this will help her escape the BOLO?" Malone said. "I'll just have it updated. Can you get a close-up of the new plates she puts on?"

Edward reversed and zoomed in. "Yep."

"Print it," Malone told him.

Edward complied.

"Thank you," Amanda said, not worried about stepping on Malone's toes. It wasn't this man's fault that Katherine's life was in danger, and he'd been nothing but helpful and cooperative.

Edward smiled and handed the printout to Malone, who passed it off to Trent.

"So, she disables the GPS and changes the plates," Amanda said. "Is she meeting up with her partner or just making off with Katherine's Mercedes?" She turned to Edward. "Can you replay all of this from the moment the car entered the lot?"

"Sure can."

Amanda watched the driver extra closely this time. "Pause it there," she rushed out.

The footage froze on the driver about to get back into the car. She stood still, facing the camera.

"She must have known she was being recorded," Trent said and looked at Amanda.

"She's staring right at the camera." Malone gestured toward the monitor. "Too bad she's still wearing the balaclava."

"Still, it goes back to our earlier conversation," Trent began. "Why would she even stop here if there was the risk of being caught on video?"

There must have been a purpose. She even took the time to change the license plates. Was it defiance or a cry for help? Her body language didn't support the former, rather the latter. Her shoulders were sagging. "Play it in slow motion, please."

The feed moved forward at a crawl.

"There. Just before she gets in the car, her chest heaves and her shoulders rise with a deep breath," Amanda said. It was clear to see despite the bulky coat she wore.

"So?" Malone looked at her, one eyebrow cocked up.

"What if she's been forced into this?" Amanda pivoted toward Trent, but the brief eye contact was awkward and he looked away. She was delusional to think he could just let their kiss go. "Given what we just saw, I suspect that's a real possibility," she added, trying to stifle her discomfort.

"Whatever the case, she's in this now up to her neck," Malone inserted.

"There are just the two exterior cameras?" Amanda was thinking if there was one that covered the exit, they might see which direction the Mercedes had gone from here.

"That's right."

She nodded. There wasn't much in the immediate area, but there were some rural properties that could afford isolation if that was the shooter's intent. But they couldn't knock on every door. It would be a waste of time. Besides, they didn't know how far they'd taken Katherine. The fact the woman changed the plates might suggest a road trip, and she didn't want the BOLO on Katherine's license causing her trouble. But as Malone pointed out, she changed them within view of a camera, putting the new ones on right where they could see them.

They left Edward with a request to send a copy of the video to CSI Blair and headed to the car.

Trent tapped the plate number into the onboard computer while she and Malone waited outside the driver's door.

Trent sat back a few seconds later. "The plates expired six months ago. They were registered to a Greg Elliott of Wood-bridge and last associated with a Hyundai Elantra."

"Go talk to him," Malone said.

Trent's phone rang, and he answered with his title and added, "Thank you for returning my call so quickly."

Malone spoke quietly to Amanda. "Keep me posted, and I will you. I'll update the BOLO and get on that GPS history."

Amanda nodded, and Malone left in his SUV. The other officer in the cruiser followed him. Shortly after, Edward came out of the marina building and got into his car and left.

Trent was waving for her to come closer and he cupped his phone. "It's Natasha Bauer."

"Put her on speaker."

He informed the woman that his partner, Detective Steele, would be joining them. Once Trent made the call hands free, he said to the ADA, "We heard that you're friends with Katherine Graves. Is that correct?"

Several beats of silence.

"Ms. Bauer?" Amanda prompted.

"That's right. We've been friends since college days. Is she all right?"

The question had Amanda's shoulders and the skin on the back of her neck tightening. It was almost as if Natasha expected an issue with Katherine. "It's hard to say. There has been an incident."

A puff of air traveled the line. "I wish I could say it's a surprise, but... What happened to her?"

Trent responded. "Ms. Bauer, two perps have taken Katherine. This came in the aftermath of shooting an eighteen-year-old girl dead."

Silence, then, "I'm at a loss for words."

That reaction surprised Amanda. As an ADA, she'd need to think quickly under pressure, but their news had made her speechless. Amanda was getting mixed signals for what that might mean and went with one. "The fact Katherine is in trouble isn't a surprise to you, is it?"

"Let's just say that Kat liked to put her nose in people's business. And, yes, I realize that's part of a cop's job. You're never going to win a popularity contest, but when she worked for the NYPD, she was a real disrupter. As much as I admired her for it, I feared it might catch up with her."

"A disrupter?" Trent asked.

"She'd push through cases with hard-headed tenacity. Her goal was always justice."

Amanda respected the intention but that ambition would have made her enemies. "Can you think of any cases that might have come back to bite her?" She'd bring up the threats but was taking things one step at a time.

"It's hard to pick one. She was involved with several dark cases. Her largest takedown was putting the Devil's Saints gang out of business."

"I've never heard of them," Amanda said, but she couldn't claim to be up on New York City gangs either.

"They were basically in their infancy but growing fast. They were already in deep with weapons smuggling and starting to dip into prostitution and the sex trafficking of minors. That's around the time Katherine made it her mission to bring them down."

Amanda's respect for the former interim sergeant just went up several notches. She could relate to Katherine since Amanda was also involved with bringing down a sex-trafficking ring in Prince

William County just over two years ago. This all explained why Katherine was so affected when a previous investigation involved the murder of six-year-old girls. While sexual assault hadn't been a factor, the murder of young children was an obvious trigger point. The case may have smacked close to her history and torn the scab.

"She was successful in bringing them down," Trent said, "so I assume the members were sent to prison."

"All of them. Most received ten- and fifteen-year sentences. Some got life."

This knowledge also resurrected their theory of a hired gun. The type of people under discussion typically had a reach from behind bars. Amanda explained this hypothetical to Natasha.

"I can request a record of their communications, though it's the ones that happen off the books that are more concerning."

And those would be the ones Amanda was most interested in being privy to. Ordering a hit wouldn't be made through legit channels. "A good start might be the names of these gang members."

"Consider it done. When we finish this call, I'll get my assistant to send over those names."

"Thank you. When did they go away?" she asked.

"Eight years ago."

Amanda's thinking returned to the basis for their arrests. Eight years might feel like a long time to hold a grudge, but Katherine had stolen their business, livelihood, and freedom. In that vein, their memories would never fade. Often time served was halved if an inmate showed good behavior. "You said the minimum sentence was a dime, but were any released early recently?"

"I'm to be notified if that happens. A memo of that sort hasn't come through to my desk."

Amanda didn't want to come across as skeptical, but the system wasn't perfect. "Could this have fallen through the cracks?"

"I mean, anything is possible. I'll follow up, but I'm more concerned that a friend or relative of a gang member may have gotten to Kat."

"Did any of them make threats against her?" Trent asked.

"Oh, yeah. She received several."

Amanda took a deep breath. With the ADA's help, they might have a real chance of saving Katherine.

EIGHTEEN

Amanda took several seconds to process what the New York Assistant District Attorney had just told them. Threats were made against Katherine from affiliates of the gang. Had they discovered a sampling of these in Katherine's drawer? "We found some typewritten threats addressed to Katherine in her home office. They were dropped off in person, not signed or dated," Amanda disclosed. Then she told Natasha what they said.

"You ruined my life. I will ruin yours."

"You owe me. I'm coming to collect."

"You lie. I will expose the truth and bring you to your knees."

"You will hurt. I will get you alone one day."

"Huh. Those threats strike me as rather simple. Each are two sentences and start with *you*. I'd say whoever sent them blames Katherine for something."

The ADA's reasoning was sound, but to hear it in so many words landed with impact. "Did she tell you about these threats?"

"No, if she had, I'd remember and would have encouraged her to report them. It's not like anyone is telling Kat what to do."

There was no advantage to dwelling on how things might have been different if Katherine had confided in someone. "You're sending a list with the names of the gang members, but if I were to ask for one name that comes to mind right away, who would that be? This person would pose the most threat to Katherine."

"Elias Rush." The name glided from Natasha's tongue. She added, "He's the older brother of one of the gang's ringleaders."

Amanda tapped the name into the notepad app on her phone. "And the name of the ringleader?"

"Ollie."

"And what was his sentence?" Amanda asked.

"Life."

"Elias get any time?" Trent asked.

"No, he wasn't directly caught up in the gang."

"But is still a dangerous guy?" An assumption as the ADA saw fit to go straight to his name.

"He's an uncertainty. He has a juvie record, if I remember, but nothing charged against him as an adult as far as I know. He takes protecting his little brother quite seriously though."

"Quite a blow then, Ollie being sentenced to life," Trent pushed out.

"Oh, yeah."

"Then you can see Elias writing these threats and/or coming after Katherine?" Putting it out there so directly had Amanda's heart racing. *Could this be the lead we're after?*

"Hard to say, and a number of years have passed."

"I thought of that, but she didn't just send them away to prison, she put them out of business," Amanda said. "Not to mention they'd have a lot of free time to plan their revenge."

"True enough, and there's not a time limit on payback. I have seen cases where people have waited twenty years to retaliate."

"Does this Ollie have a lot of power and influence over anyone on the outside besides his brother?" Trent asked.

"I'm sure he does, not that I can point you anywhere. His closest friends worked by his side and are also behind bars. They have their own connections." Natasha gave them two names, and Amanda pecked them into her phone.

"If we wanted to speak with these characters, is that something you could arrange?" Trent asked.

"Absolutely. I'm assuming you'd be interested in video conferencing?"

"That would be the most efficient and budget conscious." There was no way Malone would justify the expense of flying them to New York City, and driving there and back would take up time they didn't have.

"I'll get it taken care of immediately."

"Just before you go," Trent interjected. "Who was Katherine's partner when she was a detective?"

"Mickey Fitzgerald. Good cop. He still works as a homicide detective with the NYPD. He's a lifer. He might have some names for you too."

"Thanks," Trent told her, and the call ended.

"She was a wealth of information," Amanda said.

"That she was, and she handled the news with far more grace than I'd have expected."

"Part shock, part a career choice that demands she keep grounded." Amanda suspected the strong and fearless ADA was crumbling in her New York office right now. "Could you pull a background on this Elias Rush just quick?" He was still seated behind the wheel, the onboard computer within arm's reach.

"You bet." He clicked on the keyboard, and Amanda leaned into the car as the results filled in. She drew back when the smell of his cologne hit her, which was a blend of cedarwood mixed with notes of citrus and the sea.

Too close for comfort.

Trent said, "His current residence is in NYC. No criminal record. Looks like he got married a few years ago."

"Huh." She should have known that expecting a glaring new criminal record or a tie to Prince William County was too much.

"Dead end there, but we have Graves's partner's name. I say we call him and see what he might tell us."

She gestured for him to go ahead, and he called on speaker. "We could ask him to talk with Elias."

"Great idea."

The line was ringing, and it wasn't long before they were patched through to Mickey's extension.

"Detective Fitz." Two words, and an evident thick Bronx accent.

Trent announced who they were, namely detectives with the Prince William County PD in Woodbridge, Virginia.

"What can I do for ya?" His accent had *for* sounding like *fawh*. Despite the fact his day was probably jampacked, he didn't give the impression this call was an unwelcome interruption to his day. There was the hint of hesitancy though, as if he were weighing Trent's credibility.

Trent told Mickey about Katherine's abduction and added, "We're digging into her life to see who might have motive to do this. We thought you might be able to steer us in a direction."

"Well, she has been gone from the NYPD for the better part of two years now."

"Grudges last longer than that," Amanda said. "Surely, there's someone she put away that has it in for her."

Mickey pushed out a chuckle but stopped abruptly. "Not really the time for amusement, I know. It's just there's a prison full of people who hate Kat. But you know that's part of the job."

"We're not in it to make friends, that's for sure," Amanda

said. "We understand that Katherine had the tendency to push people, to get resolution." No matter the fact she'd worked with the woman for a while, she couldn't surrender to abbreviating her name. It struck Amanda as too informal for their relationship, but then again, Mickey and Katherine had worked as equal ranks.

"She was that. That's what makes it hard to know where to direct you. Actually— Ah, nah, he wouldn't even know where to find her."

Trent faced Amanda, and they made brief eye contact before he turned toward the windshield again.

"Here's the thing," Amanda started. "Katherine made news in the local paper, and it's also available online. She's also working with her aunt at her successful diner and has received public attention for that."

"Shit. Then he might have caught up with her."

Again with *he*. Tingles ran down Amanda's arms. "Who is this person?"

"Lowell Mooney. He's lowlife scum who just got released a week ago. He was sent away for fifteen years for killing the mother of his son when she was awarded full custody. Guy was a druggie and a deadbeat."

Amanda enjoyed how his accent flowered his words, such as transforming *mother* to *mudder*. What he was saying wasn't as pleasant. "And it was Katherine who made the collar?"

"You bet. She even testified in court against the guy. There was a history of mutual abuse. The mother was no cherry either, but she held a steady job and provided a roof over the boy's head."

"You sure he'd go after Katherine after all this time?" Trent inserted.

"I wouldn't put it past the guy. Assuming prison hasn't changed him, I can see him on the rampage to get back at Kat. He's never going to see his son again, and even though that's on him, he blamed Kat. I'll go by his place and have a chat."

The slights he'd mentioned could support the messages and tone of the typewritten threats they'd found. "Sounds like a good idea. Maybe you could also talk with Elias Rush."

"Oh, you found out about him, did ya? He's another good suspect. Has himself a dangerous brother too."

"Who we're told is locked up on a life sentence," Amanda volleyed.

"He is that, but hardened criminals have ways of working out carnage from behind bars."

This detective wasn't one to sugarcoat things, which she appreciated.

"Elias looks like he's a family man these days," Trent put out there.

"Don't let that fool ya. I'll drop by and feel him out too."

"Do you know of any written threats to Kat?" Trent asked.

"There were some over the years, not that I have any idea where I'd look for that now. She could have taken them with her or destroyed them, but she didn't seem to take them too seriously. Though she did up and leave in a blur."

That was news. Amanda had been curious what had her moving to Prince William County, before learning about her relation to May Byrd. Her previous online "research" led her to believe Katherine had been squeezed out when a relative of the police chief took over her position. If that was the case surely Mickey would have said as much. "Do you know why?"

"She said it was time, that she did all she could here. A load of crap. I mean, obviously. We're a city of nearly nine million people. We only oversee a chunk of that, but there's enough crime to keep everyone in blue busy day and night."

"Your personal opinion for why she moved?" Trent asked.

"Her mother was murdered. Maybe she felt she had no reason to stay."

"Had she lived in NYC all her life?" Amanda countered.

"From what I know, yeah."

Katherine would have sacrificed a lot by moving. "I'm sure she had friends who didn't want to see her leave." The detective might be able to give them some names. All they had was Natasha Bauer.

"Oh, I'm not sure Kat had much of a social life. She lived for the job."

That sounded like what May and Katherine's neighbor had told them. They'd also said it seemed Katherine was holding something back from them. Mickey might know what that was. "So you don't think she was running away from someone? Possibly a person who scared her?"

"If she was, she wasn't telling me. Then again, near the end, she was my boss and we didn't shoot the shit much. I wish I could be of more help."

"Hey, you're going to talk to those two people we discussed, that's a big help," Amanda said.

"All right, well, keep me posted. If there's anything else I can do that might help, I'm here. Once I have anything to offer, I'll call you." His voice was tight and full of emotion. The thought of Katherine out there with a killer obviously shook him to the core.

"Thanks, Detective Fitzgerald," Trent responded.

"Fitz. It's just Fitz to anyone who's a friend of Kat's. And there's no need to thank me, not when Kat's in trouble. I'll do whatever I can to help."

Before Trent ended the call, he left his and Amanda's phone numbers. "We go from zero leads to what feels like a hundred." Trent was looking straight out the window while he spoke. Overwhelm was written in the downward curve of his mouth, and his furrowed brow.

"I hear you." Her phone chimed with a message. "And speaking of..." She read it and shared the gist with Trent.

"Katherine's phone records are in, and her financials are expected soon. CCTV has come in from the area near the gas station. Nothing telling. There's no CCTV near the marina."

"That just gives us a fighting chance of catching up. Next stop, the owner of the expired plates, Greg Elliott?"

"You read my mind." She smiled, but he left the expression unreturned and put the car into gear. This tension was her fault. Hopefully she hadn't messed things up between them beyond repair.

NINETEEN

Despite the leads coming at them, Amanda couldn't help but notice there was one missing. She still hadn't heard back from the NYPD police lieutenant, and she put in another call to him while Trent drove to the address on file for Greg Elliott.

The lieutenant answered on the second ring. All business and treated the call as an interruption to his day. Based on initial impression, he and Detective Fitzgerald couldn't be any more different.

"Detective Steele from Homicide with the Prince William County PD."

There was a pause in which she imagined him sarcastically thinking, *congratulations*. "I'm calling about a former sergeant of yours, Katherine Graves," she told him.

"What about her?" Asked stiffly, on the defensive.

Did he even listen to his voicemail? "She was abducted this morning. During which incident a teenage girl was shot and killed." Whether or not Warren Catherwood liked things told to him straight, that's how she served the news.

"Sorry to hear that."

Four words that could be viewed as throwaway, but

Amanda detected a bit of an emotional edge to his voice. Catherwood was just good at blocking his emotions with a tough veneer. She'd wager he hadn't heard her message, which was preferable to him dismissing it. "My partner and I have been digging into her past to see who might have reason to come after her."

"Katherine was a highly respected officer of the NYPD. She put away a lot of criminals during her career here, as I'm sure she has while working with you."

From the present tense, he wasn't aware that she'd exchanged her badge for an apron. "She's no longer with the PWCPD, but she's still living in the area. I assume she reported to you before she left the NYPD."

"She did."

"Was she working any cases that may have caught up with her?"

"You suspect a perp followed her to Virginia?"

The lilt in his voice made Prince William County sound like it was some backwater and inferior to the Big Apple. It was apparent the idea of anyone being attracted to a slower pace of life was absurd. Though given the number of murders around here, the county was anything but slower paced. "That's exactly what I'm getting at."

Trent stopped for a red light and leaned his ear a bit closer to her to eavesdrop on the conversation. She hadn't put the call on speaker to avoid it being a distraction.

"As I said, she put away a lot of criminals," Catherwood said. "I wouldn't know where to start. Although there was one case she couldn't seem to let go of, but I'm talking many years ago, before she became a sergeant."

"I'm listening."

"I doubt it has any bearing on the present situation, but there was a young girl who was murdered. The leads dried up, and the case went cold. Katherine became obsessive. I told her she had to release it if she was ever going to advance rank."

ADA Natasha Bauer hadn't mentioned this case. She must not have sensed a threat there to Katherine's well-being. Or was it in the context of their discussion? For this investigation, Katherine hadn't sent anyone to prison. "How long ago was this?"

"Ten years."

In this scenario, ten years was a long time, especially when Katherine didn't pose a threat to anyone. She had been told to let the case go.

The light turned green, and they were on the move again. Trent took the next right, parked shortly thereafter, and pointed toward a white-sided house. It must be the home of Greg Elliott.

She nodded, but said into her phone, "Why did Katherine leave the NYPD?"

"She talked about a fresh start, and within a year of her mother's murder gave her resignation. Why she chose small-town Virginia, I don't know, but she seemed in a hurry to leave."

Yet another dig at the county.

He added, "I was sad to see her go. As I said, good cop."

Amanda was humble enough to admit when she was wrong. Her first impression that the lieutenant didn't care had missed the mark. "So as far as you know, Katherine wasn't scared of anyone?"

"No way. Katherine's fearless, or she was when I knew her."

Is he implying small-town living has made her soft? "Well, thank you for taking the time to talk to me."

"Don't mention it. I will pray that you find her all right, and it's awfully sad about that teen."

"Thank you." Amanda ended the call and sat there with her phone in her palm.

"Since I don't have the ears of a bat, could you bring me up to speed?" Trent turned to face her.

She filled him on what she'd learned from Lieutenant Catherwood.

"So talking to him was a bust, it would seem," Trent said.

"It doesn't advance things much, no." She butted her head toward the house. "I'm taking it this is the Elliott house?"

"Yep." He shut off the car and was the first to get out.

She followed him down the walkway to the front door, catching up only once he stopped to ring the bell.

Footsteps padded toward them, and a shadow marked the sidelight. It was the smaller frame of a woman. The door inched open. "What is it?"

Trent already had his badge held up and kept it there as he announced them as police and requested to speak with Greg Elliott.

The door was opened wider. "Greg should be at work. He *is* at work?" The woman was somewhere in her forties, and she struck Amanda as socially awkward and shy. It sounded like she was asking *them* where her husband was.

"We don't know, ma'am. That's why we're here looking for him," Trent said kindly.

"What's this about?" An edge creeped into her voice, and she narrowed her eyes.

"Who are you, ma'am?" Trent asked, again pulling out charm by adding *ma'am*.

"Greg's wife of twenty years."

"Then you might be able to help us," Amanda interjected.

Trent moved aside, and a cold front moved in.

Amanda bristled but stayed focused. "Your husband had plates registered to his name, which have since expired."

"Are we in trouble over that?"

"We need to know who might have them now." Trent pulled out his tablet and told the lady the plate number.

"Oh, those are the plates we had on the Elantra. Come to think of it, I don't recall ever getting those back. Greg got into an accident, and the car was deemed a complete write-off then and there. It was a miracle he walked away. I suppose the plates were the last thing on our minds. But we took the opportunity to upgrade." She smiled now. "Got ourselves a brand-new Toyota and some custom plates."

Depending on the severity of an accident, the vehicles involved either went to a body shop for repair or straight to a place to be demolished. Either way, Greg should have been contacted about his plates. If he didn't want them returned, the plates would have been made invalid and shredded by the Department of Motor Vehicles. Greg would have needed to sign off on that. Amanda asked Mrs. Elliott if he had.

"Hmm. Well, you'd be best to talk to Greg. Or you could just ask the place that scrapped the car? It did go right there after the accident."

"And where would that be?" Amanda asked.

"I'm quite sure it was Eco-Friendly Auto Recyclers that compacted it."

They had demolished her first jalopy, and her first case with Trent took them there. It was run by an ex-con named Simon Wheable. He was a shady character, and Amanda was starting to consider just how shady. Plates should be removed and returned to their owner or destroyed in this situation. In this case, they obviously hadn't been. "When and where was the accident?" This could help them if they ended up going to Eco-Friendly.

"It was a year and a half ago, give or take." Then she told them where the accident had happened.

License registrations were renewed yearly. The Elliotts must have just done that days prior to the accident for it to be expired for six months.

"Thank you for your help," Trent told her.

The woman didn't reply, and the door was slowly closed in their faces.

Trent put his tablet away, avoiding Amanda's eyes. There was no missing that the air between them remained tense.

Back at the car, he shut the driver's door hard, and the vehicle's chassis rocked. "I didn't need you to jump in back there."

She closed her door, did up her belt, and turned to him. She didn't even need to ask what he was referring to. His energy had changed when she inserted herself into the conversation, telling the woman she might be able to help them. "You had things under control, and I shouldn't have stepped in. You're right, and I'm sorry."

He didn't say anything in response.

"If this is also about... Well, you know what, then we need to talk and clear the air. If we can't put what happened behind us, then we'll need to talk to Malone."

She counted off fifteen seconds before he spoke.

"That's jumping the gun. It was only a few hours ago. Anyway, I can put it behind me. Can you?" He looked at her now, his gaze hardened over, and it delivered a punch to her gut.

"I can. The last thing I want is to jeopardize our relationship."

"There is no relationship, Amanda." He slowly turned his head toward her again. "Isn't that what you told me right from the start? There is supposed to be a distinct line between our professional and personal lives."

He was using her words against her. She told him this when they first became partners. At the time she was still very much reeling from the loss of her husband and daughter. She wasn't interested in forming bonds with anyone, and she certainly hadn't wanted a partner. "I was a different person then. You know that, and we've become good friends since."

"Right. *Friends.* Foremost, coworkers. If we're going to do this job effectively, we can't—" He stopped talking as if mustering up the right words to continue.

"Can't what?" she nudged him.

"Keep crossing the freaking line, Amanda," he snapped. "We're either friends and coworkers, or we put in for new partners and pursue whatever sparks are between us."

Just that proposal had her heart fluttering against her ribcage. *Logan. Zoe.* She loved Logan, Zoe loved him, he was family to them. He moved in this past spring. They rearranged their lives to make *them* work.

When she didn't respond, he said, "The woman I'm seeing is nice. We get along well." He left the accolades there, but a flicker in his eyes exposed his vulnerability.

She sensed he would end this relationship if Amanda said there was a chance for them. That's all she had to admit. Instead, she said, "I'm happy for you, Trent." It was a challenge to get her voice to work.

He sank farther into his seat and made that face guys do when they're absolutely pissed off. The cross between a scowl and the look of being constipated.

"I can't keep apologizing," she pleaded.

"And you shouldn't have to. You're not married, I'm not married. The way I see it, all that's standing in the way is our partnership."

The fact he seemed to minimize that and throw it away as if it were nothing got her back up. "You make it sound like that's not a big deal on its own." She wanted to point out how well they worked together but viewed it as volatile ground.

"That's not how I meant it, but I have received your message loud and clear. We're partners. We're friends. That's all we'll ever be."

"It's how it needs to be." *As much as that pains me to say.* She swore at the treacherous thought.

"Okay. Well, at least I know where you stand on the matter." He put the car into gear, though she sensed a lot was going unsaid.

"Are we okay?" she eventually pushed out.

"We will be. Let's just do what we do best, and that's work together and get Katherine back alive."

Her chest ached at the brutal reminder. But he was right. She had commitments and responsibilities to consider before this personal garbage. Foremost was to the badge, to her vow to serve and protect. Her thoughts turned to what Mrs. Elliott had told them. "The plates left their lives a year and a half ago. But now they're turning up. Where have they been all this time?"

Trent nodded. "And why were they never destroyed?"

TWENTY

The minutes kept passing on the clock, and Amanda and Trent might as well have been spinning in circles. It was twelve thirty, and they were no closer to finding Katherine than they had been when they'd first discovered she was taken. Just like then, they had hypotheticals. They also now had a list of Devil's Saints gang members that Natasha's assistant had forwarded over. A quick call to Greg Elliott confirmed he never gave the plates a single thought after his accident and didn't recall being contacted. It sounded convenient, but Amanda believed him. The accident must have been brutal, and his mind would have been otherwise occupied. She and Trent did have an immediate lead to follow at least.

The lot at Eco-Friendly Auto Recyclers was empty save a small inventory of older cars. Some of these had license plates, others did not. The former ones probably belonged to Simon Wheable and other employees. The others had likely escaped the compactor and were for sale. Being somewhat familiar with the owner, it wouldn't surprise her if a chunk of business took place under the table, but she wasn't with the Internal Revenue Service. The white Ford van from this morning was too new to change hands here. But did Simon illegally sell plates to his more questionable clients?

A stack of crushed vehicles towered over a tall fence that cordoned off the backyard. The clanging and scrunching of metal rang through the air confirming the compactor was hard at work.

The front door entered to a counter, an office behind it. There was also a staircase that led to a second floor. A rather robust woman was watching them over glasses that were perched near the tip of her nose.

"Can I help you?" A cool and indifferent greeting, but working here would suck a person's joy. Though Amanda's opinion may have been influenced by the *Playboy* calendar pinned to the wall in plain view.

Amanda and Trent flashed their badges, but she gestured for him to take the lead. It was the least she owed him for stepping in with Mrs. Elliott.

"We're looking to speak with Simon Wheable," Trent told the woman.

"Well, good for you, but it ain't gonna happen right this minute. He's out back crushing."

"Can you page him for us? It's very important," Trent said.

"As if what we're doing isn't?" the woman tossed back.

"Never said that, never meant to imply it. But Simon's name came up in connection with a murder investigation. So either you get him, or we will."

Go, Trent! Amanda wasn't used to hearing Trent talk to people the way he just had, but it wasn't a bad side considering the circumstances.

The woman sat back and narrowed her eyes. She and Trent played the game of silence for a few seconds, but the receptionist was the first to cave. She picked up the phone receiver, hit a button, and said, "Simon to the front desk. Urgent."

Her voice traveled through the walls from outside. The message must be being pumped through speakers in the yard.

The compactor stopped running, and about a minute later, a rear door slammed open.

"What the hell, Helen? I'm trying to work."

Simon came into view. Now nearing his mid-forties, he was starting to sport a bit of a paunch, and his face hadn't seen the business end of a razor in a few days. His brisk rate slowed when he saw them.

"What are *you* doing here?" he hissed.

"Come closer, and we'll tell you," Trent challenged.

Simon clenched his jaw. "Follow me." He turned and led them up a staircase to the second floor. There, he directed them through the first door on the right into an office. Presumably there was a desk buried under the stacks of paperwork.

Simon dropped onto a tattered leather chair that squeaked in protest and clasped his hands across his front. "What is it I'm to have done now?"

"As long as you're in a cooperative mood, we're here about a pair of license plates," Trent said. "They were last registered to Greg Elliott. We've been told they came in on his car after it was totaled in an accident."

"Okay," Simon dragged out. "Well, any relinquished plates are turned over to the Department of Motor Vehicles and destroyed."

"Well, these ones weren't," Trent pointed out. "They became your responsibility when you accepted the car with them on it."

"Whoa, now." Simon held up his hands. "I know you cops hate me, but I haven't done anything wrong here. And can you even prove I got the car with the plates?"

"We spoke to the car's owner. The vehicle came straight here after a crash."

"I don't know what to say to that," Simon replied.

"Well, I suggest you start talking. Those plates now relate to a homicide and an abduction that took place this morning. Since you were the last one to have them... Well, I think you know where I'm going with this." The way Trent was watching Simon with determination and intent, he'd be hauling the guy back to Central soon.

Simon pushed back from his desk, his face bright red. "You can't pin any of that on me."

"Then you'll open your books to us, show us the paperwork you would have received when you turned the plates in to the DMV?" Amanda pushed.

"Well, Helen's the one who's responsible for handing old plates over, making sure they are made invalid, and shredded."

"Again, as we said, that didn't happen with these ones. The car came here a year and a half ago, and the plates just fell out of registration six months ago. Where have they been all this time? I would suggest you don't claim to have no idea." Trent had his notepad out, obviously ditching the tablet for now. He tapped the tip of his pen to the page, an angry tic.

"That doesn't sound right at all. Let's go talk to Helen." Simon jumped up and led the way back down the stairs. He was hollering Helen's name the entire way.

"What?" Helen snapped.

"You don't take old plates over to the DMV? You let them sit around?" Simon launched his accusations, and it had Helen glaring at her boss. Otherwise his behavior didn't seem to shake her, so it must be the way he normally treated her. People around or not.

"Of course I turn 'em in. Get them made invalid, and the DMV is to shred them."

"Well that didn't happen, *Helen*, because these cops"—he thrust an arm with a pointed finger toward Amanda and Trent—"tell me a set was used in a recent crime. You have five seconds to explain yourself or there's the door."

"What happens once I drop them off is out of my hands. It's not like I hang around and watch 'em get destroyed."

"So you can assure me that every single plate is turned over to the DMV right away?" Simon asked.

Helen's shoulders lowered, and her eyes dipped to Amanda and Trent. Then back to Simon. "You have me doing so much around here, Simon. And you know Bill's health hasn't been the best for a long time. It can have me preoccupied."

"What are you saying?" This time when Simon spoke, he'd lowered his voice.

"I do my best, but sometimes plates can sit around for a spell."

"These ones are from a year and a half ago," Simon stressed.

"Now, I don't let them sit that long." Helen's voice lost some of its original edge, like an actor putting on a poor performance.

"If you took them to the DMV, you should be able to look that up and find a receipt from them," Amanda said.

Helen hesitated. "Oh, yeah, sure." She asked for the car type and the plate number, explaining if plates make it to them, they record that. A few seconds later, she said, "I see the car, but no plate number associated with it. As I just reminded Simon, my husband's health, that's Bill, has me distracted sometimes. I could have missed keying in the plate." She made a show of checking the physical files and shook her head a moment later.

"You didn't turn them over?" Simon's attempt at conveying disappointment fell short, and Amanda sniffed a rat. Criminals could benefit from reusing someone else's plates. If they surfaced in conjunction with a crime, police would be spinning in a circle, much like now.

"Mr. Wheable," Amanda said, earning his attention, "are you sure you didn't throw them in with the sale of a jalopy or even on their own?"

Simon and Helen didn't speak, didn't move.

"Please answer my question," Amanda pushed.

Simon's face shadowed, and he clenched his jaw. "What are you implying, Detective?"

"I think you know exactly what I'm implying, and if you don't start talking, my partner and I will need to take you to Central for a conversation."

Simon and Helen were looking at each other, clearly conveying volumes in the silence.

"You need to tell us who you passed the plates along to. Right now," she said. "If not, we'll be looking at you for the murder and abduction."

"You don't have squat."

Simon's demeanor and weak defense told Amanda he remembered Greg Elliott's name and likely his Elantra and the plates along with it. "If you have nothing to do with this, you shouldn't have a problem continuing this conversation down at the station."

TWENTY-ONE

"What do you want from me?" Simon was seated in an interrogation room at Central, his arms flailing.

Amanda wasn't in the mood to play nice with this guy. On one level or another, he was involved with what happened that morning. It was on her to determine the extent. Was it criminal incompetence or did he have an actual hand in the shooting and Katherine's abduction? "What we want from you is the truth," she put out firmly.

"Which is what I've been saying the whole time." Simon chuckled as if this was some joke and threw an arm over the back of his chair.

"I'm not sure where you've lost the thread, Mr. Wheable, but this is no laughing matter," she said. "If you were caught up in this morning's events, you will be going to prison."

"Yeah, well, I had nothing to do with murder or abduction."

"A teenage girl was shot dead. It was a *police officer* who was abducted." She wanted to put faces to the tragedy. It was also the first time she revealed the identity of the kidnap victim.

All signs of amusement disappeared. "I have no idea what you're talking about."

Amanda pointed at him. "That attitude will keep us here for hours. Instead, I suggest you start talking. Tell us where Katherine Graves was taken."

"What? Who is Katherine Graves?" He pulled his arm down from the chair, and his brow furrowed. Physical tells indicated he was being truthful, but when a person was a weasel and con artist like Simon, it made it difficult to believe anything they said whether it be verbal, body, or facial language.

Amanda gestured toward Trent, but he had already taken a photograph of Katherine from the folder. He pushed it across the table.

Simon barely looked at the picture. "Ain't ever seen her in my life."

"Take a long, hard look," Trent pressed.

"I could stare at her all day. It's not going to bring up a memory of someone I've never met."

Trent withdrew a photo captured from the marina video of the woman in a balaclava. "What about her?"

"Is this a joke?"

"No, it's not a freaking joke," Amanda seethed. Her level of frustration and overwhelm was nearly crippling her sanity. A straightforward murder investigation was taxing and required a dosage of patience but when a possibility existed to prevent harm, it ramped up the stakes and urgency. It wasn't often with her job in Homicide she had a chance to save someone, and she intended to do just that.

Trent laid out numerous photos of the woman, each showing a slightly different pose. "Look at her stature. Do you know her?"

"No, I swear, I don't."

Trent added an up-close shot of the license plate to the pile. Simon took a deep breath but said nothing.

"You're going to claim ignorance? Really? The plates *you*

had clearly ended up in *her* possession. You must have an idea as to how." She couldn't hide the skepticism from her voice.

"Maybe I should get a lawyer."

"That's up to you," she tossed out with a shoulder shrug, as if this wouldn't affect them either way, though inside she was quaking. They needed Simon to start talking, not clam up at the prompting of a defense attorney.

Simon didn't say anything, and Amanda leaned back in her chair further, striving for an air of indifference. Coming across desperate would have Simon shutting down this interview. He'd call for a lawyer before fingers could snap. It was surprising one wasn't already here. "You need to give us something, Simon, beyond claims you don't know her." She tapped a finger to the photo of the plates. "Those plates were registered to Greg Elliott. They made their way to you when Mr. Elliott's car was totaled and sent to your company to be destroyed."

"It's not like I can remember every wreck that comes my way," Simon said. "Helen told you too. There's no record we got those plates."

"But she didn't deny the car, and they were on there," she countered. There was a chance they went missing between the accident scene and Eco-Friendly, but it was highly improbable. "Helen admitted to shoddy work. What else isn't hitting the books? There may be some things the Internal Revenue Service would be interested in knowing."

Simon narrowed his eyes and tightened his jaw. "A baseless threat. I have nothing to hide."

Amanda smirked. "You know fair well you do."

Silence stretched, and she and Trent let it expand. The hope was Simon would eventually feel compelled to fill it. The reward came after at least a minute when Simon spoke.

"You realize these plates we're talking about are from a year and a half ago? That's what you told me."

She resisted smiling, not fooled by the latter bit. He knew

exactly what plates they were talking about all along. "Just a name, maybe a repeat customer? Though you'd make a lot of deals. Do all the faces blend together after a while?"

Simon glared at her.

Trent pointed at the photo of the accomplice that was on top of the stack. "Did you pass Mr. Elliott's plates on to that woman?"

"I told you, I don't know her."

"You know what? We're wasting our time with this guy. Let's just report him for his shady business dealings and get on with our day." Amanda stood, and Trent followed her lead.

Simon shimmied up straighter. "Hey, there's no need for that."

She pivoted toward him. "I disagree. You're not being cooperative or helpful." She turned back to the door again. Her hand was on the knob.

"Please, just wait," Simon blurted out. "It was just some guy."

She buried her smirk before returning to her chair. "You have a name?"

"If I do, you won't report me?"

"Name, Mr. Wheable," she put out firmly, avoiding his question altogether. "If I get up again, any chance that I'd put in a good word for you is off the table." It was best he remained in the dark that there was no chance of a good word regardless of what he said. As long as he thought there was, it might loosen his lips.

"Fine. Name's Barry, *but* that's all I know."

"You deal with this Barry on a regular basis, Simon?" One reliable thing with criminals, they were typically repeat offenders until they were caught.

"I'll take that lawyer now."

"Are you sure? This is your chance to be a hero." Normally once the request for representation was made, she left silently.

This time the stakes were too high. They could have time to save Katherine.

"*Lawyer*," he dragged out.

She and Trent left without another word. They went into the observation room next door and found Malone there.

"You see the whole thing?" she asked him.

"Yep." Malone's hands were on his hips, and he was grimacing. "That guy knows Barry's last name and where to find him. He could be our shooter and get us to Katherine. Meanwhile we're in a holding pattern because he asked for a lawyer."

"It stinks." It was frustrating as hell needing to play within the confines of the law sometimes.

Malone rubbed his beard. "There has to be another way to get info on this Barry guy."

Amanda examined their situation from different angles in her mind and landed on an epiphany. "There might be."

TWENTY-TWO

It was 2 PM, marking nine hours since Katherine was abducted. With every passing minute, the likelihood of finding her alive diminished. No request for a ransom either. Those facts haunted Amanda.

She and Trent were going back to Eco-Friendly Recyclers. In an ideal world, Helen would be more forthcoming than her boss. The only reason they hadn't dragged her down to Central with Simon was because he had primary responsibility as the owner. Helen had plausible deniability. Her knowing about plates was contingent on Simon telling her about them.

Trent breezed through a yellow to red, not even attempting to slow down.

"This entire thing is so frustrating, isn't it?" she said. "I'm clinging to the belief we'll save Katherine. Meanwhile we're just *this* close to a good lead."

"Let's put faith in that." Trent pulled into the lot for the auto recycler, and his phone rang. He parked and glanced at the screen. "It's Bauer," he said before answering on speaker. "Detective Stenson here, and Detective Steele is here too."

"This is Natasha Bauer. I've got the interviews with the gang members lined up for five PM Eastern time."

There was no need to question if there was a scheduling conflict. If talking with them could help find Katherine, it was a priority. Amanda would let Logan know she'd be home late, if at all, tonight. At the thought of Logan, a passing jab of guilt coursed through her. "Great. And it will take place via video?"

"You bet. This gives you the benefit of seeing their body and facial language. I'll be there too."

Amanda hadn't expected any less.

"Are you having any luck so far in finding her? Have you heard from Kat's abductor?" The personal toll nested in Natasha's tone rang of both hope and desperation.

"We're following one right now." Amanda told her about the plates, Simon Wheable, and his shady dealings.

"Sounds like a strong lead. Let me know where it takes you." There was a brief pause, then Natasha added, "Katherine's a strong woman, resilient. We must believe she'll be all right. They took her, so it tells me they want her alive for some reason."

"Our thinking is the same." Amanda briefly glanced at Trent, who nodded, but a dark thought creeped in. *What if the person plans to torture Katherine first?*

Before the call ended, Natasha said she'd have details for the video call sent over.

"Do you think we're still looking at someone from New York when we've been led here?" Trent gestured toward the building for Eco-Friendly.

"I don't think either are exclusive."

"Suppose they don't have to be."

They left the car and went inside the building. No one was at the front desk.

"Helen," Amanda called out. "PWCPD. We need to talk."

"Don't tell me she saw us coming and ran." Trent stepped behind the counter, glanced left and right.

Helen emerged from a side room and stopped in front of Trent. "What are you doing back here?"

"Ma'am, we have questions pertaining to one of your clients. All we have is the first name Barry," he told her. Despite the pleasant address, his tone was firm.

"I'll need more context than that." The woman hefted herself onto her chair at the front desk.

"I'm quite sure you have enough already," Amanda said.

"I've heard the name before."

Amanda smiled half-heartedly. "All right, I'll put it into more context for you. Simon sells old pieces of crap for cash. Sometimes he throws in a plate. Sometimes it's just the plates." She ran with an assumption on that last bit.

"If he does that, it's news to me." Flatlined and unbelievable. "I've nothing to do with it either."

Trent angled his head, softening his facial expression, exuding charm. "It doesn't do you any favors to lie to us, because I'm pretty sure that's what you're doing."

Helen glanced away, shifting her gaze briefly to Amanda.

"There's no reason for you to go to jail for Simon's crimes," she said. "You can talk to us." The implication was there that if she did, she'd be free and clear. Amanda wasn't going to disclose if she confessed knowledge about Simon's dealings that made her an accessory.

Helen dramatically huffed. "As I said, I've heard of Barry. Simon dealt with him."

It seemed she was already laying out her defense. Amanda would wager Helen was caught up in every bit of this.

"What can you tell us about Barry?" Trent asked.

"I shouldn't say much. He is a repeat customer."

Amanda raised her brows, trusting it would be enough to convey the implication the options were to start talking here or go with them to Central for a chat. Though the latter wasn't Helen's choice to make.

Helen batted a hand. "Nope. No way. I can't say any more, even if I want to."

Amanda picked up on the tail end of her statement. Her hesitation to elaborate might not be down to an uncooperative attitude. "Are you afraid of him?"

Helen wheeled her chair back from the counter, and Amanda considered if she was getting ready to make a run for it. She braced for that inevitability, but the woman stayed put.

"Barry doesn't need to know you sent us," Trent said. "We've got your boss at Central. It will appear that he squealed."

Helen licked her lips, looked around the front office, and finally landed her gaze on them. "His full name is Barry Holden, and I know where you can find him."

TWENTY-THREE

Bringing in a uniformed officer to arrest Helen wasn't fun. But she did even better than giving them Barry Holden's name and address. She decided to fully cooperate and turned on Simon to secure a deal for herself. She kept a secret logbook where she noted every plate crossing her desk and who Simon sold it to. Her records showed Barry Holden had bought Greg Elliott's former plates, the ones put on Katherine's Mercedes.

Helen hadn't resisted the officer's efforts to bring her in, either.

Amanda and Trent pulled a background on Barry Holden and found he had a record of drug dealing and assault. More currently, he was under house arrest, which he had been since October after being caught for drug distribution in February. Any violation would send him right back to prison. His record with the Department of Motor Vehicles told them he was six four.

He was far too tall for their shooter, but that didn't mean he hadn't facilitated the crime by providing the license plates. How they'd been used or where they were stored until today remained unknown.

The drive to Barry's house was a quiet one. Trent seemed as caught up in his thoughts as Amanda was in hers. Foremost among them was whether Barry would lead them to Katherine.

Trent parked on the street out front of Barry's house, a rundown shanty of a place, in a bad neighborhood.

She banged on the front door, and some flakes of peeling paint fell.

After two rounds, there was less paint on the door and still no answer. Barry wouldn't be the first criminal to finagle his way out of an ankle monitor. Just when she was about to call it in, the door flung open.

"What do ya want?" Barry spoke with an unlit cigarette perched in the corner of his mouth.

Amanda and Trent had their badges in hand and held them up.

"I don't need to see your shields. I can smell your stench from here, but I ain't done nothin' wrong, so beat it, pigs."

That roused her redheaded temper. She hated the expression, wishing it had long been eradicated from everyone's vocabulary. "That's where you're wrong, Barry Holden. Turn around." She wriggled her finger in a circle.

"What do you think you're doing?"

Trent grabbed his shoulder, forcing Barry to action. He shrugged him off. Trent wasn't deterred but approached him with more vigor and slammed Barry into the doorframe. Trent pulled the man's arms behind his back, and Amanda secured her cuffs on his wrists.

Barry spat out the cigarette. "You can't arrest me without cause."

"Oh, we have cause to bring you in, and since you weren't being cooperative, this is where we find ourselves," she said, as Trent closed the front door. She and Trent corralled Barry toward the road, each of them holding an arm. The timing of the police cruiser arriving couldn't have been orchestrated any better. The officer assumed immediate responsibility for Barry.

"One word," Barry said. "*Lawyer.*"

TWENTY-FOUR

Amanda and Trent hit a fast-food place for something to eat. Barry Holden had requested a lawyer, and a call was made to his probation officer. She had already been alerted to his leaving his property by his ankle monitor. Ideally, she and the lawyer would be there by the time they reached Central.

The simple act of eating had Amanda reflecting on the unfairness of life. Something so simple, often taken for granted despite so many starving around the world. But right now Amanda was mostly speculating about Katherine's situation. Was she being given food and water?

They arrived at the station at three thirty, and the probation officer was waiting in the front reception. Her professional attire of dress slacks, blouse, and suit jacket made her easy to pick out. The brunette popped up from her chair the moment the officer at the front desk bobbed his head toward Amanda and Trent.

Her heels may have pushed her to five foot four. While she was a small package, she carried herself with confidence. "You are the detectives who brought in Barry Holden?"

"That's us. I'm Amanda Steele."

"Trent Stenson," he followed up.

"Daisy Bright." Quite the upbeat name for a probation offi-cer, but Daisy wore it with pride and the woman was far from mousey. One look in her intense eyes told a person she wasn't someone to mess with. "What has the PWCPD bringing in Barry Holden?"

"Let's step into a conference room." Amanda held out a hand to guide her down a hallway.

The three of them sat at a table. Amanda and Trent took turns piecing together the steps that led them to Barry. When they finished, Daisy leaned back and clasped her hands in her lap.

"Based on what I'm hearing, he's linked to the shooting of a teenager and the abduction of a former police sergeant. Is that right?" Her face was sharp lines.

"He's our strongest lead at the moment," Amanda said.

"It's impossible to ignore that he was the last person known to be in possession of plates used by one of the perps," Trent added.

"Well, if so, he's going back to prison. No way around that." Cool and unsympathetic to Barry's fate.

"As I'm sure you can appreciate, our primary concern is this morning's events." A poor choice of words for what had actually transpired. "A witness has come forward and is willing to testify that Barry Holden bought the plates under discussion."

Seconds ticked off the clock on the wall.

Eventually, Daisy spoke. "I'll tell you how it is. Barry Holden is a dangerous man. He has his hands in many things. Most can't be supported with enough evidence to lay charges. The original arresting officer in his latest offense has been trying to flip him and turn him into a CI. So far he hasn't been amenable. He knows the officer can't back up all their suspi-cions, and Holden's associates aren't exactly fans of snitches."

That scenario presented a win-win. "This could give the

134 CAROLYN ARNOLD

other investigations some leverage. It all depends how things shake out once we speak with him." If Barry turned out to be innocent of that morning's crime, they could offer him a pass on possession of the plates in exchange for him turning confidential informant. If he was guilty, the mood for favors would be gone.

"You said this guy's dangerous," Trent started. "Then you wouldn't put it past him to take part in murder and abduction?"

"I don't know if anything surprises me anymore. But typically Holden grants favors then draws on them down the road. He doesn't want to know people's business."

"He takes their money in exchange for facilitating crimes?" Trent inserted.

"Exactly. He's out for himself. Always. There's no big picture unless he's in it. Trying to pull on his humanity, even about a murdered teen, will get you nowhere. Instead, stress how his cooperation benefits him."

Amanda nodded, unable to fully comprehend being so self-serving, even if the job brought those types across her path regularly.

Daisy continued. "He already knows that just by being questioned in relation to a crime, he faces the real possibility of winding up behind bars. Push on that. Put the fear of God in him, if you'll pardon the expression."

Amanda was surprised by how forthcoming Daisy was in advising them on how to handle Barry. Typically, probation officers didn't get this involved, but Amanda was grateful for the insights. "I'm open to suggestions on how to get him to talk."

"He has old buddies in prison who think he put them there. They would be all too happy to get payback. Remind Barry of this."

Playing up the snitch angle could work. "I appreciate your advice."

"Don't mention it, Detective. Barry Holden is a liability to society, and he deserves a solid stint behind bars. I've seen the results of his actions. He beat a man unconscious once."

"Which makes me question why he's able to serve time under house arrest," Amanda said. "It sounds like he should be living full-time in prison."

"It's those connections that gives cops faith they can turn him into a CI yet."

Amanda glanced at the clock. 4:05 PM. They had less than an hour to make Barry talk before interviewing the NYC gang members.

TWENTY-FIVE

Amanda and Trent sat across from Barry Holden and his lawyer, a man by the name of Alan Gaines. He was a two-bit defense attorney who worked for his own firm and employed about five people. They had a reputation of being willing to sink as low as necessary to get their clients off. The law practice was the equivalent of the school bully who sucker-kicked to the groin if it took down their opponent.

"You pulled my client in without even stating the charges against him," Alan said, straightening his tie as he spoke.

"Your client isn't currently under arrest by us," Amanda began, "but he is suspected of being involved with a murder and abduction that took place this morning. His resistance made it necessary to bring him in forcibly."

"In cuffs, you mean," the lawyer said.

Amanda didn't respond to that.

"You've got this all wrong," Barry snapped. "I am not involved with any murder."

Alan laid a hand on Barry's arm and gave him a reprimanding look. "You may need to be reminded, but my client is currently under house arrest. That means he needs to wear an ankle monitor twenty-four seven. If he so much as leaves his property, it alerts his probation officer. He can't be involved in what you suspect him of."

"We're well aware of Mr. Holden's situation." She leveled her gaze at Barry. "Do you have regular dealings with Eco-Friendly Auto Recyclers?"

Barry turned to his lawyer for permission to speak, and he gestured to him to go ahead. "Yes."

She pulled a photograph from a folder of the license plates affixed to the Mercedes. "Do you recognize these plates?"

Barry leaned forward, putting his nose to within inches of the picture. Then he sat back. "Nope."

"Huh." Amanda looked at Trent, and they played as if they were having a silent conversation about Barry and his future.

"Wait, why are you so interested?"

Again, Alan admonished Barry to keep quiet. "Get to the point, Detectives." The lawyer's tone was impatient and condescending.

"These plates went to Eco-Friendly, where your client just admitted he conducts business," Amanda said.

"So what?" Alan volleyed back.

"*So what* is the owner of this company has a side hustle of selling license plates. The ones put on a stolen car this morning were purchased by your client."

"Oh, please, how could you ever prove that?" the lawyer said.

"We have a witness who has gone on record," she tossed back.

"*Pft.* I doubt that. They'd risk jailtime themselves."

"You doubt me, we can move forward with your client going before a judge in the morning."

"I didn't do anything wrong," Barry blurted out.

Alan took a deep breath. "Let's say my client bought those

plates. There's no proof that he was involved with what happened this morning."

"Please. Those plates were last known to be in his possession," Trent interjected. "That makes them, and how they are used, his responsibility in the eyes of the law."

"We'd like to believe you're innocent," Amanda told Barry, leaning across the table, playing Good Cop. "But unless you can tell us who you passed the plates on to, you'll be going back to jail."

"I'm *not* involved," Barry hissed.

Amanda stared him down. "The plates you purchased were used in the commission of a crime. Possibly one or more before today."

"Oh, please, Detective. Are you stooping so low as to threaten my client?" Alan shifted his chair to face Barry and spoke to him. "They have nothing against you that will hold up in court."

"Hmm. That's where you're wrong, Mr. Gaines. I told you about the witness. You must also know that if your client even falls under suspicion of a crime, he can face jailtime."

Alan cleared his throat, and his cheeks flushed.

"If your client cooperates, this will go much smoother for him." She drilled eye contact with Barry and came at him with her words. "We heard you like to facilitate things. Let's be honest, that really means you help people carry out crimes. That's no secret, and your future behind bars is certain. It's just a matter of when. A windowless cell will make house arrest look like a dream."

"What is it you need from him, Detective?" Alan asked.

Amanda pulled out a photo of Katherine, and pushed it across the table to Barry. "Do you know her?"

Barry lifted it, and a few moments later, shook his head.

"What about the name Katherine Graves?" she asked.

Another shake of his head.

She believed he was telling the truth, as his reaction was calm and level-headed. She put the photo away. "What happened to those license plates, Barry?"

He traced a pattern on the table, watching his fingertip as it moved. "I don't know. And that's the truth." He looked pleadingly at his mute lawyer.

"We'll need more than that. Let's start with the reason you got the plates in the first place," she said.

Barry didn't respond.

"Mr. Holden," she pushed.

Barry met her gaze. "I got them for someone."

"For what purpose?" she countered.

"I don't ask questions I don't want answers to. Besides, that was a long time ago. Why the plates are kicking around now, I have no clue. You've got to believe me."

Amanda took a few centering breaths, detesting Barry's expression, but slapping it back in his face wouldn't be conducive to gaining any forward traction. "We're going to need a name."

"I don't have one."

She narrowed her eyes. "Come on, you expect me to believe that?"

"I don't get involved with names. It's better that way."

"All right, I get that. Then you can't be accused of being a snitch." She'd laid out the label to get a bite, and she got one.

"I'm not a snitch," Barry seethed. "Never have been, never will be."

"Not how we hear it," she said nonchalantly.

He lunged across the table, and his lawyer reached out to settle him back down.

Trent glanced at Amanda as if to ask if she was okay. She nodded.

"Intending to assault me isn't going to help your cause." Her instinct would typically have her bringing up the teenage girl in the morgue or the fact a police sergeant had been abducted, but Daisy's words were ever-present in her mind. "Give us a name, or we'll arrange a reunion for you in prison. You'll be able to meet up with some old friends."

"You can't just threaten my client," Alan pushed out.

Barry sat still and from the look of his chest, he might have suspended his breathing. Amanda recognized the rock and the hard place between which he found himself. He detested being a snitch, and that's what she was asking from him. If he refused her request, he'd be face to face with old friends who already pegged him as one.

She peacocked her stance and ignored the lawyer, keeping her focus on Barry. "It's not a threat."

"I can't tell you who they were!" Barry's yell would have reached past the thick brick walls to reception.

"Yeah, I'm not sure I believe you." She had said it calmly, antagonizing him.

Barry's nostrils were flaring. "I don't get names, and I'm no snitch!"

She held his gaze, and his eyes penetrated hers, threatening, but she wasn't one to back down. She stared back just as unrelentingly. "Name."

Barry smacked the table, and she buried her instinct to react and flinch. She just continued to watch him. *One second, two, three...* She stopped counting and left the room.

In the hallway, she said to Trent, "He's not going to give us anything."

"Nope, and I don't think he's behind what happened this morning either." The admission was devastating and put them right back to square one.

TWENTY-SIX

After Amanda and Trent left Barry Holden, only fifteen minutes remained before their video interviews with the NYC gang members. They returned to their desks and found that Malone had left them a note that Katherine's call history had come in, along with her main financial accounts, and GPS history on her Mercedes. The app gave them three months' worth of her travels. He'd also left word that Detectives Hudson and Ryan had exhausted all possibilities within the county and surrounding areas and hadn't had any luck tracking down the white Ford van. Uniformed officers had also canvassed Katherine's neighborhood and no useful tips came back.

Trent slapped the folder from the interrogation room on his desk. "This is all so frustrating. So close, yet so far away."

"I hear you. But we're not without other leads. We need to stay focused on our goal of getting Katherine back alive. We also have those interviews starting in a matter of minutes— Oh. Shit. Logan." She dropped into her chair.

Trent raised his eyebrows and sat down at his desk.

She hadn't called Logan yet to let him know she wouldn't be home until late. He'd need to take care of Zoe. She pulled out her cell phone, but hesitated before hitting his name. Guilt spiked through her, taking her breath.

So much had changed since she'd kissed him goodbye this morning. Foremost, she'd kissed another man! How would she ever make that up to him? Or did she just discount it and put it from her mind? After all, it was one moment of weakness. It wasn't like she was carrying on an affair with Trent. Logan might be better off never knowing. It would save a lot of uncertainty over how he was going to respond. Would he leave her and Zoe? That would give the eight-year-old another father to grieve. Her first had been murdered along with Zoe's biological mother. There would be a lot less upset to their lives if Amanda kept this from Logan, but she doubted her conscience would allow that.

"It looks like we have an email from Rideout with his autopsy findings too," Trent said, breaking through her thoughts.

"What's he saying?"

"As we know, the bullets used were nine mil. He pointed out that often rounds of that caliber don't fragment unless they are designed specifically to do so. This particular round was mostly intact."

"Which should make it easier to determine the lands and grooves and link us to a specific gun," she added.

"Yep. Rideout said the autopsy was quite straightforward. Cause of death was the gunshot wound to the aorta. Shot to the heart," Trent said quietly.

It was heartbreaking to quantify this as *straightforward.* Amanda thought of the girl's parents and her great-grandmother, recalling she was set to turn one hundred this week. That was assuming she didn't die of a broken heart.

"I also have a message from Digital Forensics," Trent said. "They are in Katherine's laptop, but there's nothing much there except for budget and financial portfolios. Turns out she has a doorbell cam."

"That could be helpful. Browsing history?"

"Quite clean. She wasn't on any social media that they can see either."

Amanda nodded. A low profile, or a nonexistent online presence was typical of most cops. Those who did venture onto social media usually avoided doing so under their real names to protect themselves and their families. "I still wouldn't mind looking at the doorbell footage myself. Can you get them to forward it over?"

"Yep."

She opened her email and saw another joint message sent to her and Trent from CSI Blair. It was a breakdown of the evidence collected at the Fill N Go, and it was sparse.

- 9mm bullet casings UPDATE no prints. Gun type confirmed: Glock 19
- Broken silver necklace and locket UPDATE: since confirmed as belonging to Katherine Graves
- Blood spatter and saliva—found on gum packaging on shelf UPDATE: type O-positive
- Cigarette butt ringed with pink lipstick—found in the lot, being tested for DNA
- Blood spatter on paperback, same type as victim
- Smashed cell phone UPDATE: also Katherine Graves's

Blood on the gum packaging and pink lipstick on the cigarette were all that stood out as new tidbits. The former could have happened when Katherine hit the shooter. Though he was wearing a balaclava, he could have spit blood when she'd struck him. The blood type was the most common on the planet, so not exactly a huge help.

Blair also confirmed the shooter was five eleven. She concluded this from the security tape on the door just as Amanda had. But the investigator included the estimated height for the woman as five six. This was most likely determined by a series of comparisons and calculations based on surrounding structures.

Still, none of this got them anywhere quickly. DNA typically took weeks, if not months, to process. New technology could trim this down to one or two hours, but it hadn't come to the county yet. That left them needing to root through every other possible lead until it either gave up a diamond or a lump of coal.

The phone records, GPS history, and financials could help, but they had an appointment to keep. If she had faith in a greater being, this would be the time she'd pray for a break in the case.

TWENTY-SEVEN

The video interview was taking place in the conference room of Central. Amanda was always self-conscious about seeing herself staring back from the small window in the corner of the screen.

Trent was seated next to her, a sliver of elbow space between them. The tight quarters were necessary for them both to fit into the frame of the camera.

On screen was Natasha Bauer. She was late forties and the well put-together package expected of an ADA.

It was just a few minutes to five and they were waiting on prison guards to escort in their first interview subject. It gave them enough time to get acquainted and for the ADA to offer her bits of wisdom.

"I figured we'd start with Ollie Rush, and then hit up the other two," Natasha told them. "Both have narcissistic leanings. Also a reminder, these guys are hardened from life on the streets. They follow one code, and it's not blue. Don't tiptoe around them, and don't bother feeding them a sob story. They won't care. If anything, they'll find it amusing."

That advice mimicked Daisy Bright's about Barry Holden.

These were gang members from a huge city though. They'd be more anti-cop than any thugs here and had been tied up in sex trafficking. Their humanity had died a long time ago. "We have experience in dealing with these types," Amanda pointed out.

"Yes, I apologize if I am coming across as condescending in any way, Detective. I read about you online. I know you and your partner were involved in taking down a sex-trafficking ring there in Prince William County two years back. I just want this to go as smoothly as possible."

A metal door clanged open.

Natasha turned from the camera, then back to them. "Mr. Rush is here with his lawyer, Quinn Gray."

Natasha sat in another chair that put her back to the camera, allowing Trent and Amanda to face Ollie and Quinn.

"This is a waste of time, Ms. Bauer. As you know, my client can't be involved with what you mentioned over the phone." Quinn was slimy and slick from his designer suit to his gelled black hair.

"Save your breath, counselor. No accusations have even been made. These are Detectives Steele and Stenson with the Prince William County PD, stationed out of Woodbridge, Virginia."

"That's a long way from New York City," Quinn said dismissively.

"The modern world is quite small, Mr. Gray," Amanda retorted.

Quinn didn't bother to respond and glanced over at his client. Ollie Rush was in his thirties, of pale complexion, but most of his skin was covered by various tattoos. They stretched over his face, neck, and portions of his arms and chest that were exposed. The ink likely continued under his clothing. He had a piercing in his left eyebrow, three on his left ear, two on his right. His face was a blend of chiseled lines and sunken cheeks. His nose sat crooked, as if it had been broken and never set right. His shoulders were broad, and it would seem prison hadn't been a cause for him to forego his workout routine. His mouth was set in a grimace and his eyes peered into the camera, the intent behind them unmasked. He was trying to be intimidating, and he wasn't exactly failing at the endeavor. He certainly wasn't someone Amanda would want to confront in a dark alley.

Amanda's respect for Katherine Graves shot up knowing that not only did she go up against this guy, she brought his network down. Talk about ballsy.

"Let's get to the point of this circus, shall we?" Quinn practically groaned as he sat back in his chair and crossed his arms across his chest.

"Let's," Natasha said firmly. "Katherine Graves was abducted this morning."

Ollie cast a side-glance at the ADA. A smirk toyed on his lips.

Amanda nudged her head subtly toward the screen for Trent's benefit, and he nodded. He'd seen it too. Ollie took pleasure in what he'd been told. Was it personal pride from a guilty man though?

"Did you arrange for this, Mr. Rush?" Amanda cut into the interview. The sooner they could find out who was responsible for Katherine's abduction, the faster they'd be able to rescue her. *Assuming it isn't too late already.* The thought crept in, but she pushed it aside as quickly as possible. The prospect of saving Katherine was what fueled her to keep going.

"I'm behind bars, lady," Ollie deadpanned, his eyes leering into the camera, again trying to intimidate.

He had no idea who he was dealing with. She sat straighter, hardened her gaze, and stabbed at his pride. "Katherine Graves was responsible for taking down your little gang."

Ollie's lips curled, like the jowls of a rabid dog.

His *bark* didn't scare her. Maybe if she was in that hypothetical alley with him. But not while he was secured in New York City. "Did you order a hit on Katherine Graves?"

Ollie slumped in his chair, leaning to the left, and he laughed. He laughed so hard, he snorted and pinched the tip of his nose.

"Inform your client of the seriousness of this interview, Mr. Gray," Natasha jumped in.

Despite the ADA's reminder, the interview was slipping away. They had no proof that Ollie had contacted the outside world to order the job.

Quinn looked at Ollie. "Just amuse them. Then we can get out of here."

"I'm in no hurry to return to my cell. Tell me"—Ollie leaned forward to look deeper into the camera—"was she hurt and made to bleed during this abduction?" He sat back with a resting smile in place.

Forget fear. Any iota of that was gone. Amanda's temper had been ignited, and she wanted to reach through the camera and throttle the man. She'd been up against a huge opponent before and had lived to tell the story. She leveled an unblinking gaze at Ollie. "Are you curious if the job you commissioned was accomplished?"

Ollie's smile disappeared.

"Did you order Katherine Graves's abduction?" she barked.

He slowly moved in again. "If I was behind this, she'd have been dead on sight."

TWENTY-EIGHT

The lawyer hung around for two more rounds of interviews. They went about as well as the one with Ollie, leading to dead ends.

"Well, that didn't exactly go according to plan." Natasha ran a hand through her long hair, and her face was drawn. The experience had clearly taken a toll on the woman.

"We'll figure out who did this." Amanda was at best a rosy optimist, at worst a fraud. She had nothing to back up her words.

"I should leave before the warden kicks me out."

"Like that will happen," Amanda told her, and added, "We'll keep you updated. Sorry that you are going through this."

"Don't apologize to me, just find her safe and sound. Please." With that, Natasha ended the video conference, and based on her gravelly voice, she was fighting tears.

"That's that. Back to digging in. We're safe to rule out any of the other Devil's Saints members too. If the leaders aren't behind this, there is no reason they would be." On the plus side, they had one thing to strike off their list. She continued. "We've got Katherine's call history, GPS history, and her financials."

Trent stood and pushed his chair in. "I'll even give you first dibs."

"Doesn't much matter. You pick." She got up and caught a look at the clock. 6:30 *PM*. "Shit."

Trent stopped at the door and turned. "What?"

She didn't want to tell him why she swore, but he had asked. "I forgot to call Logan."

"Yeah, you might want to take care of that." He left the room, likely headed to his cubicle.

She pulled out her phone and saw that Logan had tried her twice and left a voicemail. Taking a deep breath, she pressed his name and listened as the phone rang.

"Amanda?" Logan answered. "I've been worried sick. I was about ready to call your boss to make sure you were okay. You are okay?"

His genuine concern just layered on the guilt. She'd been so absorbed in the investigation she hadn't even considered that he might be worried. The fact her job was dangerous wasn't new territory for them to cover, and it had broken them up before. She pulled out a chair and dropped down. "I'm so sorry, Logan."

There were a few seconds of silence.

"You're all right, that's all that matters," he said. "Another late night?"

A pointless question considering the time. "More than that. I'm not sure when I'll be home."

"What does that mean?"

Maybe it was her guilty conscience, but he'd replied as if she wasn't planning to return at all. "A case came up today, and it needs my full attention. All the PWCPD is working together on it."

"Wow. But surely, you can take a break, get some rest. You deserve that much."

She loved that he was concerned for her welfare, but he'd

never been a cop so there's no way he could fully understand. "I promise I'll get home when I can."

A few beats, then, "All right. What should I tell Zoe? Or did you want to talk to her?"

The thought of Logan and Zoe settled in at home warmed her heart and made her envious at the same time. The three of them had a good thing going, and her stupidity threatened to destroy all of it. "I'd love to."

"I'll get her."

"I love you," Amanda blurted out, and the absence of a response or acknowledgment seared her chest. He just might not have heard her.

"Mandy?" Zoe's chirpy little voice traveled the line and buoyed Amanda instantly.

"Hey, sweetheart. How was your day with Libby and Penny?" Zoe was on school break for the holidays and had spent the day with them. "Aunt" Libby was Zoe's chosen family from her life before. Penny was Libby's girlfriend.

"Great. I made a Santa out of cotton balls and a Popsicle stick."

"I'd love to see it."

"I have it here. When will you be home?" Zoe's smile traveled over the line, and the thought of being the one responsible for stripping the girl of her joy splintered Amanda's heart.

"It will be late."

"Oh, why? More bad guys to catch?" Zoe didn't sound as disheartened as Amanda had anticipated. Maybe it was because Amanda disappointed the girl so often, she expected it and the impact grazed off her.

"There are always bad guys, Zoe, but you know you're my special girl, right?"

"Yeah."

"Good. I will look at your Santa Claus as soon as I can."

"All right." A sense of sadness traveled the line.

"I love you, Zoe. Be good for Logan tonight."

"Will you be home to read to me?"

Amanda had a habit of reading to Zoe from the very beginning. It was something that Zoe's biological mother had done, and with Zoe having already lost so much, there was no way Amanda would let her lose that part of her routine. She was thankful that Zoe hadn't outgrown it like she had so many other things. This habit warmed Amanda's heart, though she realized this pastime would soon be in the rearview mirror. "I don't think so, baby, but Logan can—"

"He doesn't do the voices as good as you."

The line went dead before Amanda could respond. Either Zoe had hung up on her intentionally or it had been a slip of her finger. Her heart begged for it to be the latter. She was about to call back when her phone rang. "Detective Steele," she answered.

"Fitz here, from the NYPD, and I've got something you need to hear."

TWENTY-NINE

Amanda was quite sure she was holding her breath while she listened to the NYPD detective.

"I popped by and had those chats I said I would," Fitz said. "Elias Rush and Lowell Mooney. Well, Elias, we can rule him out. He still spits at the mention of Kat's name, but he's not behind her abduction. Either himself or commissioning it."

"Same for his brother," she said.

"You spoke to Ollie in prison?"

"Over video. He said if he got to Katherine, she'd be dead." Just repeating the incarcerated gang leader's words had goosebumps rising on her arms.

"I got the same impression from Elias. Well, more than an impression. He might have said it in so many words too. The hatred is certainly alive and well, but he has no interest in stirring up trouble with the law. Surprisingly he was doting on his young son when I was there. Don't see him messing up his home life, no matter how much he hates Kat. But Mooney. He's why I really called."

Her skin pricked at this. What he had must be good.

"He's nowhere to be found, but I was able to get authorization to track his phone. Detective Steele, Lowell Mooney is in Prince William County. More specifically, Woodbridge."

Amanda popped up from the chair she'd been in, and the motion bounced it off the wall behind her. She hustled to Trent's cubicle. They needed to move on this ASAP. "Send me the address," Amanda said into the phone.

"I'll text it the second I hang up. Just keep in mind that Mooney is a dangerous guy. Unhinged doesn't begin to describe his mental state. Obviously, he can't register a gun as an ex-convict, but I wouldn't put it past him to have armed himself with one from the street."

"Noted. Thank you." She ended the call and walked while holding her phone out in her hand. Waiting for Fitz's text was agonizing.

She entered Trent's cubicle and found him leaning forward looking at a stream of information on his monitor. At a quick glance, Amanda saw it was Katherine's financials.

"Trent," she said, and it was enough to break whatever spell he was under. "Fitz just called, Detective Fitzgerald from NYPD." She found irony in being uncomfortable with shortening Katherine's name, while she easily did for a detective she'd spoken to a grand total of two times. Then again, she'd never reported to Fitz.

Trent straightened up. "What is it?"

"Lowell Mooney, who Katherine put away for murder, is in Woodbridge. Fitz is sending me the address."

"Let's go."

She looked at her phone. No text. "Let's go bring Malone up to speed."

Their fast, even strides took them to the sergeant's office in no time. Malone was behind his desk, his door wide open. He waved them in when he saw them.

"You get something from the call history or financials? Just tell me you have a solid lead."

Amanda looked at Trent.

"I started on her financials," Trent said. "Nothing flags."

Malone bobbed his head.

"We just got a solid lead." Her phone chimed with a message. *Please be Fitz with that address.* She checked and confirmed that's what it was.

"Hey." Malone snapped his fingers to get her attention. "Over here."

He hated being ignored in favor of an electronic device. "Sorry, it's just..." She held up her phone, the screen facing him, though it wasn't like he could see it from there or make sense of the message without narrative. "A killer Katherine put away in NYC was released a week ago, and now he's in Woodbridge."

"And that message?" Malone pointed at her phone.

"Where his phone last pinged."

Malone wriggled his fingers, and she held the phone so he could read off the address and then peck it into his computer. "It's the Sunny Motel."

Life must be playing a sick practical joke on her. The place was impressed upon her memory. Under prior ownership it was tied to the sex-trafficking ring that she had brought down. She turned for the door without saying a word, hearing Trent's steps behind her.

"I'm getting backup to follow you," Malone called out.

Amanda kept moving. She had this acid in her gut, a churning telling her that Katherine was running out of time, if she already hadn't. It was unlikely Lowell was holding her in his motel room.

THIRTY

The clerk at the Sunny Motel parted easily with Lowell's room number and told them he should be there. His cooperation would have been encouraged by the fact three squad cars, six uniformed officers, and two detectives pulled into the lot at roughly the same time. Three officers evacuated the other occupied rooms as a precautionary measure. SWAT wasn't on site, but Mooney was still being approached as armed and dangerous. Two uniforms covered the rear door and Amanda and Trent went to the front.

Once it was confirmed all was clear, Trent knocked on room 8. They stepped to the sides of Lowell's door in case they were greeted with a muzzle. They both had their guns drawn and ready.

A television blared inside, so it was impossible to hear footsteps to determine Lowell's whereabouts. One thing was certain, unless he was passed out or dead inside, he was awake.

"Mooney! PWCPD!" Trent banged on the door again.

The door flung open, and Lowell stood there in jeans and a tee. The handle of a gun poked out from the waistband of his pants.

Amanda raised her weapon on him. "Put your hands in the air," she told Lowell. He gave her this deadpan look, and it sent shivers through her. Fitz had warned her he was unhinged, and those were the eyes belonging to a madman. In a flash, a shadow crossed over his face. Amanda lunged forward just as he started to reach for his— "Gun!" she screamed as she steamrolled into him.

Lowell stumbled back, air whooshing from him. Three uniformed officers came up behind Amanda and Trent, their weapons also drawn.

"You've got five guns on you," Amanda said. "You might want to surrender. This doesn't have to end badly." She wished it wouldn't. Lowell could be the link to finding Katherine alive.

Lowell squared himself as if he were a wrestler urging his opponent to make the first move.

"Hands in the air!" Amanda yelled.

Lowell smirked, just the glimmer of one, seemingly finding it fascinating to be bossed around by a woman. Slowly, he complied and raised his hands, but there was the slightest hesitance.

Trent must have noticed too because he rushed forward, beating her to it, and threw himself at Lowell. He slammed him to the floor, and the two of them struggled for dominance, writhing, punches being thrown. One of Lowell's jabs connected with Trent's face and had him arching back. Lowell used this moment to topple Trent, rolling himself on top of him.

Stupid mistake.

Amanda yanked Lowell's hair back and pressed the nose of her gun to his skull. "I said, *hands up!*"

Lowell snarled but consented. His arms in the air, Amanda holstered her gun, drew his wrists together and slapped on cuffs with the speed of a seasoned veteran. She tugged him to his feet, and Trent got up, touching his cheek and wincing. He was going to have a shiner.

She disarmed Lowell, removing a Glock 19 from his person, which she held pinched between two fingers. Their prime suspect had the same gun type used to kill Leah Bernard, but it was one of the most popular around.

"I'll take him from here, Detective." A uniformed officer stepped forward, and she transferred Lowell to him.

Amanda cleared the chamber of the Glock, removed the magazine, and handed over the gun too. Lowell was patted down to make sure he wasn't concealing any other weapons, and loaded into the back of a cruiser.

She and Trent would catch up with Lowell back at Central. And he better be talkative.

THIRTY-ONE

Amanda watched the skin around Trent's left eye changing color before her eyes, or so she'd swear. There were cuts at his brow, not deep enough for stitches but they were bandaged on site by a paramedic, despite Trent's protests that he was fine.

"Usually it's red noses at Christmas, not black eyes," the paramedic had said. Amanda wasn't sure if he thought he was witty or what, but Trent hadn't appreciated his attempt at humor. He'd mumbled something incoherent, which Amanda was quite sure included an expletive or two.

Before they left the scene, they looked around Lowell's motel room. It turned up some cocaine and an almost empty bottle of whiskey. She didn't recall smelling it on Lowell, so she'd wager he hadn't been drinking when they'd arrived. One small mercy. Interrogating an intoxicated suspect was the worst.

The coat worn that morning and balaclava weren't found, but they could have been discarded. He also didn't have a wrist tattoo, but there was no way Lowell was in Woodbridge to see the sights. His hatred for Katherine and the glaring fact he was holding the same gun type that killed Leah Bernard told them that. Maybe the tattoo had been a temporary one he'd since wiped off.

Crime scene investigators would follow up with a thorough sweep of the room to search for any trace of Katherine. He might not have brought her here, but he could have gotten transfer from her person onto his.

Amanda and Trent got on the road to Central after Blair and Donnelly arrived on scene.

"Thanks for stepping in back there," Trent said, taking the turn into the station's lot.

"Don't even mention it."

A stillness fell between them, a peace that took her back to before she'd made the impulsive decision to kiss him. This level of comfort was a relief to fall back on.

It was nearing eight thirty by the time she and Trent walked into the observation room next door to where Lowell Mooney was awaiting interrogation. He wasn't an impressive looking fellow. Average height, average looks, Caucasian, brown eyes, brown hair. The background they had pulled while waiting to move in on his motel room told them he was forty-two. His son would be seventeen now and mostly finished growing up without his father in his life.

"Whoa. Look at you." Malone stepped back when he saw Trent's eye.

"Yeah, it looks worse than it is."

Amanda sensed Trent was being macho about it and putting on a bold front. His eyes told of a pounding headache, but he must have a high threshold for pain. This wasn't his first time injured in the line of duty. He'd nearly died before. Back when he was an overeager uniformed rookie with the Dumfries PD, he had inserted himself into an FBI investigation. They were hunting a serial killer in the area, and Trent's impulsive actions earned him two bullets. That case turned out to be fateful not just for Trent. Amanda's best friend, Becky Tulson, met Brandon Fisher, a member of the Behavioral Analysis Unit assigned to the investigation. They started seeing each other, and it had been over four years now.

"Is it right what I heard? You pulled a Glock 19 off the guy?" Malone said.

Amanda nodded. "Yep. The same type of gun used to shoot Leah Bernard."

"He's also the right height," Trent put in.

"Just no tattoo," Amanda said. "Unless it was a temp one he has since cleaned off."

Malone nodded. "And his partner in crime?"

"No visual indication a woman had been in his motel room. But CSIs are processing it to see what they can find," Amanda told him.

"A dive like Sunny, they'll find an overwhelming number of DNA profiles to process."

All Amanda did was nod, though she was disgusted by his statement. There was a time her heartbreak drove her to have regular one-night stands in sleazy places like Sunny. In fact, sometimes *at* Sunny. She shuddered at the thought she'd been in such a painful spot that she'd sunk so low as to give herself over to strangers. Her motto had been the less emotional tie, the better. That went sideways with Logan. He was the last one-night stand she ever had.

"No request for a lawyer, so you're good to move in whenever you'd like." Malone turned toward the window, his motion doing as much as saying, *get on with it.*

Amanda and Trent looked at each other. Usually Malone liked beefier updates than the one he'd received. Not to mention this time he had done most of the talking.

They went next door, and Lowell Mooney didn't shy from making eye contact with them. Like Ollie Rush, Lowell seemed to get a kick out of being of interest to the police. He clearly viewed it as a game of who could outsmart who.

"Lowell Mooney, we didn't get a chance to introduce ourselves," Amanda began. "Detectives Steele and Stenson."

Lowell lassoed a finger in the air as if to say *whoop-de-doo*. The gesture sparked Amanda's anger. It took her remaining willpower to clamp her mouth shut. She'd already demonstrated restraint.

Amanda turned to Trent to proceed. He pulled Katherine's photograph from a folder he'd brought in with them. The same folder of "goodies" they'd used during interrogations earlier today.

He put the pic on the table and pushed it across.

Lowell swept it off the table with gusto, and it danced on air currents as it descended to the floor and landed several feet away.

"Katherine Graves." Amanda set her name out there as a lure, let him fill in the ensuing silence. Narcissists loved hearing the sound of their voices.

"Bitch." Lowell made the *B* pop, and the rest of the word followed as an afterthought.

"Why are you in Woodbridge?" she asked him, not giving him the satisfaction of reacting to his language.

"Just hanging out in a motel room watching TV." Lowell shrugged.

She casually leaned back in her chair, though she would have preferred to lunge for his neck. "Where were you this morning?"

"Depends what time."

"Early. Five to six AM."

"Asleep."

"Can anyone testify to that?"

"I wouldn't think so."

Trent pulled another picture from the folder. This one was of Leah Bernard in the aftermath.

Lowell looked at it and didn't give any visual reaction.

"This your work?" Trent asked him.

Lowell didn't answer.

"Did you shoot this teenager in cold blood and proceed to abduct Katherine Graves?" Trent's voice took on a firmer tone with every syllable.

"Quite the shiner you've got there." Lowell pointed at Trent's injured eye and snickered.

Trent pushed against the table and shot to his feet.

Lowell's grin faltered, just a crack.

Trent stood, heaving for breath, but eventually dropped back into his chair. "Where is Katherine Graves?"

"Wouldn't you like to know."

"This isn't a game, Mr. Mooney," Amanda said. "You have a history with Graves and are on record as wanting revenge. Now you're here in Woodbridge where she lives, armed with the same gun used in a murder this morning." Amanda stabbed a fingertip to Leah Bernard's face, refusing to be sidetracked by looking too closely herself.

"I didn't kill her."

"Here's where I can't suspend disbelief. The evidence is stacked against you. My partner asked this already, and this time you're going to tell us. Where. Is. Katherine. Graves?"

THIRTY-TWO

Katherine woke with her chin hanging forward. Her eyes were unfocused, and pricks of light danced across her vision. She must have a concussion. The last things she remembered were being pushed into a room and hit on the head.

She tried to move her arms, wanting to touch the injury and assess, but she had no range of motion. She concentrated and tried to summon her eyes to focus. It took opening and shutting them several times to clear her vision, but it still did little good.

Is the sack still over my head?

But she didn't feel fabric against her face. Looking to her left, she saw the moon outside a window. Its cool light seeped into the room and netted a soft glow.

The last time she'd been conscious it had been daylight. Hours had passed. Days too? She had no way of knowing. But the faint light still allowed her to see she was in a classroom, likely in an abandoned school. A heavy coating of dust lay atop empty shelves that ran along the wall, and there were no desks.

She looked down at herself.

Her wrists were bound to the arms of a chair by zip ties.

These were impossible to break without having a way to compromise the plastic.

She tried to move her legs, but she couldn't get them to go far. Leaning forward, she couldn't see her ankles, but something hard was cutting into her flesh. They must have them secured with zip ties too. Unless her captor released her or she was rescued, she wouldn't be going anywhere.

Her head was groggy, and she was disoriented. Like her mind was floating above her, unattached, unfettered.

There was no one around though. *Why?* Was the plan to leave her here to die of starvation?

Katherine screamed, her voice striking her ears at a far quieter volume than she'd have expected. She called out again, mustering all the strength she could. Even then, her shouts did little.

She considered herself resilient, able to face difficult times with strength and grace, but she couldn't handle the thought of starving to death. Just withering away, enduring the searing pain and agony. That was just the physical. The passing hours of suffering would inflict emotional and mental torture, the living over and over again of things she wished she'd done differently in life. The list was short but simple. She should have listened to the advice of her aunt and her neighbor and put herself out there, found someone special to spend her life with. But at this sad reflection, where would that leave that person now? It would just be someone else dragged into this drama and made to suffer.

Tears fell for the young gas station clerk. If only there was a way to bring her back to life. The inability to do so, or prevent her death in the first place, haunted Katherine. The girl's blood was on her hands. It was a regret that would play on Katherine's conscience until her final breath. Whenever that would be.

She'd rather face a bullet to the head. Get it over with quickly.

Suddenly, she flashed with rage as thoughts of that poor teenager drowned her. Her entire body pulsated as adrenaline raced through her veins.

"What do you want?" She hurled the words, and this time they were piercing, desperate, belonging to a woman who demanded answers. Now if only someone would hear her and respond.

"Well, well, someone finally woke up."

She turned in the direction of his voice. "Why are you—?" Her throat stuck together, parched from thirst.

He moved closer, and he was alone. She wanted a good look at him, but in the faded light, it wasn't possible.

"Who are you?"

A bright flash caught her in the eye, and she squinted in response. He chuckled as he fussed with something in his hand. Her mind pieced the limited clues together to mean that he had taken her picture with a phone.

"It seems you're worth a bit more money than I'd first realized."

"If this is about money, I'll pay you whatever you want." She was trembling.

He smirked. "I have no doubt. What if I told you I know all about your precious Aunt May and the success of her diner?"

Katherine remained quiet, not wanting to reveal how much his words were affecting her. It would only fuel his God complex.

"Guess she owes her success to you." He held up the screen of his phone, but her eyes were blurry.

She blinked, concentrated.

"Let me help you. You're famous. Some article hit this morning and gave you your fifteen minutes of fame, Katherine."

Her name coming from his lips gave her chills.

"This wasn't the original plan, but I'm nothing if not adaptable. Your Aunt May would do anything to get you back."

"Leave her out of this!" she screamed.

"Before you so rudely interrupted," he said calmly, "I was going to say she's worth a lot of money, and I'm sure she'll pay whatever I ask. That's if she wants to get her niece back alive."

He could shoot her right now if it would save her aunt more stress. Katherine was quite certain she was a dead woman anyhow.

THIRTY-THREE

Amanda stared down Lowell Mooney, willing an answer out of him, but he was gazing back at her with a blank expression on his face. "You don't have to talk to us, but you're going to," she challenged.

"And why would I?"

"Because you're in this up to your neck. You cooperate with us then we might be able to work something out."

"I don't need you. I need street justice," he spat.

"Like when you killed the mother of your child?" Trent hissed.

"I served my time for that, and that bitch deserved it."

Trent flinched, but Amanda shook her head. He stayed put but hissed, "No woman deserves that."

Amanda admired Trent's restraint. Violence against women was a trigger point for him. His aunt had cut herself off from his family at the prompting of an abusive husband.

"She took my son from me."

"Because you are a cokehead and a loser," Trent seethed.

"You have no idea what you're talking about."

"I'm pretty sure I do. We found your little stash, by the

way," Trent tossed out, his words a weapon.

Lowell shook his head. "Not mine."

Trent smirked. "It was in your motel room."

Lowell chose to observe his right to remain silent. For a few seconds. "Whatever."

Amanda's mind hadn't really left Lowell's earlier words, *I want street justice*. It sure sounded like he was involved with this morning's events. He obviously justified the murder of the woman who'd birthed his son. Logically, he'd have less compunction about taking out the cop who sent him to prison. "Did you take Katherine Graves to right the scales, to get *street* justice? She obviously didn't understand your side. You murdered your former lover because she must have crossed a line. You wanted to make it right."

"Uh-huh. That's right." Lowell emphasized his words with a hand in the air, index finger pointing down like he was preaching from some soapbox.

Amanda passed a side-glance at Trent. Had she heard Lowell correctly? "Is that an admission? You took Katherine?" The loss of Leah Bernard was never far from her mind, but she kept her focus on a life they could potentially still save.

Lowell rubbed his jaw and slouched. "Nope. Never took her. Never shot that kid."

Trent pulled a photo of the woman and slid it across the table.

"Who is that?"

"She's your partner. You tell us," Trent pushed out.

"I don't know who she is. Where is this?" Lowell's forehead wrinkled up, and Amanda tended to believe him, but she wasn't letting her guard down. Criminals said and did whatever necessary to keep a charade alive as long as it benefited them.

"Captain Ron's Marina in Lorton, though I'm sure you know that," Amanda said.

"Never heard of the place."

All of this back and forth was wearing on Amanda's patience and nerves. Most of the volleying wasn't getting them any closer to Katherine. "Detective Stenson, a minute?"

They left the room, ignoring Lowell's protests for release.

Trent tucked the folder under an armpit and crossed his arms, standing with his back to the door. "The guy's giving me a headache."

"You and me both. What's your read on him?"

"He's full of himself, hasn't provided us a reason for being in Woodbridge, dodgy as hell. And then there's all his talk about street justice. He thinks he had the right to kill the mother of his child. Based on his terms, I could justify strangling him, which I'm strongly resisting the urge to do."

Amanda reached out to put a hand on Trent's shoulder to calm his temper but retracted, thankfully, catching herself before making contact with him. "We can't put him at the Fill N Go."

"Though he's the right height, had the same gun on his person that was used to kill Leah Bernard."

"Which ballistics will need to test to see if it is *the* one."

"There is the possibility he hired others to do the work while he sat back and vegged out to reality TV and awaited word the job was done."

"Lowell doesn't seem the type to 'sit back.' He strikes me as a man of action, especially where his perception of justice is concerned."

"True enough. In the least he'd want to witness Katherine's suffering."

"We obviously have more than enough to hold him. We'll look at his call history and see if he was in touch with anyone to commission all this. We also need to press Lowell on where he got the gun, and why he's in town."

"All of which will take his cooperation and time."

She sighed with frustration. "And we're short on both."

THIRTY-FOUR

Amanda considered Lowell's priorities, his warped sense of justice, and his hatred for Katherine. There must be a way to use those things to get him to talk. She gave it some more thought and told Trent her attack plan.

"Could work," he said.

"Let's go see." She led the way into the interrogation room.

"And you're back. Lucky me," Lowell said drily. "Did you find the hero behind Katherine's abduction?"

A bolt fired through Amanda. It was like he'd just dismissed the murdered teenager. But his reaction to them would fit well with how she intended to proceed. She sat down. Trent was already situated.

Amanda clasped her hands on the table. "The three of us are alike."

"How do you figure that?"

As suspected, this approach had thrown him off. "You have a high regard for justice. So do we."

"Yeah, right. Our viewpoints on that are completely different."

"Not really." Somehow, she managed to keep herself calm

and her tone even. "We both take a situation and break it down. Right and wrong, black and white. There are no shades of gray."

Lowell shuffled up in his chair. She had his attention.

"I can see how much you loved your son, and his mother came between you." It sickened Amanda to put any onus on the woman he'd murdered. To get him talking though, he had to see her more as an ally.

"She lied about me to a judge. She said I was never there for Tyler, but I was."

"I have no doubt you were."

Lowell narrowed his eyes. Her comment had been too fast, too familiar, and he'd taken it as patronizing.

She rushed to repair the damage. "All I know is my father did everything for me. Dads are an important figure in a kid's life."

Lowell's shoulders lowered, his arms and hands less tense. "Not mine. That's why I vowed to do better by Ty."

She resisted the urge to coddle Lowell, not about to make the same mistake again. "Katherine would have never understood that though."

"What would you know about that?"

"I used to work with her. You get to know a person."

Lowell didn't blink. Katherine having worked with the PWCPD wasn't news to him.

"She was a real witch too, wasn't she, Detective Stenson?" She shifted in her chair to face Trent, and he was bobbing his head.

"Real witch," he reiterated and looked at Lowell. "She was all about appearances, how she'd look to the bosses. She didn't care about anything else. Certainly not justice."

Trent's words skimmed close to the truth of Amanda's first impression of the woman, but in the ensuing months, Katherine had clawed her way back to Amanda's favor. "I know, right? She was willing to sacrifice whoever to get someone put away for the crime."

"See?" Lowell gestured emphatically with his arm. "So whatever she has coming to her is due."

Amanda stalled on his reaction, unsure whether it was an expression of guilt or an admission he was in the dark about Katherine's current whereabouts. "It's an exciting time for you to be in town. You get a front-row seat for all this."

A shadow passed over his eyes that Amanda took for Lowell erecting a wall around himself.

She held up a hand. "Not saying you're behind this. I'm just thinking if she wronged me like she had you, I'd want my own revenge." A play at his pride.

Lowell's gaze fell to the photograph of Katherine that was face up on the floor. Amanda retrieved it and put it back on the table in front of Lowell.

Time ticked past in silence, as he stared at the picture, clenching and relaxing his fists in a repetitive rhythm.

"When did you get into town? Just curious," she tossed out. A switch in topic might unsettle him enough to lower any guard he had raised.

"Two days after my release."

"Why?" One word, just keeping it simple and non-confrontational.

"I mean, I can think of one reason," Trent cut in, according to their plan. Cut down to the basics, it was to present themselves as Lowell's ally.

She looked over at him. "What's that?"

"If it was me and she made me lose my kid, I'd want to confront her and force her to apologize."

"She didn't get it!" Lowell roared. "She doesn't have kids. Ty was everything to me."

Amanda resisted the urge to point out his track record that

led to his losing custody of his son. Their method seemed to be working. Lowell was talking and reacting.

"And that's why I'm here," Lowell said. "I wanted to talk to her, but I haven't gotten a chance yet. Now you tell me she's gone."

Amanda stiffened. He spoke as if he were innocent, but madmen often got caught up in their delusions and took them for gospel. "And you picked up the gun off the street, so you had it for what reason? Were you going to threaten her? Shoot her?"

"I just needed a way to make her listen."

Amanda shook her head. "You must take us for fools. You want us to believe you got a gun with no intention to use it?"

"Only as a prop."

"A prop with live ammo," she countered.

"Believe or don't. Whatever."

"Did you plan to resort to that because your written threats didn't work?" Amanda produced copies of the ones found in Katherine's home office.

Lowell read each and put them down and laughed.

"Is this all a joke to you, Mr. Mooney?" she asked.

"It is funny. Lady has so many enemies, who knows who got to her?"

"Did you write these?" Amanda wasn't letting herself be distracted. The evidence lined up against him. He made no secret of having it out for Katherine, he was in town, and he was in possession of the same type of gun used that morning. That made him their prime and only suspect. Also their only possible link to Katherine.

THIRTY-FIVE

There was a knock on the door before Amanda had her answer from Lowell Mooney. Malone was on the other side, and his face was pale. She motioned for Trent to join her in the hall.

"What is it?" Her entire body was quaking. It wasn't just his complexion but the energy he was giving off. Something bad had happened. "Is it..." She rubbed her throat, as if the physical movement would coax Katherine's name to her lips.

Malone nodded but quickly added, "Though it's not what you might think." He guided them to the observation room but didn't shut the door. "May Byrd received a ransom demand fifteen minutes ago."

This had been something she'd half-expected all day. Now that it had come, that expectation hadn't made it easier to hear. "It wasn't from Lowell Mooney obviously, but it could be he's working with someone. That's the angle we're looking at, but I need to go, Sarge. I need to be with May." She swallowed roughly, mustered the courage to ask, "Did the kidnapper provide proof of life?"

"He emailed a picture to May, but it's not good."

For the second time in less than two minutes, her entire

body trembled as chills passed over her. Her mind slowed as thoughts fired through. "What do you mean 'it's not good'?"

Malone took out his phone and brought up a photograph. He held the screen toward her, and Trent moved closer to look too.

Katherine hardly looked recognizable. The flesh beneath her eyes was puffy and darkened crescents. Her eyes themselves looked widened in terror and were bloodshot, her pupils dilated.

Amanda trembled. "She's been struck, possibly suffering from a concussion. And the picture doesn't offer up any clues where she is being held. It's dark though. It may have been taken tonight. What does the kidnapper want?" She was braced to move, but her legs seemed to have her grounded to the floor.

"One hundred thousand dollars by tomorrow morning at ten."

Amanda put a hand to her forehead and paced in a circle as she ruminated on the number. "Does May even have that kind of money? What are we going to do?" The downward spiral was real and made her head spin from the lack of control. It was made worse because this nightmare involved someone she loved. May Byrd was a mother figure of sorts to her. She'd been there for Amanda while she was growing up.

Malone slowly shook his head. "I don't know, but we'll figure this out."

"Where's the exchange to happen?" Trent asked, his voice comforting her. He was managing to keep his emotions compartmentalized, his focus objective.

"At Prince Park, near the playground."

Thankfully, her adrenaline had finally kicked in and was helping her mind focus. That park was used as a burial site in a past case. It had been the one that had touched close to home for Katherine. Was the choice of location made based on that or coincidental? Her father would say nothing was a coincidence, but this time, Amanda didn't see how it was anything but. That investigation had been stitched shut.

The park did make for an odd choice though. It didn't draw crowds for the shooter or his accomplice to fade into, but it would also be more difficult for them to stay hidden. "Could it mean they're holding her somewhere nearby? There could be some light in that. Right?" Though she was grasping to accept it. The neighborhoods in the surrounding area were heavily populated. It wouldn't be easy to hold Katherine hostage in one of the homes, though not impossible. They could have snuck her in through a garage and been holding her in a soundproofed room. Amanda pinched her eyes shut. There was no easy way to narrow any of this down.

"Maybe, maybe not," Malone said. "You need to know there are some stipulations to this request."

"Hit me." She set aside her sensibilities, dipping into the present for the sake of a good outcome.

"It's not to be a person-to-person exchange."

"What do you mean?" she spat. She wasn't an expert at kidnappings and ransom demands, but her common sense told her that if Katherine wasn't there and the swap made live, the likelihood of getting her back was slim. "I want to hear this request for myself."

Malone gestured toward the one-way mirror. "And this guy?"

Amanda glanced at Lowell Mooney. He was slouched in his chair and staring defiantly at the mirror. "He's facing unrelated charges, but we're not done with him."

"Fine by me."

Malone summoned an officer to wrangle Lowell back to holding, and the three of them headed out to May Byrd's house in Dumfries. Malone went in his SUV, while she and Trent took a department car. May's home was a few blocks from where Amanda lived and was a brick bungalow much like her place. The difference was while she had updated the interior with Kevin to make it open concept, May left the original blueprint of the home intact.

May's yellow Volkswagen Bug was in the driveway. The color she would have chosen to denote her cheery approach to life, which somehow in the light of recent events struck Amanda as mocking.

Behind May's car was a bright-blue Ford Mustang, which Amanda recognized as belonging to May's best friend, Dee. Presumably, May would have had her support when the call came in.

One cruiser was parked on the street out front, currently unoccupied and there was no sign of the uniformed officer. He or she was likely inside. An unmarked cop car was in the driveway. It most probably belonged to the detective responsible for standing by in case of a ransom request. He came from another unit of the PWCPD, but Amanda hadn't had any run-ins with them before.

Amanda was the first inside, Trent right behind her, and Malone following him.

May's voice traveled to the entry, and Amanda headed for her. When she rounded the doorway to the dining room, May was talking to the detective and uniformed officer seated at the table. Dee was standing behind May, a hand on her shoulder.

May stopped talking at the sight of Amanda. Her chin quivered, and tears pooled in her eyes as she stood. Amanda rushed over and swept the older woman into a hug. She didn't let go but let May end the embrace.

"They have her, Mandy. They are going to—" She slapped her hand over her mouth and sobbed.

Amanda hugged her again, rubbing her back in a way she'd soothe a baby. "They're not going to kill her. They want money. We pay them, then she comes home alive. Okay?"

"They've already hurt her." May palmed her cheeks. "Did you see her picture?"

Amanda glanced away briefly, finding everyone else's eyes were on her and May. "I did see it," she admitted. "But Katherine's strong. We'll just get the money together and do as they say." She was just about to request that the detective play the ransom demand so she could hear it when May started whimpering. "We'll get her back." Amanda laid a reassuring hand on her forearm.

May shook her head. "You heard how much they want? I don't have that lying around. They want it by ten tomorrow morning. It's ten PM now. I don't know what I'm supposed to do."

Amanda squeezed May's arm, trying to stop her downward spiral. "We will figure this out."

"How?"

Amanda had been thinking about this very thing from the moment she heard the amount. When her husband, Kevin, had died he had a life insurance policy on him, and Amanda came into a substantial amount of cash. She'd refused to spend it because of how she had received it. It didn't stop her from putting some in a bank account, for a possible future rainy day, and squirreling the rest into investments as recommended by a financial advisor. He managed everything from watching the stock market to selling and buying. Sometimes, she opened the statements that came in the mail. She'd watched the money continuously grow over the last eight and a half years. It brought her little satisfaction as she viewed it as blood money, but it was set to be passed on to Zoe when Amanda died. "Don't you worry about it at all."

May met her gaze, and a light flicked in her eyes. She bobbed her head slowly. There was an unspoken understanding, a telepathy of sort behind them. "You are like a daughter to me." May hugged Amanda, and it took all her willpower and determination not to cry. But she was no good to May if she didn't retain a strong front.

Amanda dipped her head at Dee, and the woman came in for a quick hug too.

"It's nice that you can be here for her," Amanda told her.

"My girl needs me, I'm here," Dee said, straightening her pharmacy-store bifocals that were hanging on a chain around her neck. She was a classy older woman, who was inclined to be frugal with necessities and freewheeling with discretionary items. Having flashy cars topped the list. The Mustang out front was her winter wheels. In the summer, she had a sixty-nine Corvette.

"And that's why you're an incredible friend." Amanda smiled at the woman.

"Detective Steele." A gentle prompting from Malone. "Detective Greenway is ready for us."

Amanda realized that he meant the ransom request was cued for replay. She considered May next to her, and thought it might be hard for her to hear it again. Turning to Dee, Amanda said, "Maybe you could take May to the living room. She might appreciate the soft cushions of the couch." It was more than a suggestion, but Dee complied, and May didn't fight it either.

Once both women had left, she walked over to the detective who was holding out a set of old-school headphones.

Malone held up his hands and stepped back. "I heard it already before I collected you at Central. You two go ahead."

Amanda looked at Trent. They'd need to get close to share the headphones, which would be uncomfortable.

"You go first." Trent bobbed his head at her, possibly thinking the same as she had.

"Thanks." She took the headphones from the detective, and he hit play.

"Is this May Byrd?"

A mid-baritone voice belonging to a man.

"Yes. Who is this?"

"Don't concern yourself with who I am, but that I have what you want."

May gasped loudly. A few seconds.

"Do you have my Katherine?"

"I do." Smug, sounding almost as if he were smiling at the admission. "And if you ever want to see her again, you'll do as I say."

"Proof of life." May blurted this out, her voice quaking.

He laughed. "Sure, I'll send you proof of life."

There was a chime. A few moments of silence.

May cried out. "You hurt her."

"Yes, but you will see that she's still very much alive. See the light reflecting in her eyes."

May sobbed, little jagged exhales giving her away.

"Now, do I have your attention?"

"Yes."

"Good. From what I see, business is doing well, so how about we say one hundred thousand?"

"I can't. I don't have that sort of money."

"You will find a way to get it, or your precious Katherine will die in the most painful way. Her fate is up to you. What will it be?"

"I'll do whatever you ask."

"Good. Cash, unmarked bills, tomorrow morning, ten, at Prince Park, near the children's playground. Do you know where that is?"

"Yes, I... I do."

"No police. If I see any, I will put a bullet in her head."

"I... I understand." May was calmer now, likely riding endorphins and slipping gracefully into shock.

"Good. You put the money in a bag and drop it into the garbage can near the swings by ten AM. I'll be there to collect it. Don't be late."

"Will she be there? Will I get Kat... Katherine, then?"

"You leave the money, and she will find her way home to you."

The click of the call ending.

Amanda took the headphones off and passed them to Trent. No one prompted her for her thoughts, and she was thankful for the reprieve. The caller wasn't Lowell Mooney, which was expected. The call came in at nine thirty when she and Trent were questioning him. But Lowell could be working with this man. Regardless, none of what she had just heard was any good. She might be plucking the man's words apart, but the underlying message sent chills through her. Not once did the shooter promise Katherine's *safe* return, just that May would see her again.

THIRTY-SIX

Amanda impatiently waited as Trent listened to the ransom demand. There were several times that he met her gaze and adjusted the headphones. She'd guess he wanted to throw them across the room, as if that would somehow make it so the call never happened.

When he finished, he handed the headphones back to Detective Greenway.

"So?" This prompting came from Malone after a brief period of silence.

"It's not good." They were the only words she could initially push out. "But why Prince Park? It's not a hotspot. There's no way for him to blend in."

"I don't think he's concerned about that so much," Greenway said. "This is essentially an open-ended drop."

"Meaning?" Trent asked.

"He gave a deadline for the money drop, but he can show up at any point after that to collect."

Amanda lowered her voice and said, "In your experience, does he have any intention of returning Katherine alive?" Her question had the energy darkening in the room, and it became darker still when the detective shook his head.

"Not from my experience," Greenway amended. "That doesn't mean it won't turn out differently in this case."

Amanda wasn't one to put faith in optimistic thinking, but she wasn't about to give up either. If only for that sweet older woman in the other room, she'd get Katherine back safely. She tore the man's words apart from another angle. "Ten AM. He stressed that time. Why, if he isn't intending to be there to collect around then? And he mentioned if he *saw* police. That suggests he'll be there and watching."

"It is possible," Greenway said. "We will need to watch our steps, take precautions."

"Does it concern you that he didn't bother to disguise his voice?" Trent asked. "Is that something we should worry about?"

Amanda watched the detective, curious about the answer.

"It's not necessarily good or bad, but it might be telling us that he doesn't fear being identified by voice or getting caught. The call came into Ms. Byrd's cell phone. I was informed it's unlisted, unlike her landline."

"He forced Katherine to give it to him," Malone concluded. "Possibly threatened her aunt's life if she didn't comply."

At times like this, Amanda's life was surreal. For most people murder, kidnapping, and ransom requests remained in the realm of fiction and entertainment, not reality. Amanda envied others' ignorance.

"No matter how he got Ms. Byrd's cell number, he did," Greenway said, as if putting a lid on the discussion. "We need to deal with what's in front of us now. His number was blocked, but we will be doing what we can to run it down. Moving on, we have a time and place and the request for a hundred thousand dollars. I don't suggest we try to pull anything under-handed—fake bills, marked, or ink bombs—or we will have as good as signed Katherine's death warrant. With all that said, we'll have undercover officers dispersed among the park in the area near the playground. Others will be posted on the surrounding roads and streets on the lookout for a white Ford van. Now, it comes down to the cash. Do we have it? Can we get it?"

Amanda squared her shoulders. "I'll handle it. No problem at all."

Malone and Trent looked at her.

"You'll be able to get that together in time?" The detective sounded skeptical.

"I am certain of it." She had that much money in a high-interest bank account. The turnaround was dependent on the institution, but she was certain if she flashed her badge around enough and threatened to move her business to another bank, they'd move on it.

"Sounds good," Greenway said and bobbed his head. "We also need to talk about sending someone undercover in place of Ms. Byrd. We can assume the caller knows what May looks like and will be watching that garbage bin. We'll need an officer about May's size. Then we'll make her up to look like May."

"Oh, no, you don't." May breezed into the room and gave all of them a look through narrowed eyes. She'd gone past grief and progressed to rage. "He said no police."

"May," Amanda beseeched. Her name dangled out there, carrying the weight and implication that May simply couldn't go. PWCPD protocol would never allow for risking the life of a civilian in this way.

"You heard that man. No police," she reiterated again. "I'm not risking that guy smelling a rat and killing my niece. You all hear me?" May jabbed a pointed finger at everyone in the room.

A chorus of hollow "yes, ma'am" circled the room. Not one of them came from Amanda.

"I can't let you do this," she told May.

"It's a good thing, then, that I don't need your permission, Amanda Steele." May stared her down, and it had her catapulting back to when she was a teen and being reprimanded by her mother. Only then, it would involve the use of her middle name, Julie, also her mother's first name.

"I strongly advise that you don't do this, ma'am," Greenway said and earned a steely glare.

Amanda put her hands on May's shoulders. "Please, don't do this. Let us handle it."

"I thought you, of anyone, would understand why I *need* to do this, Mandy." The softened appeal tugged at Amanda's heart. "Kat is family, and you do anything for family." Her voice caught on her words.

"I still highly recommend that you let us take care of this," Amanda told her. "We can give you a bulletproof vest, keep an eye on you, but if this guy catches a whiff of trouble, what's to stop him from aiming for your head?"

May flinched and nodded, her cheeks flushed, and she appeared to melt into the closest chair. Amanda had resorted to laying out a cold, dark possibility, but there was no way in hell she could let May go in and jeopardize her life. Call it tough love, but she had no choice. They didn't know who they were dealing with here. It had taken nearly seventeen hours before a ransom demand was even made. Almost as if it had been an afterthought. Then other words the caller had said struck. "We have an opportunist here. We've been trying to figure out the endgame in taking Katherine and have speculated a lot, but I don't think money was initially part of the original plan. He said, 'from what I see, business is doing well.' As if it was a new discovery and then he stated the amount. How did he *see*?" She followed a hunch and checked the internet on her phone. Before, when she'd searched Katherine's name, Amanda had been interested in how the shooter had found her. Now it was to determine how he saw a payday.

Was he simply placing all bets on the grieving aunt or something more concrete?

She searched Katherine's name and Hannah's Diner again. As she waited for the results to load, this was one time she'd be fine if her suspicion was wrong. Her stomach formed into a lead ball when she saw the title of the first article.

"Former PWCPD Police Sergeant Taken in Abduction That Left Teen Dead"

The byline identified the author as Fraser Reyes. "That son of a..."

Everyone in the room was watching her, as if waiting for her to finish her sentence. Her finding was just as she'd feared. Along with the news of that morning's events, Fraser included a bio bite on Katherine. It said that due to her efforts, the diner had gone from strength to strength.

"Listen to this," she said. "'Hannah's Diner is no longer the go-to spot for just Dumfries locals, but is a must for anyone within driving distance who wants an excellent cup of coffee and a slice of apple pie. Within the last six months, the trajectory of the diner's success makes it legendary, with much credit to the founder's niece, Katherine Graves.'" She took a few heaving breaths. "I might strangle this man with my bare hands. Wasn't a media ban put in place?" She leveled a look at Malone.

"I'll get an officer to bring him in, put some fear in him," Malone said.

She threw her arms in the air. "What's the point? He'll walk. He'll claim some freedom of the press bullshit and throw the constitution in our faces. But if his article results in Katherine being murdered, I will make it my mission to watch him and prosecute him for any little misdemeanor he does."

Eventually, Malone said, "You'll have the support of the entire PWCPD."

"Mandy," May said. "Please, just help me get Katherine back alive."

Amanda sat next to May and gestured toward the PWCPD members in the room. "We will do just that." It was a promise she had no right to voice, but she'd make good on it if it was the last thing she did.

THIRTY-SEVEN

8:59 AM, TUESDAY

Missing for 28 hours, 9 minutes

61 minutes until ransom drop deadline

Amanda had barely slept and beat the sunrise to a new day. CSI Blair had emailed to advise there was no trace of Katherine in Lowell Mooney's motel room. It wasn't enough for Amanda to shake her suspicions of the guy though. Someone with a murder record and a vendetta doesn't travel all this way just to talk. With any luck, by midmorning they'd have their shooter and his accomplice in custody and Katherine back safely. The attack plan was laid out before everyone went home last night.

Officers would be hidden in the woods at a few points surrounding the playground. They'd be dressed in camouflage to blend into the cedar and other types of evergreens. The soft- and hardwood trees had lost their leaves, rendering them pretty much useless for providing cover. A few other officers would pose as hikers passing through, dressed appropriately. They found the perfect May substitute in Officer Sophie Bennett, a third-year cop, just enough past being a green rookie to make the success of this exercise possible.

It was 9 AM, and Amanda had already handed the cash over to Officer Bennett. Amanda had called the bank last night through their twenty-four-hour customer service line and got her call elevated to a senior manager. They woke the local branch manager at home, and the money was ready for pick up at eight thirty. This was before the bank even opened to the public.

Everyone was on the move to the park, as were she and Trent.

It was a brisk and overcast day, making the local news weatherwoman right for a change. If her prediction held out, at least they wouldn't have to contend with drizzle or any white stuff.

"How are you holding up?" Trent asked as he drove.

They were about ten minutes out in his Jeep Wrangler. They were dressed as hikers and posted to a parking lot a half mile from the playground.

"Are you looking for the truth or some bullshit?"

He looked over at her, his black eye looking worse than yesterday, and took a turn down the road for the park entrance. "Always the truth."

"Scared, worried, freaking out that if something can go wrong it will." That about covered her emotions relating to the money drop. She was also still contending with guilt about kissing Trent yesterday. Nothing like a fresh day to intensify one's regrets.

"At least you are holding on to a positive outlook." He laughed, and given how easy it came and went, it told her his nerves were frayed too.

"You're feeling the same as me. Admit it."

"You know it. I'm not sure we'd be good at our jobs if we didn't consider possible outcomes."

"And after you gave me a hard time?" She sarcastically mocked him and smiled.

"They say you preach what you most need to hear."

She nodded. "Valid point."

"Besides, you think positively, you manifest positive outcomes."

"I think there's a lot more to it than that." Logan was a big believer in the law of attraction, mantras, affirmations, and while she'd like to give herself over, life's bitter hits made that difficult. If all a good outcome required was positive thinking and prayers, her husband and daughter would still be alive. Same too for her unborn baby, and she would still be able to have children.

"Well, here we are." Trent turned into the lot, and they settled in for the wait.

They each wore an earpiece tuned to the same frequency as the other members of the PWCPD on this mission. It rankled Amanda that she wouldn't have a front-row seat to the drop or pickup. The latter might not even happen for hours, and today had the potential of being a long one.

They were allowed out of the vehicle but had been encouraged to stay put in case the perp parked in their lot. The last time she was part of a sting was back when she wore a uniform, but the experience had stuck with her. It was why she'd brought snacks and some water.

The earpiece crackled to life with the voice of Officer Bennett. "Going in now."

"Acknowledged." This came from the detective leading the operation.

Trent turned to her. "It's getting real."

She let out a steady breath. *Real* began for her when she felt the weight of that cash. It wasn't money she had earned but had come into because of tragedy. But the fact she could use it as a tool to save a life despite that made it the right thing to do.

Each minute that followed progressed in slow motion. Sporadic updates fired in, like little missives connecting them to the action unfolding about a mile away. The money had been dropped, and everyone was in position watching the garbage can.

A couple of civilians were cleared from the playground area and asked to leave the park. Only undercover and camouflaged PWCPD officers remained.

"We should have brought coffee," Trent said when the clock on the dash read ten after ten.

"No coffee. Worst thing when you're just sitting around. It's a diuretic. You don't want to be peeing in a bush when it's time to chase down a suspect. Because trust me, the timing rarely works in your favor."

"That pesky call of nature never gets it right."

"There's someone moving in on the garbage can. Over." An officer's voice traveled through the earpiece.

"Describe? Alone?" This came from Detective Greenway.

"Alone. Small build, wearing a winter coat and balaclava."

"You said small build?"

"Yes. A woman, I'd say."

Amanda spoke to Trent. "The shooter sent his partner."

They continued listening as it was confirmed from which direction she came, and other officers chimed in there was no sign of a white Ford van or the Mercedes in the immediate area.

"Suspect has the money and is moving east through the trees."

Amanda and Trent sat straighter.

"That's us," he said. "She's coming our way."

Amanda looked around them, but there wasn't a vehicle in sight. *Where are you going?*

Then Amanda saw the woman emerge from the trees. White coat and balaclava.

She nudged Trent's arm. "There. We've got to move. Remember, we're hikers."

Amanda stepped out of the car with guarded movements. Her impulse was to bolt into a run, but that would risk spooking the woman and jeopardizing everything. The ultimate goal today was to get Katherine back, whatever form that took.

Trent walked around to Amanda.

The woman was within fifty feet of them now.

"Gorgeous day, isn't it, sweetheart?" he said as he held out his hand for hers.

She wanted to take it, could feel her hand folded in his. Her mind chastised her, but this wouldn't be considered cheating on Logan, this was an act. But all her thinking had her hesitating, just a hair's breadth too long.

The woman must have sensed something was off and started to run. She was fast too.

Amanda and Trent took after her, him talking over the radio to inform the others of the situation.

They pursued her through trees and down paths, dipped toward the river and then she swooped back toward the road.

Amanda was panting, and her calf muscles were burning, but she pushed through. Trent was breathing heavily too but keeping even strides.

The sound of snapping twigs cut through the air as other officers moved in to assist.

"Suspect just made off in a white Ford van," an officer said over the comms.

"You have to be shitting me," Amanda said to Trent.

"Officer Brandt in pursuit."

Sirens cut through the woods, piercing the air.

"Suspect dropped the money bag." This update was from the same officer who had called out her getaway a moment prior.

Trent turned to Amanda with raised eyebrows. "Oh, this is not good. Why the hell would she do that?"

"Plates aren't visible, and the driver is driving erratically," came another update across the comms.

More sirens wailed to life, and Amanda was left on the sidelines, panting for breath and fearing she'd just signed Katherine's death warrant. All because she hesitated to take Trent's hand.

THIRTY-EIGHT

"What the hell happened to stand back, watch, follow at a distance?" Malone was pacing in front of Amanda and Trent. The fact they were outside, and there was a cold breeze, did nothing to delay the dressing down.

They were still at Prince Park, and she was holding on to her bag of money. The Ford van was lost as the officer driving couldn't keep up, and even others that joined in the pursuit had failed to apprehend the shooter and his partner. No one ever had eyes on Katherine.

"Talk to me," Malone barked.

Amanda deserved the brunt of his anger. "She got spooked. We had to move."

Malone's cheeks and high forehead were flushed, a sure sign he was about to really lose his temper. "And why did she get spooked?"

Amanda said. "She must have sensed something was off."

"Talk to me, Steele, or so help me."

She flinched. His tone, his look, all of it was scalding her, as if she wasn't putting herself through enough hell already. If only she'd taken Trent's hand right away, then they might have

Katherine. "Trent and I must not have sold ourselves as a couple." The sentence scraped from her throat, and she found herself giving Trent a side-glance. He only met her gaze briefly before turning away.

"This isn't all on us, Sarge," Trent said, speaking up. "We didn't burn out after her in the car."

"You're kidding me, right? Your defense is pointing the finger elsewhere? Sure, there were a few officers chasing her on foot, but once she got in that van, there was no choice but to pursue. The shooter won this round. We can just pray our incompetence doesn't come back to bite Katherine. We might have just—" Malone snapped his mouth shut, clenched his jaw.

Prayer had failed Amanda before, so that wasn't her go-to. If Katherine was going to be saved, it would be at her hands. But Malone's strong reaction was understandable. They had taken a bad situation and made it far, far worse. "We'll get her back."

"Yeah? How do you plan on doing that, Steele?" Malone snapped.

"We, ah, still have Lowell Mooney in custody. We push him."

Malone shook his head. "He wasn't here today."

"He couldn't have made the ransom request either," she countered, "but that doesn't mean he's not behind all this."

"Spit out your point."

"Lowell could have hired people to take Katherine. They could be acting on his orders now, or their own," she said.

"The caller's wording, as Amanda pointed out last night, indicated that a ransom may have been a change of plans," Trent inserted. "It sounds like this guy saw an opportunity and took it."

Amanda nodded. "It still doesn't rule out Lowell's involvement. The person he hired to take Katherine may have simply gotten greedy."

"Talk to him, and get to the bottom of this. I'm afraid the clock has just sped up."

Amanda wanted to rush to obey, but one thing held her back. "I request permission to make one stop first."

"You just heard what I said?"

"I know, Sarge, but May deserves to hear what unfolded here today from me." Tears formed in her eyes, and she tried to blink them away. "Please."

She felt Trent's and Malone's eyes on her, but couldn't bring herself to meet either of their gazes or she'd crumble apart. And she needed to stay strong.

"Permission granted," Malone eventually said.

THIRTY-NINE

May had her front door open by the time Amanda and Trent walked up her driveway.

"Tell me you have my Kat," May said.

There was still an officer present with her, but he was out of the loop on that morning's outcome. Amanda had ensured that before heading over.

Dee came up behind May and put a hand on her shoulder. "Let them inside, May."

She complied, but her steps were unsteady. Normally such a robust woman for her age, regularly bustling around the diner, May appeared fragile and old.

"I'll put the kettle on." Dee disappeared down the hall toward the kitchen.

May settled on the couch in the living room, and looked at Amanda with sorrow-filled eyes. Her chin quivered, and she fussed with the hem of her shirt. The skin on her hands was nearly translucent and speckled with age spots, something that Amanda hadn't noticed before today. May usually kept herself so busy moving, this was one of the rare times she was still.

"You have bad news for me, don't you?" May stiffened,

pushed out her chin. "Just tell me, Amanda. We've known each other far too long for you to pussyfoot."

Amanda used her imagination to project the current scenario onto fictional characters. To think of all this affecting real-life flesh and blood was too much. "We were unsuccessful."

May gasped out but didn't cry. Dee returned, sat next to her friend, and took her hand.

"They got away. Officers pursued but were unable to keep up." Amanda doled out the bad news in bite-size pieces for her benefit and May's. "The good news is they never made off with the money."

"How is that a good thing?" Dee asked.

"It means that they'll likely be calling again and making another request for an exchange, ma'am," Trent said.

"But he specifically said, 'no police' or..." May's voice faded to nothingness. Then, "This is all my fault. I should have handled this." She cried surprisingly gently and rather controlled.

"This is not your fault," Amanda offered quickly, resisting the urge to assume the blame herself despite guilt curdling in her gut. Trent might even blame her as he'd hardly said a word from the park to here.

"The only person responsible is the man and woman who have your niece," Trent added with conviction.

Amanda looked at him and blinked slowly, striving to communicate a silent "Thank you." She gingerly touched May's shoulder. "Detective Greenway is on his way back here. He'll be around when you get another call."

As if responding to her cue, said detective walked into the house.

Amanda and Trent took this time to excuse themselves. She hugged May tight before leaving.

In the car, she turned to Trent. "What's eating at me, is why did she leave the money? She had it and was so close to getting into the van."

"I've been bothered by the same thing, and I can't see her partner being too happy about her choice. He's proved himself willing to kill for less."

"The woman may have signed her own death warrant. But all this brings up the suspicion that came up for me yesterday. Remember I suggested she got in over her head and wanted out when we were watching that video at Captain Ron's Marina? That might explain why she left the money."

"Still a stupid move, if you ask me."

Her phone chimed with a text message, and she checked it before Trent got them moving to Central. She could hardly believe what she was seeing.

FORTY

Just after leaving May's house, Amanda and Trent were armed with a crucial lead. It came via text and informed them an officer snapped a picture of the woman's face when the van tore past. He must possess the trigger finger of a professional photographer because he'd nailed it. But it wasn't all luck. The woman had removed her balaclava. She was in her late twenties with dark blond hair and green eyes.

"I just don't understand why she'd do that before they fled the area unless it's as you say, and she wants out," Trent said as they walked to their cubicles. It was just after noon when they got back to Central.

"It has to be." Amanda put the bag of money on her desk.

"Are you just going to keep toting it around?" Trent asked. "You should lock it up someplace."

He was right, of course. It was a substantial sum but simply a tool. Even so, she ended up securing it in a locker in the station's restroom. After all, she had some time before they would be able to speak with Lowell Mooney. He was being brought up from holding, and that would take a few minutes.

When she returned to her desk, Trent was hard at work at

his. She sat at hers. With the excitement of that morning, she hadn't had a chance to check her email.

It would be nice if good news was waiting there, like a fast hit on the female accomplice. Malone told her the lab would be running her photo through facial recognition databases.

"Amanda." Trent dragged out her name and seemed to be having a hard time taking his eyes off his screen.

She got up and joined him in his cubicle.

"Digital Forensics emailed, and you're not going to believe this. They were able to clear up the license plate on the van."

"We have a number?"

"Not that clear, but they can tell it was issued from New York State."

"Lowell Mooney is from New York."

"Didn't escape my notice." A slight tug of a smile.

"How do they know it's from there?"

"The detective was able to discern it's a custom plate because it has the logo for the New York Giants on it, along with a swipe of blue along the top."

"New York plates. All right, well, this gives us some leverage." She couldn't get in to talk with Lowell fast enough now. "But we also had local plates pop up. Are we looking at someone from New York working with someone local, as occurred to us before?"

"Seems we might be."

She moved to leave.

"Hold up. There's more. Apparently, they also cleared up the tattoo on the shooter's left wrist. Let's see what we have." He clicked on an attachment, and she leaned in toward his screen to take a look.

The graphic was distinguishable despite being somewhat grainy from being enlarged. "It's a snake," she said, knowing it made her Captain Obvious.

"Yep."

"Print that and the picture of our female perp too. I look forward to seeing Lowell Mooney's reaction."

"You and me both."

They took their printouts and stopped by Malone's office to bring him up to speed.

"Finally, a break." Malone let out a deep breath.

"You going to watch the interview?" Amanda asked.

"I wouldn't miss it."

The three of them left his office. Malone went to the observation room, and Amanda and Trent headed next door to speak with Lowell.

Thankfully, he wasn't insisting on a lawyer, telling the officers in the cells the last one didn't do him much good. This could be of benefit to her and Trent. Lowell's best interests were the last thing she was concerned about.

Mooney was seated at the table, facing the door. He looked up at them, a glimmer of amusement dancing in his eyes. "You find her yet?" Like before, he appeared comfortable in a police interrogation room, as if he were at home.

Amanda dropped into a chair and pulled out a photograph of the female perp. "We found her," she said, slapping the picture on the table.

Trent sat next to Amanda and leaned across the table. His eyes held a deep intensity as he stared at Lowell, and the lines of his jaw were sharp.

Lowell looked at the photograph, and then blinked, brow furrowed. "That's not Graves."

"Nope. It's your partner in crime," she put out there nonchalantly. "Though that's something you already know."

Lowell shook his head and drew back into his chair. "Never seen her before in my life."

"Forgive us if we don't believe you. When did you get to town?" She remembered what he'd said before and was curious if his story would remain intact.

"Two days after my release. I told you this."

"About a week ago. But doing what, exactly? You never exactly said. Graves was around for you to confront that whole time, but you insist you didn't get around to it. So what got in the way?"

Any confident demeanor seemed to evaporate. His eyes darted around the room. "Nothing that concerns you."

"That's where you are wrong. Let me tell you what we think. You came to town with revenge on your mind. You wanted to get back at Katherine, and you hired local people to help." Rage over the effect all of this was having on May propelled Amanda forward as much as saving her former sergeant. "Where is Katherine Graves?" she hissed. If time was sand running through an hourglass, the last grain was about to drop.

"I had nothing to do with any of this. I've never seen this woman before." He pushed the picture back across the table, this time with a swoosh that sent it flying, but Trent caught it smack between both of his palms.

"Yet you traveled here all the way from New York. Speaking of, how did you get here?"

"Bus."

"Can you prove that?" she countered.

"I had the ticket but threw it out."

"That's convenient. You're here, where Katherine lives, and you have a vendetta against her. Before coming down, you took the time to arm yourself with a Glock 19. It was the same gun used in the murder of a teenage girl." She exaggerated the *same gun* part but was confident Lowell was involved. "And now, you're telling me you took a bus? You must think we're idiots." She simpered and set out a photo of the NY plate. "Explain this."

"It's a plate from New York."

"A friend of yours drive down with you?" she volleyed back.

"You've lost it, Detective. You've got nothing against me."

She slapped down a picture of the snake tattoo.

Lowell barely glanced at it. "What's that supposed to be?"

"Your friend's left wrist. Quite elaborate ink," she said.

"Whatever. I've never seen it before."

She sat back in her chair, frustrated. If only there was a legal way to force people to talk. Regrouping, she resumed by showing him the typewritten threats again.

"Here we go. I never sent them, but you're obviously not believing a word I say. It's time for that lawyer."

FORTY-ONE

Amanda and Trent had left Lowell Mooney and directed the uniformed officer at the door to escort him to holding. The Glock 19 was confirmed unregistered, and he faced charges for that and the possession of cocaine. His exit from prison into the free world would be a brief tour. They still hadn't asked him about Barry Holden or the license plates either.

They found Malone in the observation room. He was on the phone, talking rushed and animatedly, his arms flailing all over the place. She collected drips of his conversation. *You're sure? Where? Stay put. Don't touch anything. Call everyone in.*

That last phrase set Amanda on edge. In her world that signified bad news. Usually a dead body. Suddenly she found herself chilled as shivers tore through her. Trent looked at her, as he must have noticed her trembling, and his eyes held concern but also mirrored fear.

Malone ended the call, palming his phone, and rubbing his beard.

"What is it?" Amanda was surprised she managed to get her voice to work. Her mind served up the image of Katherine's dead body. "Is it Katherine?" That question ripped from her throat, as if it took blood and flesh along with it.

He shook his head. "It's her Mercedes."

"All right." Amanda still wasn't breathing easier. Had they ditched the car because Katherine was dead?

"Officer Wyatt found it out on rounds. It came back on the BOLO I had issued with the updated plates."

"Where is it?" Amanda asked.

Malone told them it was on a country road north of Gainesville, south of Catharpin. "It's fifty minutes out. I'll send the GPS coordinates to you."

"You're not going?" she asked.

"Nope. You two can take this from here. Keep me posted."

As they walked to the lot, they talked it out. "Why choose now to ditch the Mercedes?"

"I'm not sure you want to hear my answer."

"I don't think I do, but it changes nothing. Katherine could be dead."

FORTY-TWO

Amanda found herself practically holding her breath the closer she got to the Mercedes. Could she and Trent expect leads that would take them to Katherine? Or were they too late? Would they be finding her body?

Trent parked behind a cruiser at the rear of the Mercedes. Another one was lined in front of it.

Their strobes added color and light to what was a rather overcast day.

Somehow coming this close to Katherine's car made all the events of the past thirty-three hours that much more real. Images crashed in her mind. Those of Leah Bernard getting shot and going down, Katherine being shoved into the back of a van, running after the woman who'd collected the ransom, losing her... *Losing Katherine?*

She and Trent joined the two uniformed officers who were chin-wagging next to the ditch.

"Detectives." Officer Wyatt dipped his head. She didn't recognize the other officer, possibly new to the PWCPD, but he wasn't a rookie as he'd obviously been entrusted with his own squad car.

"I don't believe we've met," she said to him. "I'm Detective Amanda Steele."

"Detective Trent Stenson," he chimed in.

"Officer McRoy, Jerrod. I joined the department last month."

"Any word on when CSIs are going to get here?" She would have thought they'd have beaten her and Trent there. Their office was half the distance they'd just traveled.

"Don't know."

The breeze kicked up, and she caught a familiar odor. It came and left so quickly, she wasn't sure if she'd imagined it. If so, that would be good news. But her instincts had her moving closer to the trunk, and she was sniffing at the air like a blood-hound. Another breeze danced through. *Unmistakable.* "Do you smell that?"

Trent came over. "Oh yeah. Blood."

"We need in that trunk right away, fellas." Amanda pointed toward it. Every nerve ending in her body was at high alert. Her mind was locked on the smell of blood and fear that Katherine's body was inside.

Officer McRoy hustled to his cruiser and returned with a tire iron.

"No keys left inside the car?" Trent asked, stepping back to make some room.

"Nope. Ah, just a bit more space, please."

Amanda shuffled aside, and Trent gave him more berth.

The officer slipped the tire iron under the lip. Amanda cringed at the sound of the paint job being scraped and dented. If Katherine were here, she'd have something to say about the damage to her beloved Mercedes. The thought came and went, its presence futile.

Officer McRoy heaved on the tire iron. With several more attempts at wedging it along the trunk line, the lock finally gave way.

The lid was cracked open, and the smell of blood became stronger.

Please no. But her silent plea did no good. They had found a body.

FORTY-THREE

The woman was on her side and facing away from them, a bullet hole in the back of her head. But her stature was about the right size for the accomplice.

"It's not Katherine," Amanda verbalized, the announcement only easing her breathing some. She needed a few moments to get her bearings, to realize what this meant. Presumably Katherine was still alive. But for how much longer? She was at the mercy of a man who was a proven killer.

Trent stepped up next to her, his elbow grazing hers, but she didn't move hers out of reach. "Are you all right?" he asked.

"Uh-huh. You?" She looked over at him, and his eyes were wet.

"Yeah. Quite a jolt though. Unexpected."

"Yeah." She took more time to compose herself, to realign her thinking. It hadn't been Katherine, but the killer had claimed another victim. That woman cried out for justice too. Rage pummeled Amanda. The killer had just bloodied his trail even more, but the joke may be on him. Criminals often messed up when they were in a hurry. This case could provide a clue that would break the entire investigation wide open.

Trent leaned over the trunk, not giving any indication of being affected by the smell of blood. In fairness, decomp was much worse. "It looks like this is also the scene of the murder."

The blood spatter and some brain matter on the underside of the lid and other parts of the trunk supported that. "So the shooter had her get in the trunk, had her turn away from him, and then shot her?"

"Seems like. Does that mean he's developing a bit of a conscience? That he didn't want to look in her eyes when he took her life?"

"I doubt that. The method is still brutal and short range." She wished to see the face, but the body couldn't be moved until the CSIs did their thing, starting with snapping a myriad of photos. *If I could somehow reach over her...* Amanda pulled her phone from a pocket, held her arm out as far as she could, angled the screen down, and essentially took a selfie of the victim.

Trent stepped up next to her and looked at the photo she had just taken. "It is the man's partner." He released a deep breath. "We talked about all the ways she was sabotaging things. But leaving the money behind and removing her balaclava must have been the last straws."

"Still, he chose to shoot her from behind. The woman and the shooter may have history."

Trent nodded. "Ask me, and she meant something to him."

She was going to respond when the van from Crime Scene pulled up. There were two more people who needed to join the "party." She put in a call to the Office of the Chief Medical Examiner and requested a medical examiner, adding that she'd prefer Hans Rideout. He was on a call but would be sent out.

Now that aspect would become a waiting game. A *painful* one. Amanda's mind was inundated with concerns about Katherine's well-being and whereabouts. Was she still alive or were they too late?

"We got a surprise when we opened the trunk," Officer McRoy told the investigators.

Amanda listened as he told them what they'd done. Blair and Donnelly responded by setting down their collection kits and getting to work. Blair snapped photographs, and Donnelly dusted for prints.

Amanda and Trent stood by, watching the activity. If it served a purpose, she'd floor it back to Central and have Lowell Mooney hauled back into an interrogation room. But until they had more information, that endeavor would be pointless. He'd already denied knowing this victim from the photograph, but she wanted to witness his reaction to her lifeless face. It might jolt him to talk.

Amanda nudged Trent's arm, encouraging him to join her in talking with Wyatt and McRoy.

"You found the car," she said to Wyatt, knowing this from Malone. "At what time?"

"Would have been about twelve forty-five."

It wasn't a high traffic thoroughfare, but surely the Mercedes hadn't sat on the roadside all day. They already knew the woman was alive and running around at ten that morning. "How often do you roll by this stretch of road?"

"Honestly? Not often. First time this shift."

Amanda and Trent thanked the officers and walked back toward the CSIs.

Amanda turned to Trent. "I'm trying to make sense of why her partner killed her in Katherine's Mercedes and left her here to find. Also, why here of all places? Was he holding Katherine somewhere nearby? Is he still?"

"Could be, but without a way to narrow it down, we have no idea where to start looking." Trent kicked the toe of a shoe at the gravel on the shoulder. "I realize you want to think Katherine's alive, but we need to face the real possibility she might not be. The shooter could have killed his partner and ditched the car to clean up loose ends. He hasn't tried to reach May again."

If she were viewing this from an objective standpoint, then yes, she was with Trent that Katherine was dead and buried. But she tried to remind herself that Katherine was a fighter. "I just can't think that way. I can't."

Trent let out a sigh.

"I'm surprised you can. If there's only a glimmer of possibility we can save Katherine, I'll hold on to that."

Trent held up his hands.

"Let's think this through from the start," she said after a few beats. "Motive, we can only speculate. We figured ransom wasn't the original plan."

"Okay, well if Lowell is behind this, he's after pure payback."

Her eyes widened. "Lowell. Let's say he paid these people to get Katherine and hold her for him. If the man kills her, Lowell wouldn't be too happy. Trent, there's a good chance that she's still alive."

He smiled, but the expression faltered. She read it as a means of pacifying her. Not because he was holding faith.

Tires crunched on the gravel of the shoulder, and Amanda turned to see it was Rideout and his assistant, Liam, in their van. They'd made short work of getting here, for which she was thankful.

Brief greetings were made all around, Rideout checked the CSIs had finished taking their photos and processing the immediate area near the body, and Rideout and Liam gloved up.

Rideout stood back, angling his head left then right. "Preliminarily, COD is a gunshot wound to the head." He motioned for Liam to step forward, and together, the two of them worked to hoist the woman onto her back. "Rigor is just barely beginning. Time of death is less than four hours ago."

Amanda did the quick math in her head, after taking a

glimpse at the time on her phone. It was 2:20 PM now. The woman was last seen in the car chase at 10:40 AM. Wyatt found the car at 12:45 PM. She shared these details with Rideout.

"There you go then. TOD is between ten forty and twelve forty-five."

Amanda glanced at Trent. The timing confirmed the shooter had executed her not long after the botched ransom. "Caliber of bullet?" she asked.

Rideout took a close look at the entry point, pushing hair aside. "I'd say nine mil."

"Like that used on Leah Bernard," she said.

"Is there any ID on her?" Trent asked.

"Let me take a look." Rideout buried his hands in the pockets of her jeans and none of them gave up anything. "Nope."

"Again, that would be too easy," Amanda muttered. If they had her name and address, they could use this to track down the shooter, especially if they did indeed have history.

"Not sure if you two noticed this, but she suffered from abuse. She did a pretty good job covering the damage with makeup, but there is bruising around her orbital sockets and on her cheekbones," Rideout told them.

Trent took a heaving breath and stared straight ahead. Amanda let him have his space.

Amanda hadn't picked up the bruising in the crappy photo she had taken. "From recent assault?"

Rideout shook his head. "Spanning a few weeks."

Trent was still eyeballing the trunk, his eyes glazed as if unseeing.

"That supports our theory about there being history between her and the shooter," she said to him.

"Yep." It wasn't much more than acknowledgment, but Amanda took it.

"And speaking of bruising," Rideout started, flicking a finger toward Trent's eye. "You've got yourself quite the shiner."

"At least I'm getting the last laugh. The guy responsible is in holding."

"Do you think he might be behind all this?" Rideout waved a hand over the car, but his question took in the bigger picture of Katherine's abduction too.

"We suspect he's got a hand in it," Amanda said.

"Then throw the book at him."

Blair stepped forward, and the ME and his assistant stepped back. It was like a choreographed dance to allow the investigator space to take her photographs.

"Could you email me one of those?" Amanda asked her.

"You got it. Right away, I'm guessing?" Blair said.

"That would be great. Trent and I need to have a little talk with our suspect."

FORTY-FOUR

It was four o'clock by the time they returned to Central. Liam had texted that the autopsy was scheduled for tomorrow at 11 AM. Amanda had called ahead to have Lowell Mooney put in an interrogation room. She'd also briefed Malone. A lot of expletives had flown across the line.

They joined Lowell in Interview Room Two and found that he was alone. Surprisingly, it would seem, he had waived having a lawyer again.

"You come to personally tell me that I'm free to go?" Lowell asked.

"Not even close," Trent said. He'd requested to take the lead this go around. Prior to that, they had discussed their approach. Time of death ruled out Lowell for the woman's murder. He had been behind bars, but he didn't have to know every detail if holding some back would get him to talk. Otherwise, Trent had been rather introspective on the drive, which Amanda attributed to the abuse the woman had suffered.

They both sat across from Lowell. Trent wasted no time pulling out the photo Blair had sent of Jane Doe. "Look close." Trent pushed it under Lowell's nose.

"Don't know her, like I told you before. Just in this picture, she looks a little *deader*." Lowell licked his lips as he stared at the photo as if deriving some sick pleasure from it.

"Do you think this is some freaking joke?" Trent asked. "That it's funny? Well, neither of us is laughing or even amused. She was shot to the back of her head with a nine mil. We think you're caught up in that."

"It wasn't me."

"I never said you pulled the trigger, but this is on you." Trent thrust a pointed finger toward the picture. "She was stuffed into the trunk of Katherine Graves's Mercedes, the one your goons stole when they abducted her. She's been beaten for weeks."

"My goons? You've got *nothing* on me. Let me go or the next time there will be a lawyer present."

"A lawyer? Really?" Amanda said. "That's starting to feel like your fallback. But for someone who claims their innocence, you seem to find pleasure in what you're seeing." She'd shared her observation for shock factor and to net a reaction.

Lowell smiled. "It makes me think of how Nancy looked after..."

Nancy was the mother of his son, who he'd murdered and served prison time for. Apparently, the sentence hadn't been long enough to make him reflect on his crime and regret what he had done. Then again, rehabilitation may just be the delusion of humanitarians.

"What about this? Does his voice sound familiar?" Trent played a segment of the ransom request.

Lowell was grinning the entire time.

"You proud of your cohort's initiative?" Trent put out there. "I wouldn't be. He's leaving a trail that is going to lead us straight to you."

"It hasn't worked yet."

They showed him Barry Holden's picture and the plates, but neither netted a reaction.

Amanda stood and Trent followed, slowly gathering up the photos.

In the hall, Trent said, "He's shady as shit. He's stringing us along, wasting time."

"I agree, but we can't make him talk. We need to build our case against him. His gun's already being tested to see if it's a match to the bullets that killed Leah Bernard. Obviously, it wouldn't match Jane Doe as his weapon is with us. But we'll get a warrant for his phone records, see if we can prove he commissioned Katherine's abduction."

"And if we're barking up the wrong tree with Lowell?"

"We're nowhere." She didn't even want to think about that.

FORTY-FIVE

Katherine had been drifting in and out of consciousness but had bolted awake when the man and woman returned. He was screaming at her, and things were being thrown and crashing into walls.

"How stupid can you be?" he hurled at the woman.

"I—"

The sound of a hand hitting flesh. "You left the cash behind."

He'd struck the woman again, her cries penetrated Katherine's skull, and there was nothing she could do about it tied to this blasted chair. That had taken place a while ago. Hours maybe, and Katherine hadn't heard the woman since. But shortly after their altercation, they'd left, and Katherine breathed some relief. She'd be alive for at least a little longer.

It had already been two full days. She'd seen the sun set and rise through the one window in the room that wasn't boarded. All they had provided her with was the odd protein bar and sips of bottled water. Bathroom breaks were infrequent and accompanied. The man stood over her at gunpoint while she evacuated her bladder and bowels. It was humiliating and demoralizing.

If only he'd entrusted the task to the woman. Then Katherine might have found some way to turn her against the man. There was obvious tension between the two, him always bossing her around and hitting her. But she was quite sure the woman wouldn't be coming back.

It was obvious that things had gone sideways with the ransom exchange. She was surprised she hadn't received a bullet to the head. Poor, sweet May, who had welcomed her with open arms. She'd never thrown the past in her face once, that her mother and May had been estranged for years. Katherine only wished there had been time for the sisters to reconcile.

Heavy footsteps stomped down the hallway toward the room that Katherine was in. When he entered, she got her first real look at him. Her vision was clear enough, and with sunlight streaming in, she racked her brain trying to place him, but she couldn't.

He was holding his gun and came at her. "Your fucking aunt messed up everything!"

Before she could utter a word, he pistol-whipped her across the face. Her teeth clamped down on her tongue, filling her mouth with the bitter taste of blood. Her jaw throbbed. Had he cracked it?

It took all her willpower to raise her head and confront her attacker. "Good."

He snarled and hit her again. With each consecutive blow, she wondered which one might be her last, when death would claim her and sweep her away for good. She'd join her mother and be happy and at peace.

"Who are you? Why are you doing this?"

His face fired red, and his nostrils flared. "You really have no idea how much I've suffered because of you."

"I... I don't, but I can—"

He lunged toward her, and she flinched, hating herself for it, but it was on instinct like a beaten dog withdrawing from an abusive master. He latched his hands around the arms of the chair. An elaborate snake tattoo wound around his left wrist. Leaning in close to her face, he said, "Take a good, long look."

She took in the hardened contours of his face, his wild eyes, and inhaled the stench of beer and cigarette smoke. No matter how hard she concentrated, she couldn't place this man.

He must have sensed she had no idea, and he pushed off the chair, nearly sending her flying backward. "You really don't know who I am. You carried on with your life, not giving me a single thought."

A lie might help him feel better. She certainly was lost for who he was, and people didn't think of those they didn't know. To admit to this would only anger him further.

"Let's try this again. I'm going to make a little video of you with my phone. You're going to say this: 'He will kill me next time.'"

She shivered, her entire body trembling. As much as she contemplated death, she really didn't want to die.

FORTY-SIX

"Lowell's obviously hiding something here. As you said a moment ago, he's shady as hell." Amanda paraphrased, but the point was made.

"I have no doubt. Now whether he's behind all of this or not, he's conceded his intentions weren't pure coming down here." Trent slapped the folder they had taken into the interrogation room onto his desk.

This case was clearly getting to him like it was her. It was four fifteen Tuesday afternoon and nearing thirty-six hours since Katherine was taken. It had been silent since the botched ransom, and the odds of getting Katherine back alive were slipping away. Even if Lowell hired the shooter, he'd shown initiative before. It was possible he would again. He might have developed a love for killing. They needed something substantive to shake Lowell into talking to build up more against him. "Okay, we're going to get on Lowell's phone history, especially now that we believe he may have commissioned all this. His criminal record and his public grudge against Katherine should help get that approved." She spoke with a confidence she didn't necessarily feel. "We ask the front desk clerks at Sunny if they ever saw a white Ford van in their lot since Lowell checked in. Better still, if someone came to visit Lowell in one."

"I like that angle. We can't prove he took the bus. He threw out the ticket. What's to say he didn't get a ride with a friend from New York down here?"

"Exactly."

"Glad to find you guys here." It was Malone, and he'd aged years in the last few days. Though she wouldn't be surprised if the same applied to her too. She'd been too busy to look at herself much in the mirror.

"The bad news keeps coming," he said.

And there was that lead weight again, sinking in her gut. She didn't even have the energy to form the question.

Malone wet his lips. "May received another call, and he emailed a video. Katherine's alive, but it's not good. She looks quite beaten up, even worse than before."

"If I get my hands on this guy, I'm going to—" Trent clenched his jaw and balled his hands into fists.

"Get in line," Malone told him as he brought up the video on his phone for them to watch.

Amanda had to fight turning away at the sight of Katherine's bruised and bloody face. She barely had a voice when she said, "He will kill me if you don't do what he says."

"There's nothing there to give us any indication where he's holding her," Trent said. "Other than it's dark like with the photo."

Malone shook his head. "This person seems determined to keep his location a secret."

"What did he say on the call?" Amanda's breathing slowed, as if her next inhale was contingent on what Malone was going to say.

"He wasn't happy about the police presence. Said if May doesn't do exactly as he says the next time, he won't hesitate to put a bullet in Katherine's head." Malone paused, his cheeks flushed. "He says he'll be calling May within a couple of days and telling her where to drop the money."

"Within two days?" she spat. "We're supposed to spin while he does God-knows-what to her?"

"No. We use this time to find her and bring her home."

It wasn't like they hadn't been trying that all along, but Amanda kept her mouth shut. With every passing hour, a happy outcome became more elusive.

"Where are things with Lowell Mooney?" Malone asked.

"Hitting a wall." Amanda told him where they were, how they wanted to get his phone records and check with the motel staff.

"Not sure there is enough to get the warrant on his phone."

"I was afraid you might say that," she said.

"I can see about getting officers over to Sunny Motel to inquire about the van."

"That would be great." She and Trent could do it, but they had other work ahead of them.

"Keep your chins up." Malone turned to walk away, but she called out.

"Before you leave, have we had any luck tracking the phone behind the ransom request?"

He shook his head and retreated down the hall.

"Just one dead end after the next," she vented.

"There has to be something in front of us we're missing."

Her partner—the beacon of hope. "We do have Katherine's phone and GPS records, and we haven't had a chance to look at either."

"Very true. Both fell to the side. Along with the mystery key from her office drawer. We were going to check if the GPS history would give us a clue where that belongs."

"It's hard to believe it was just yesterday we found that. It feels much longer ago." The same time period must have been an eternity for Katherine.

"As they say, no time like the present." Trent gestured to his computer, the implication being the GPS tracking.

"You do that. I'm taking a quick look at her phone records." She did that for the next several minutes, but nothing flagged.

"You'll want to see this." Trent popped his head over the divider.

She joined him in his cubicle.

"Look." He motioned toward his screen where the GPS log from the Mercedes was on display. He pointed to one line, then another, and another. They had the same coordinates on different days, at different times.

"Where is that?"

Trent keyed into an internet search window. The result came back, and he said, "You don't think that...?"

"I do. Let's move."

FORTY-SEVEN

The GPS coordinates led them to U-Store-It. They rented out storage units of various sizes with roll-up doors. A blinking neon light in the window advertised they were open twenty-four hours a day.

A man in his fifties was behind the counter, and Amanda took out her badge. "Detective Steele, and this is Detective Stenson. Does this look like a key that would belong to one of your units?" She gestured toward Trent, who held up the key she had found in Katherine's drawer.

"It could be. It's about the right size."

"Do you show a record of renting to a Katherine Graves?" she asked him.

"Do you have a warrant?"

She smiled at him. "I don't think it's necessary we leap right there, is it? I'm sure you want to help the local police."

The clerk hesitated, but then started tapping away on his keyboard. "We have an Amy Graves." The clerk pressed his brows. "But you said Katherine?"

"Uh-huh." It was possible a woman by that name, with the

surname of Graves, had a unit here but the odds would be too great. "We'll need to see Amy's unit."

"Now, I will need to insist on that warrant." He squared his shoulders, and there was a glint in his eye that disclosed he was having fun being the one in control at the moment.

"We'll get you one, but one thing first. We need to see if this key fits the lock on unit number...?" She left the end dangling, anticipating he'd fill in the blank.

"Three-oh-nine."

"Right, so can we just see if it fits the lock? If it does, I'll be happy to get you that warrant."

"Okay, before you go in, I will need to insist on it."

She smiled at him. "Understood."

They followed him out to a golf cart parked at the side of the office building, and he hopped behind the wheel. "You can join me or follow in your car."

They got on the golf cart, and he took them through rows of storage units. After the fourth turn, he parked and pointed toward the number posted next to the door. 309.

The three of them left the cart. Trent stuck the key in the lock.

"Perfect fit," he said, twisting it.

"Hey, wait, warrant, remember?" The clerk stepped in front of them holding up both hands and waving them frantically.

"The warrant," Trent said, "is coming right up."

She had been fully prepared to make the call, but Trent already had his cell to an ear and was walking away. From the sounds of it he called Judge Anderson directly.

"What's going on anyway? What did Amy do?"

Amy probably did nothing, but Katherine renting a unit under a fake name was suspicious. People with something to hide pulled stunts like that. Combine that with the existence of the burner phone. But why had Katherine chosen *Amy*?

Katherine's middle name was June. Her mother's name was Tori Hurst. Unless it was her mother's middle name?

"Detective?" the clerk prompted when she hadn't responded to him.

"It's an open investigation," she offered in an off-the-cuff manner to shut down the conversation.

Trent returned to them, phone in hand. He spoke primarily to Amanda. "A warrant will be coming through."

"I can let you in once I see it," the clerk said, nudging out his chin, again riding a power high.

Trent's phone chimed, and Amanda held back her smile, having a hunch it was the warrant.

"Here it is." Trent held the screen of his phone so the clerk could see it. This would be the digital version to support a verbal authorization. She and Trent would still need to submit the supporting paperwork.

The clerk squinted, as if the print were too small, but pulled back a few seconds later. He hadn't even bothered to scroll down. Amanda guessed if he'd read much, he hadn't understood it. Still, he said, "Guess it's all yours." The clerk gestured toward the unit.

Trent lifted the door.

"Whoa. That's intense." The clerk stepped forward, about to go inside, but Amanda and Trent blocked his path.

Amanda said, "We need you to stay back." Once he complied, she added for Trent, "We need to call this in, let Malone know what we're looking at here."

FORTY-EIGHT

Photos of a young girl in several poses were pinned up on marker boards that lined the storage unit. Among them were pictures of five men. Beneath them were their addresses, alibis, and motives. All but one man had a name.

"Lieutenant Catherwood mentioned a case about a murdered girl that Katherine had been obsessed with," she said, recalling that conversation. "He thought she'd let it go."

"Guess it's safe to say he was wrong."

"And he certainly didn't mention it was Julie Gilbert." Amanda moved through the space, shocked and impressed. In one way, relieved. If all Katherine's cloak-and-dagger of having a burner phone and mystery key tied back to this, it provided an innocent explanation for both. The cash may have factored in somehow too or just been a safety net. But at least Katherine wasn't involved in something criminal, rather trying to bring one down.

Ten years ago, six-year-old Julie Gilbert's brutal murder had made country-wide news. She'd been tagged America's little angel. The case had more impact on Amanda because of the girl's name being her own. Sadly, this Julie had been raped

and found beaten and strangled in an outbuilding on the property of her family home in Brooklyn. Her parents, close rela-
tives, and family friends had been looked at but released of
suspicion. The case had gone cold, and while Katherine had
been told to stop obsessing over it, she obviously hadn't. What if
she had provoked the wrong person? Amanda might have been
too quick to dismiss *the murdered girl* case as irrelevant. Then
in all fairness, she hadn't known about this storage unit
before now.

"I had no idea Katherine worked this investigation," Trent
said.

"Me either." If the lieutenant hadn't let it slip that
Katherine had been obsessed with a case involving a murdered
girl, they'd be left with assumptions. The name of the investigating detectives had been kept out of the media. Amanda fixed
on the girl's face and was stabbed by grief at the loss of someone
so young, in such a tragic way. What sort of monster could rape
a child? *Murder* a child?

In most of the photos, Julie's cherubic face was plastered
with makeup, and her neck adorned with chunky pieces of
jewelry. Her light blond hair gave her an ethereal glow. Her
blue eyes looked into the camera with a certain defiance and
utmost confidence. She had seen a lot for her short time on
earth, being carted around the country to beauty contests from
the time she was a baby. How would her life have turned out?
Would she have developed substance-abuse problems as many
people do when the spotlight finds them at a young age?

"It must have been horrible for Katherine, being on scene
and seeing Julie's lifeless little body," she said.

"Sometimes I ask myself how I do this job. *Sometimes.* But
it's the wins that keep me going. Someone needs to get these
violent offenders off the street."

"That keeps me going too. Well, that and coffee." She
winked at him, in an effort to loosen the tension.

Trent walked over to the board of suspects' faces, but she paused in front of a desk, where another laptop sat ready.

No wonder there was nothing of interest on her home one...

She joined Trent at the board. Her primary interest was in the unnamed man. His photograph was a candid shot. It appeared to have been taken at some event, possibly one of those beauty contests. He was in the background, lingering at the edge of the frame. The focus, front and center, was Julie captured mid-twirl with a hula hoop. Katherine must have come into this picture somewhere along the investigation.

"What in the world is all this?" Malone's voice pulled her from her thoughts. He had just stepped into the storage locker and was taking it all in. Sheer horror marked his expression, his jaw slack and eyes wide.

She had called Malone the moment they cracked the unit door. "Exactly our first reaction."

"Why the heck did Katherine have all this? And don't answer with some smart-alecky response. She was obviously looking into the murder of the Gilbert girl, but why?" Malone kept looking around the space, but it was a lot to absorb.

"We figured she must have been there from the start," Trent said.

"We'll need to verify that." Malone barely glanced at Trent. He pointed at the suspect board. "By the looks of it, these people had her interest. How does any of this tie in with Lowell Mooney?"

"If it does, it's far too soon to say." Amanda hated not having answers. She held herself to some high standard of needing to have one at the ready for every possible question, despite that being unreasonable.

"Well, if this isn't connected to Katherine's abduction, you need to let it go."

"You must admit all this looks, well, intense. What if

Katherine got close to the killer and they reacted?" Trent painted one scenario.

"They'd have killed her and destroyed all of this," Amanda said, playing devil's advocate, even though she wasn't willing to simply release this find either.

"Assuming they knew about *all* of this," Trent countered.

Amanda took a few deep breaths, the burden of overwhelm landing squarely on her shoulders. "We can't just ignore this, Sarge."

Malone was rubbing at his beard, tugging on the shortly groomed hairs. "We'll need to reevaluate distribution of manpower. And where would we even begin?"

Amanda gestured toward the marker board of suspects. Five faces, names or no names, they were all strangers to her, but one of them could belong to Katherine's abductor.

FORTY-NINE

7:30 AM, WEDNESDAY

Missing for 2 days, 2 hours, 40 minutes

The items in Katherine's storage unit were left as they were. Malone posted an officer to watch over it and sent Amanda and Trent home. She woke up the next morning to the smell of coffee and bacon, at seven thirty. That might as well have been the wee hours after only three hours of sleep.

The buzz of low chatter permeated the bedroom too. Zoe was an early riser, but Amanda was curious if that would change once she was a teenager. But no sense rushing time when it already flew.

She found Logan and Zoe in the kitchen. He was at the stove, tongs in hand, and Zoe was sitting at the peninsula.

"Look who finally decided to get out of bed." Logan smiled and set down the tongs. He walked over to her, hugged her, and kissed her. "Good morning."

"They usually start off that way." The words tumbled out, and she wished she could retract the negativity. No one needed that first thing, but her sleep had been choppy. She'd suffered a barrage of strange dreams, and Freud's diagnosis would put them down to helplessness over Katherine's abduction. "But, good morning," she added.

The bacon was sizzling madly, but he didn't return to tend to it. Instead he held eye contact with her and brushed a hand to her cheek. "Let's intend it *stays* that way."

Logan's loving, intimate touch had her transgression with Trent flooding back. She hadn't just kissed Trent but had initiated it. "Let's."

The toaster kicked up two pieces of toast.

"Well, that's my cue." Logan went to butter them. "Are you going to hang around for breakfast? Ouch." He tapped the tips of his fingers to his lips. "Hot toast."

"As it should be, but yeah, I'll stay." Running off would be the easy way out, and she had no valid excuse to leave. The fact it was torturous facing Logan after what she'd done didn't qualify. She came up behind Zoe and squeezed the girl, then swept back her hair and planted a kiss on her forehead. "Hey, sweetie."

"Morning." Zoe squirmed and turned to the side to face Amanda. "Do you want to see my Santa Claus?" Her eyes lit at the prospect of showing off her craft project to Amanda, and it had her heart swelling with gratitude. Life really was a series of ups and downs. Some of these veers were such drastic course corrections, they were as dizzying and nauseating as they were exhilarating.

"You know I do."

"Can we wait until after breakfast?" Logan dropped two more slices of bread into the toaster and turned to the stove. There, he lifted the pieces of bacon out and placed them on top of paper towel and dabbed off the grease.

"We can do that," Amanda answered, and Zoe pouted. "But *right* after, not a second longer." She smiled and patted Zoe's head, then took over duty at the toaster.

"Okay." Zoe was placated but not entirely happy to be

put off.

It turned out to be a nice, calm, and relaxing breakfast. Amanda did her best to stay in the moment, as Logan was always reminding her to do. And he had a point about wasted energy. No amount of worry about the future or regrets about the past changed a thing. If only. Then that blasted kiss never would have happened!

The pinch of a headache jabbed her left temple, and she winced.

"You got in pretty late last night," he said.

"This morning. Technically." She tagged on a brief smile. "But, yeah, it was almost four."

"Any leads?"

"Possibly too many."

"How is that possible?" He was smiling and not under-standing, but there was no reason he would. He'd never been a cop and never would be.

"It makes it hard to know where to concentrate your efforts." She left out the frustration that every wrong choice they made left Katherine out there for that much longer. "I should go. You got all this taken care of?" She referred to the dishes. Logan already had work at eight thirty ahead of him. He'd also volunteered to drop Zoe at her friend Maria's for the day and a two-night sleepover. "If not, I'll take care of it later."

Logan didn't jump on *later*, but she sensed judgment. His eyes seemed to ask, *when later?* "I'll handle the cleanup," he eventually offered.

"Mandy." Zoe was glaring at her. "You were supposed to look at my Santa Claus."

"Of course, sweetheart. Show me." She smiled at the girl. The big fella in red had been the furthest thing from her mind. It was overridden by thoughts of Katherine and whether they'd be too late to save her. Her heart and mind betrayed her with memories of kissing Trent and stirred up both regret and desire.

How she wished she could completely squash the latter. Logan was a good man and proving himself an excellent father figure for Zoe.

Zoe hopped off her chair and reached for Amanda's hand. She led her to her bedroom where she pulled her Santa Claus from the bookshelf.

"So? What do you think?" She held up the glued and lovingly crafted Santa. He was sequined, and his beard was made of cotton balls. His red suit, boots, and black leather belt were made from felt.

"He's fantastic. And you did this?" Amanda was grinning, as was Zoe.

"Uh-huh. All by myself. Libby just told me what to do. But *I* did it." She was beaming with pride, as she should be.

"You're such a talented girl, Zoe." Amanda reached out to hug her, but the girl pulled back, her face serious.

"Be careful. Don't hurt him or I won't get any presents." Her serious expression gave way to laughter as she returned Santa to the shelf where he had been. Zoe turned around to face Amanda, her expression all serious. "Okay. Now you can go."

"Why you little..." Amanda lunged across the room. Zoe squealed, but, for all the noise, she didn't try to get away. Moments like this, that were shared between them, were a balm to Amanda's spirit.

Logan joined the action, and the three of them wound up on Zoe's bed laughing. Amanda was looking at the ceiling. How had she gotten so lucky twice in one lifetime? She rolled to her side and kissed Logan.

"Oh, man," Zoe groaned and bopped up. "Don't you have work?"

Amanda and Logan laughed and shook their heads. Another cycle of play and, like all good things, it had to come to an end.

FIFTY

It was strange for Amanda not to stop at Hannah's Diner. They were open for business, but with May not there, it would have been too much. Amanda made a mental note to check in on her today, to make sure she was hanging in there. When that time came, Amanda had every intention of having answers too. Even better, be returning Katherine safely home.

Trent wasn't at Central when Amanda got there.

"Steele?" It was Malone, and he was coming toward her cubicle. He patted a hand on the top of the partition at her doorway.

"Good morning, Sarge." She tried to ground the swirling energy in her gut that rose in contrast to her cheery greeting.

"Where's Stenson?" He made a dramatic show of looking over at Trent's desk, as if he'd magically manifest in front of his eyes.

"Not here yet."

"No, no, he's here somewhere." Malone glanced over his shoulder. "There you are."

Amanda caught sight of Trent walking over, a coffee cup in

hand, and she'd be lying to herself to say her heart hadn't bumped off rhythm a bit.

"Morning," he said to her, but it was low volume and close to a mumble.

"Good morning."

"Now that's out of the way, can we get to work, please?" Malone asked, exasperated. "Come with me to the meeting room." He headed in that direction, not giving them a passing glance backward. He expected they'd follow.

"No Hannah's this morning for you either?" Trent lifted his mug, filled with station brew.

"I couldn't bring myself to go inside."

"Same here."

"You guys coming?" Malone huffed and flailed his arms.

She smiled at Trent and shook her head. "We better get a move on before he flogs us in the public square."

He smirked but buried the expression in the lip of his mug.

Amanda was wishing she'd thought ahead to bring a traveler of coffee with her, but she'd rushed from home.

Trent held back and gestured for Amanda to enter the conference room ahead of him. It was standing room only. Several uniformed officers and the other detectives from Homicide were jammed inside. The man commanding the room was Police Chief Jeff Buchanan.

"Now that everyone is here, let's get started." The chief continually paced, working the front of the room the way any good speaker would, using the space to draw in his audience's attention and to hold it. "As you all know we're facing an urgent situation. Katherine Graves, a former Homicide sergeant with the PWCPD, was abducted on Monday morning during a shooting that resulted in the murder of an eighteen-year-old girl. Graves may no longer be at the PD, but she remains a part of our family. Most of you have been working tirelessly to find her and her abductors. I applaud you for this, but the fact remains we still haven't brought her home."

Amanda glanced at Trent, who was standing next to her. They were both positioned rather close to the door. Buchanan hadn't made the purpose for this meeting clear yet, and the uncertainty had her insides twisting into knots.

Buchanan continued. "It's time that we buckle down, determine who is behind this attack. Detectives Steele and Stenson have apprehended a potential suspect, Lowell Mooney of New York City. It's not yet been confirmed if Mooney is involved or not. Therefore, we are no closer to our goal. We don't even know if Katherine is still alive."

The chief's words drilled in the direness of the situation, and the room became quieter than before.

"This is why I've decided to take drastic action," Buchanan said. "The Public Information Office will be sending out an official statement to the public asking for their help. It will include a picture of our Jane Doe, appealing to anyone who knew her to come forward. News of her murder will stay out of the news, but it will be stressed she may be in danger. A photo of Katherine will also be shared. Our desire is someone will recognize the woman or will have recently seen Katherine. A tipline is being set up for this purpose. I have every intention that we will bring Katherine back to us alive."

"Then don't do this." The words slipped out of Amanda's mouth, and all eyes were on her. She held up a hand. "I apologize for interrupting. Go ahead." Everyone was slow to pry their gaze from her, except the police chief kept his fixed on her. His mouth twitched like it did whenever he was in deep thought or being challenged.

"This is a unique situation." The chief eventually tore his gaze from her to take in the room. "I called this meeting so that none of you will be blindsided by the news today. That is all. You are dismissed."

When everyone started dispersing from the room, he beelined for her. "Detective Steele."

"Chief." She offered him a pressed-lip smile, doing her best to tamp down her anxiousness. His decision was the wrong one, but she wasn't hinging this on some premonition. Rather, on precedent.

"You don't agree with my decision to appeal to the public?" Buchanan asked her, and Malone and Trent shrank back.

"I don't. You're aware of what happened the last time any of this hit the news." She shouldn't need to list the repercussions one by one. That it had ultimately led to a ransom demand and another murder.

Malone popped his eyes, standing out of the chief's view, as if to caution her to stop there.

"That was an unapproved piece, Detective," Buchanan said coolly. "The department will be drafting what the media is to share this time. We don't even know for a certainty if Mr. Reyes's article resulted in the ransom demand. That's an assumption. Far as I'm aware, we haven't even landed on a concrete motive for the shooter yet."

"All the more reason to play this close." Her heart was thumping rapidly, and breathing was becoming more difficult. One false move, and Katherine would pay the price because of their error.

"And you're well experienced in this type of situation?"

She couldn't claim she was, so she remained quiet.

"What I thought."

"I'm coming at you from a purely logical standpoint, Chief. Whoever took her is under enough stress, whether they put it on themselves, or it is being applied by a third party." Her thoughts dipped to Lowell Mooney and if he'd hired the man. "They've had her for two full days already. Katherine's standing in this community and background is no secret to them. But by making her current situation public, this intensifies the pressure this person must already be under."

Buchanan bobbed his head. "And who wants an anxious person's finger on the trigger."

"Exactly. We already suspect the shooter detoured from the original plan with the ransom request. What's to say this statement you intend to publish won't cause that to happen again, possibly with fatal consequences?" She didn't say it in so many words, but she was thinking they could find Katherine's dead body next.

Buchanan appeared to consider her words, then parted with, "No. The statement goes ahead. Katherine is out there. The public could help us find her. I'm all ears if you have a better idea."

The offer was there as if he were open-minded, but she wasn't swallowing it.

"Where are we with Mooney anyway?" Buchanan straightened his tie, as if he were suddenly being strangled by it.

"He is clear of the ransom request and Jane Doe's murder. He was in custody at those times, but Trent and I believe there is a possibility he may have commissioned the people responsible."

"Hired the shooter and his partner? Tell me about that third-party theory you mentioned?"

Malone must not have passed along their thinking on this aspect to the chief. "Ideally we could get a warrant for Mooney's phone records and financials."

"I don't think there's enough to support that from what Malone's briefed me on, unless I'm missing something."

Amanda highly doubted Malone would have overlooked passing anything along. "I can appreciate your position, but this guy makes no secret of hating Katherine. He's been in town for a few days and still hasn't told us how he's spent his time, just that he intended to confront Katherine. To *talk*," she added with finger quotes.

"I don't like that, but our hands are tied unless we get solid evidence against him. Though, I understand that he was in possession of the same gun type used in the shooting. Yet you don't believe he is the shooter from the gas station?"

"He's not. No tattoo," Trent inserted.

"Right, so I say we cut Lowell Mooney loose."

"Just give us a few hours longer," she pleaded.

Buchanan regarded her with impatience.

She rushed ahead. "If we could talk with the employees at the Sunny Motel, ask if they saw a white Ford van there for Mooney, then..." Malone was going to see to this, but it would make Buchanan feel like he was calling the shots.

"Hmm. That might give us something to support a warrant for his phone and financials."

"Yes, sir."

"Okay, well, let's do it."

This was where she hesitated to speak, to point out that Lowell Mooney wasn't her only focus. "Thank you, sir. But, of course, we are still considering other possibilities."

"You're now referring to the burner phone and the mystery key that led to that storage unit."

"Mainly the last aspect," she said.

"I heard about all of that." Buchanan gestured toward Malone. "But that avenue could quickly become a time-sucking rabbit hole."

"Can we risk being choosey?" Trent spoke up, earning everyone's attention. "We should push Mooney more, but I also don't think we can dismiss Graves's storage unit and her obsession with the Julie Gilbert case either. It's easy to see how she could have gotten herself into trouble if she pushed the wrong person."

Buchanan squared his shoulders and puffed out his chest,

his body language challenging. "Fine. I'll assign officers to speak with the employees of the Sunny Motel. You try the Gilbert angle. *But* if I get the sense it's a waste of time, I'll shut it down. Am I understood?"

"Yes. Thank you, Chief." She dipped her head, and Buchanan reciprocated before leaving the room, his cell phone pressed to an ear.

As Amanda and Trent headed to the storage unit, she wished for just one thing that would break the case wide open.

FIFTY-ONE

Officer Brandt was the one charged with keeping an eye on Katherine's storage unit, and he let Amanda and Trent in with no more than a greeting.

She headed for the marker board with the suspects on them and photographed them. "We start here. See if we can place any of these five men in Prince William County recently."

"Simple but efficient."

"I'm not about to waste time, Trent." She wasn't sure why his comment had her so riled up, but it was her instant reaction to his words. It could have been residual emotion from her standoff with Buchanan or the pressure bearing down on her shoulders. While they debated their next course of action, Katherine remained in captivity. That is, if she wasn't already dead.

"I didn't mean to imply otherwise." He walked over to the laptop that was still on the desk. They hadn't touched it last night. "We should crack into this and see if there's anything useful on here."

"I bet there is. The laptop at her house served her personal needs and having one here, well, it speaks for itself."

He nodded. "Her research notes."

She hit the power button, and the computer turned on. "It has battery life, so it hasn't been sitting unused for long." The password screen came up. "You don't happen to know the password that unlocked her other one, do you? It could be the same."

"Yep. Just a second." Trent pulled out his notebook.

"How do you keep track of what you note where?" He switched from old-school to his tablet so often it was dizzying.

"I'm just that good." He smiled at her and continued flipping pages. "Ah, here we go. Badass."

"Thanks. I like to think I am."

Trent was smiling. "It's the password."

She grinned. "Of course it is. It kind of goes with ninja." She typed in the password and got nowhere.

"Speaking of ninja, let's not knock it till we've tried it."

She gave that a go and was granted access. It was a good thing for them that Katherine reused her passwords, even if she didn't keep them consistent across her laptops. "What do you know."

Trent tucked his notepad away again.

She sat at the desk and opened the file directory. There were a lot of Word files, and they were organized under folders named *Julie Gilbert, The Gilberts, Extended Family*, and then there were ones labeled with the four named suspects from the board and one as *Suspect Five—Unidentified*.

"Lots of reading ahead of us," Trent said.

"Thank you, Captain Obvious." She smirked at him and turned her focus back to the screen. She knew better than to expect a starred document to point them to Katherine's top suspect, but she would have taken it.

"Where should we start?"

"I'm going into Word and opening the last document she

worked on." It was a thought that occurred to her, and she followed the nudge.

"Sounds smart to me."

"I have them sometimes." She smiled, and the expression held while she clicked on a document called *Master Notes*, but the expression disappeared when she started reading.

FIFTY-TWO

Amanda kept reading the document, most of it in her head, the odd sentence out loud. Trent was hunched next to her reading too. The document contained a play-by-play account of the steps that Katherine had taken during her investigation into the Gilbert case. Katherine seemed to cover events in chronological order. The most recent entry at the end was from last Wednesday.

> I feel like I'm getting so close. I just need the evidence to prove it, to finally track down this unknown man. He haunts my dreams at night, and sometimes it feels like I'm being watched. But it has to be paranoia, and all in my head. If I don't know who he is, he doesn't know me.

"That was just a week before her abduction." Trent turned to Amanda, placing their faces within inches of each other, but neither of them pulled back. Rather they lingered in discomfort and demonstrated an admirable display of self-restraint. *Who will turn away first?* Trent did. Eventually. The pending seconds had her heart pounding like a jackhammer. "And why would she assume paranoia? She received those threats we found."

"Maybe they are from a while ago."

"Whatever the case, this guy Katherine suspected of raping and killing Julie Gilbert could have come for her."

"Eliminating Lowell Mooney from suspicion. In the least, he's not the mystery man in that photo. He also wasn't in town yet to be watching her."

"True enough. Though it seems Katherine had two people stalking her."

"Yep. Going back to the mystery man, it wouldn't seem Katherine managed to identify him. Really, how much of a threat could she have been to him?"

"She didn't need his name for him to be a threat. If she ever got close to him, that could be enough. Maybe she asked the wrong person about him and word reached him."

"Back in New York though? And when? Also, what prompted him to act now? His left wrist isn't visible in the photo, so I can't tell if he has a snake tattoo." Frustration sank in but gave way to an idea. She brought up the search function within Word and keyed in *Prince William County*. Nada.

Next, she tried *Woodbridge*. Bingo.

It took her to the one-and-only mention, which dated back a year ago.

Thad Coffey moved to Woodbridge. But why come all this way? A change of pace or running to escape his guilt?

"That's this guy." Trent pointed to a middle-aged man on the board with a high forehead, bouncy white hair, wild eyebrows, and a dominant, if not a slightly crooked, nose.

"Coffey was Julie's talent manager." Amanda recalled the name from the media coverage, without needing to refer to the brief note on the marker board.

"She thought he did that to Julie."

"She's not the only one if you remember the news from the time. There was a lot of heat directed his way, but he was cleared. There wasn't any evidence against him that would stick in a court of law."

"He moved to get away from the limelight then."

"Except he waited long enough, didn't he? Katherine's entry is only from one year ago. Surely, Coffey would have been old news by then."

"One year ago." Trent's eyes widened. "That's about six months after that article disclosed that Katherine was in Prince William County. Did he come out here for her?"

Amanda looked at Coffey's photo again. He hardly fit the image of their shooter ten years ago or whenever that photo was taken. Though it didn't mean Coffey hadn't hired someone. She continued to read.

Coffey left the beauty pageant world. Again, I ask myself why? Was Julie's murder just too much for him to stomach? Had his grief consumed him? Is he wanting to put space between himself and what he did?

"Is Coffey's name mentioned anywhere else? Do that search function again," Trent said.

Amanda brought up the tool and typed in the talent manager's name. His name appeared fifty-five times. "Katherine must have really suspected him." She scrolled to the most recent entry among the results. She pressed a fingertip to the screen.

"From Friday two weeks ago," Trent said.

She read the entry.

Coffey was right there. I could hardly believe what I was seeing. In my grocery store, and he didn't seem surprised at all to see me. He didn't say a word as I made myself walk past him. Is he why I've been feeling watched? Like my skin is crawling? Just when I think I have my mind fixed on a suspect, it's as if they shuffle and rearrange themselves, each one fighting for priority.

Amanda backed out of the document, powered down the laptop, and shut the lid. "I say we have our next stop."

FIFTY-THREE

Amanda had called Malone and briefed him while Trent drove. Now they were walking up to the house on file for Thad Coffey, retired talent manager. He was sixty-two and married to a woman named Noreen, who was sixty. The house was all decked for Christmas. Lights were strung along the eaves and wrapped a cedar tree on the front lawn. A blowup Santa Claus lay collapsed on the ground. The fan blower was likely on a timer that ran it during the night and early morning hours.

A wreath with red and gold baubles and pine cones adorned the front door. When Trent stepped onto the *Merry Christmas* doormat, Santa bellowed, "Ho ho ho!"

All the decorations made Amanda feel insignificant if she drew up her own beside them. There was no comparison. Zoe's Popsicle-stick Santa was all that smacked of seasonal cheer at her house. Amanda would turn that around, after she got Katherine home safely, and once she talked with Logan.

Trent rang the doorbell and a rendition of "O Holy Night" radiated from inside the home.

"Nice touch." She regretted her compliment when she

thought of the inhabitant. The man who lived here might have raped and murdered a young girl. He may also be behind two more recent murders and Katherine's abduction.

A foot propped the door open, and a woman tucked her head out. "Thing sticks like crazy." She was wearing a red apron, and the house smelled of gingerbread.

Has she no shame in making me feel like Scrooge? The thought whizzed through Amanda's head.

Trent held up his badge. "Prince William County PD, ma'am. We'd like to speak with Thad Coffey. Your husband, I presume?"

"He is, but why do you want to speak with him?" Her forehead furrowed.

"It's a police matter, so it would be much better if we could speak with him directly," Trent said matter-of-factly.

"Very well. Come inside, you're making my house cold." She stepped back and allowed them room to enter.

The warm house amplified the smell of gingerbread. It had been heavenly on the doorstep but was intoxicating inside.

She called up the stairs, "Thad! You have company!" Back to them, she added, "He should be here in a minute. I must go check on my cookies." With that, she was off to the rear of the house.

While waiting, Amanda took in the decorations from the entry. The staircase was tucked on the right side, and the railing was wrapped with garland speckled with spray snow, pine cones, and red berries.

Thad stomped across overhead and started down the stairs. "Who is it, Noreen?" He stopped at the sight of them. "Who are you?" He'd aged since the picture on Katherine's marker board. The passage of time had drawn his hairline back and thinned out his eyebrows. Wrinkles carved deep grooves around his mouth and eyes.

Amanda and Trent both held up their badges.

Thad's head dipped forward, lifted up. "Please don't tell me you're here about Julie Gilbert."

"We're not here about her." Trent was doing a good job of going with the flow of conversation and not showing any surprise. Though the fact Thad mentioned the girl's name could be a good assumption on his part. But it was his delivery that made his statement seem almost threatening.

"What if we were?" Amanda put in.

Thad huffed. "Just get to the point."

"We're here about Katherine Graves," she pushed back.

"Oh, bother. She's been determined to ruin my life ever since that child was murdered."

His callous indifference woke up her fiery temper. "You say that like it's nothing. She was six years old. Her murder ruined *your* life? I'd like to know how." She might be coming across hot, but violence against children was her trigger.

"You make me sound callous."

"You did that yourself," she volleyed back.

"It wasn't her murder that ruined my life. Heck, I hate to think what that poor dear suffered, but I had nothing to do with it. Katherine didn't let up though. She put me through endless hours of questioning even after my alibis checked out."

Amanda wasn't going to delve into it, as she recalled Trent saying that not every case was for her to solve. Otherwise she might point out that alibis were subject to manipulation. And if Katherine still considered Thad a suspect, Amanda put faith in the fact she had her reasons.

"Well, as I said, Mr. Coffey, we're not here about Julie Gilbert," Trent said. "But we do have questions for you about a recent investigation."

The man's shoulders relaxed some. "Very well, but let's go in here to talk. My knees act up if I stand around too long." He took them to the living room off the entry.

She would guess he hadn't seen Fraser Reyes's article or Chief Buchanan's press release, or he'd be more on guard about discussing Katherine. Amanda stepped forward at the same time as Trent, and they found themselves squeezed together in the doorway.

"Oh, you have to kiss." Noreen was back from the kitchen and wiping her hands on her apron. She jabbed her gaze above their foreheads.

A sprig of mistletoe.

You've got to be shitting me! Amanda smiled at Noreen. "We're work partners, and that would be inappropriate." As she spoke, she made brief eye contact with Trent. In that moment, she wasn't sure how to read him. She'd guess he was going to comply, but he looked away.

"We're here on business, ma'am." Trent walked into the room.

Thad was in a recliner, and Amanda and Trent parked on opposite ends of a couch.

Noreen stepped into the room and perched on the arm of her husband's chair. "What is this about?"

"Katherine Graves was abducted at gunpoint Monday morning. You might have heard this on the news?" Trent waded right in.

"We try to avoid the news," Thad said. "Ever since, well, I made headlines."

Thad rolled past the main soundbite and responded only to the question. Amanda said, "Katherine Graves is still missing. What do you know about this?"

"Me? Nothing. But that woman is relentless. She's convinced that I killed Julie. But I did not." He reached for his wife's hand and squeezed it, running his thumb over the back of it. "She's part of the reason we left New York. Go figure my luck winding up in the same town as her."

"You didn't know she lived here when you moved?"

Amanda found it hard to believe though he did say he avoided the news. All this was contingent on his word being trustworthy.

"Not until we got here," Thad said. "Noreen came across archived news at the library where she works part-time. She saw Katherine worked as a police sergeant."

"Have you had any contact with Ms. Graves since you moved to town?" Amanda asked.

"I saw her a couple of weeks ago at the grocery store," Thad told them.

According to Katherine's note that was true. "And that's all? You saw her and walked away?"

"That woman..." Thad seethed.

"That woman, *what*, Mr. Coffey?" Amanda pressed.

"She never left well enough alone. I thought for sure when I saw her she was going to come after me and pick up her harassment." He flailed the hand that wasn't holding on to his wife's, and his cheeks flushed bright red.

Amanda chose to withhold that Katherine knew Thad Coffey had moved to Woodbridge long before they bumped into each other at the grocery store. Though her not confronting him could suggest she had relinquished her suspicions about him. How did that reconcile with her notes? Maybe she was searching for more to use against him before coming at him again.

A timer chimed from deep within the house, and Noreen attended to it.

"Were you angry when you saw her?" Trent asked.

"You bet I was. Everything came flooding back. Even though my alibi cleared me, she was having none of it. Told me I was a liar so often that I lost count. She certainly made no bones about coming out and accusing me to my face of hurting that poor girl."

The man's anger wasn't far beneath the surface, and if he was innocent of such atrocities, he'd be justifiably insulted and defensive. But how far would he go to quiet Katherine's allegations? Was he willing to hire someone to get rid of her or do with her as they saw fit?

FIFTY-FOUR

Amanda couldn't shake the fact that Thad Coffey had bumped into Katherine two weeks ago. Just the mere mention of her aggravated him after all this time. His home made it evident that he'd have the means to pay someone to do his dirty work, but that was where their suspicion ended. They didn't have enough to justify continuing with this angle.

She and Trent grabbed lunch before returning to Central. Amanda also called May, who told her she was hanging in there but was understandably exhausted. At the station, they updated Malone on their visit to Thad Coffey. He had news for them too. The officers had no luck with the staff from the Sunny Motel. None had seen a white Ford van in the lot since Lowell Mooney had checked in. His Glock 19 wasn't the one that killed Leah Bernard, which was a result they had expected at this point. He was still being charged with possession of an unregistered gun and cocaine but as of now, he was cleared of suspicion regarding Katherine's abduction.

She and Trent went to their desks. He was going to watch Katherine's doorbell camera footage, while she pulled backgrounds for the three other names Katherine had in her storage unit. She also called Detective Fitzgerald and asked if he considered Katherine to have a borderline obsession with the Gilbert case. He did. When Amanda inquired about Katherine's top suspects, he only told her Katherine tried to secure several search warrants for Thad Coffey's residence. None of her efforts in this regard met with success. Apparently, from a legal standpoint, there wasn't enough to authorize the intrusion into his life.

Amanda had hung up finding some empathy for Thad. Once Katherine had her mind set, it was next to impossible to change. If she was convinced Thad was guilty, she wouldn't be quick to be swayed.

"Amanda, you need to see this." It was Trent, his head popping over the partition.

If his words weren't enough to get her moving, his pallor certainly was. "Whatcha got?"

"Look." Trent clicked play.

The view covered the front of her house to the street. A few cars drove by, but that wasn't exciting. Then a man came shuffling down the sidewalk and turned toward Katherine's house. "Is that Lowell Mooney?"

"The one and only. This wasn't the only time he strolled by Graves's house though. The timestamp puts this one from Sunday afternoon, but he was also there Saturday, and last Friday."

"Guess we know what he's been doing in town since he got here."

"And why he didn't want to tell us."

"It doesn't look good, but there's nothing we can do about it. We need to move on."

"I know."

Her desk phone rang, and she hustled to answer.

"This is Officer Radcliffe," her caller told her. "I'm assigned to the Graves investigation tipline."

Amanda waved for Trent to come over and hit the speaker button.

Radcliffe continued speaking. "We received an anonymous call from a man who identified Jane Doe."

Amanda snatched a pen from a holder on her desk, prepared to write down the name. "I'm ready."

"Lynnette Johnson, twenty-nine years old."

Amanda put pen tip to paper, but the pen was dry. She tossed it into the garbage can next to her desk and tried another one. This one worked, and she hurried to write down what the officer was telling her. She stopped when it came to the address. "Can you repeat that again?" she asked.

The officer did, and Amanda wasn't hearing things. She and Trent had already been there once during this investigation.

FIFTY-FIVE

Amanda and Trent were seated across from Malone. "The tipline came through, boss," she said. "Lynnette Johnson, and you're never going to believe where her address takes us."

"Barry Holden," Trent snaked in, and she gave him a narrow-eyed glare for taking that from her.

"The man who had the plates that were put on the Mercedes?"

"Uh-huh," she said.

"That can't be a coincidence."

"Trent and I don't think so either."

"Where's this Holden guy now? Wasn't he headed to jail?"

Trent looked at her, and she gestured for him to respond.

"I called his probation officer, and she said he was sent home, still adorned with his ankle monitor. There was a deal worked out."

"He turned confidential informant," Amanda said, grinning at Trent, considering this payback for him swooping in a moment ago.

"Changes nothing. We do this by the book. That means a residential search warrant, and SWAT will clear the home before you move in. Holden very well may be a willing accomplice in all of this."

"Agreed," both Amanda and Trent put in.

"We'll secure an arrest warrant for him too," Malone said. "We do have him on record as confirming he had the plates in his possession?"

She thought of the recorded interrogation, and she didn't recall him admitting as much in so many words off the top. "We have a witness willing to testify to that, possibly two." Simon Wheable might be harder to get on board, but his cooperation could lessen the sentence he'd be facing for fraud.

Malone reached for the phone on his desk. "Then let's move."

FIFTY-SIX

Warrants and arranging things with SWAT always took time. Strategic Weapons and Tactics needed to analyze the best approach and be prepared for several scenarios. Among those was that the shooter might be inside the house with Barry Holden.

It was nearing five o'clock by the time Amanda and Trent parked near Barry's home. His street had been cordoned off to limit traffic and avoid possible casualties, which was a necessary precaution considering the circumstances.

Amanda and Trent, wearing Kevlar vests, were positioned behind the vehicle, using it as a means of cover.

SWAT officers approached Holden's front door, guns at the ready, looking like they were loaded for warfare. Other members of the team advanced on the rear of the property.

Their roar of "Prince William County PD" echoed through the neighborhood and shook Amanda's core, infusing a fresh dose of adrenaline into her bloodstream. Moments like this weren't black and white and could turn deadly quickly.

No one answered their cries, and officers stepped back to let one through who had a battering ram. He forced entry, and the officers swarmed into the house like a bunch of angry ants.

Thumping and shouts traveled through the air, but so far, no gunfire. If that continued, it was a good day.

Shortly after, two officers came out with Barry Holden, each one with a firm grip on his arms. His hands were cuffed behind his back. He struggled against their hold, but to no avail. These SWAT guys could bench-press the man without breaking a sweat.

"I didn't do anything. What the hell?" Barry's fight seemed to leave him when he caught sight of Amanda and Trent walking across the street. "I should have known."

Amanda smiled, pleased they made a lasting impression.

Barry snarled. "What is this?"

"I would think that's quite obvious," Amanda said. "You're under arrest for your involvement with the murders of Leah Bernard and Lynnette Johnson and the abduction of Katherine Graves."

"We've been through all this. I'm innocent. As for the plates, I don't know who I passed them on to. You released me."

"Apparently our mistake. New evidence has come to light that implicates you."

"How is that possible? Wait a minute. You said Lynnette Johnson? She was murdered?"

"You should know since you're in this up to your neck," Trent said.

A uniformed officer came to retrieve Barry and load him into the back of their squad car.

"Hold up," Barry said. "What's going on exactly? Lynnette was murdered?"

He wasn't exactly smart, but not all criminals were. The officer motioned to ask if he were to take Barry now or hold off a moment. Amanda shook her head, and he retreated a few steps.

The SWAT team were already headed for their command vehicle.

Barry's forehead was beaded with sweat despite the fact it was below zero. His anxiousness did nothing to waylay Amanda's suspicions.

"We need to have a talk down at Central," she put out in a firm tone.

Barry looked from her to Trent. "I know how I look on paper. I've got a record, and I admit to having those plates you mentioned, but please talk to me. Lynnette is dead?"

He seemed stuck on this point, his reaction genuine. It had her taking pause. "Lynnette Johnson has been identified as one of the perps involved with the murder and abduction earlier this week. And, yes, she is dead."

The uniformed officer stepped forward again, and she held up a hand to stop him from taking further action.

"How?" Barry asked.

"Gunshot to the back of her head," she told him.

His eyes welled up. "Lynnette didn't deserve that."

"No, she didn't." *No one does.*

"She was so broken."

Maybe it was a case of it takes one to know one. From the outside, some might describe Barry as broken. "What makes you say that?"

Barry didn't respond but toed the floorboards of his front porch.

Amanda motioned to the officer.

"Wait," Barry said. "Lynnette was down on her luck, but she struck me as someone very familiar with the landscape, if you know what I mean."

"Let's assume that we don't," Trent interjected.

"Bad life, poor childhood. She held a deadbeat job at some dive bar in town. And don't ask me the name. We weren't slumber buddies, but she needed a break. It's why I let her stay in a room upstairs."

Amanda doubted Barry was some selfless, helpful Samaritan. Even his probation officer told them Barry was out for himself. "It had absolutely nothing to do with her being young and beautiful?"

"It wasn't like that."

"Very well. How long did she live here?"

"Six months, give or take. But I haven't seen her in a few weeks."

"Why is that?" Her patience allowed her to play along some. It wasn't far from her mind that the man before her could be wrapped up in this mess and know Katherine's whereabouts. The fact his name had surfaced twice in this investigation certainly didn't work in his favor.

"I kicked her out."

She struggled with the decision of moving the conversation back to Central. So far, Barry was talking. If they put him in an interrogation room, that could stop with one demand for a lawyer. "And why was that?"

The uniformed officer gave her another look as if to ask whether he should take Barry. She shook her head, and he sighed.

"Why did you kick her out?" Amanda asked.

Barry's expression blanked.

"I asked you a question, Barry, and if you don't want to continue this conversation here, we can move it back to Central," she pushed out.

"It's just— Wait. It's all coming together for me."

"What is?" The dance was exhausting. While they stood here, who knew how these precious seconds affected Katherine?

"Those plates being used in that murder and abduction Monday. I didn't put it together until now."

She glanced at Trent, and he shook his head, obviously

tapped out of patience. She debated whether to rush Barry along to get to the point, or remain silent. She opted for the latter.

He met Amanda's gaze. "Lynnette must have lifted them from me."

And here we go, down story lane.

"Because you gave them to her to use?" Trent tossed back.

"Noooo." He glared at Trent. "I just had them kicking around in my garage. She must have seen them, decided they could be useful and lifted them."

"What happened to you getting them for someone else, a person you didn't know by name?" she pushed out.

He shrugged. "I might have lied or made an assumption."

"You lied then, but not now?" This guy was a piece of work.

"Yeah."

"Any wonder I'm having a hard time believing you? Let me tell you what we think." She reached the end of her patience. "You assisted Lynnette and her partner in executing Monday's plan by giving them those plates. That makes you an accomplice." She lassoed a finger in the air and the officer grabbed Barry's arm.

"I did no such thing. But wait... partner? Is it *that* guy?" he blurted out.

She put off the officer again. "What guy?" While she waited for Barry to answer, her heart beat wildly in her chest. Were they finally going to find out the identity of Katherine's abductor?

FIFTY-SEVEN

"He gave me the willies, I'll tell you that." Barry mocked shivers.

"I asked you, what guy?" Barry was exasperating, and sucking Amanda's goodwill dry.

"Do you have his name?" Trent asked, sounding about as fed up as her.

"I don't, but—"

"Barry, if you want our help, want us to buy any word of what you're telling us, you need to work with us." She was tired, cold, and emotionally frayed.

"I can tell you that he's been sniffing around Lynnette for a good two months. He's why I finally kicked her out a few weeks ago."

"What does he look like?" Surely, he could provide that much, or *this guy* was a fictional creation.

Barry gave them a rather vague description. Brown hair, brown "crazy" eyes, a chin dimple, late forties, early fifties. "Oh, and he had a snake tattoo on his left wrist."

That can't be a coincidence!

"This the one?" Trent had the enlarged shot of the ink up on his tablet and held the screen toward Barry.

"Yeah, yeah, that's him, man." Barry bounced up and down.

"You need to tell us where we can find him," Amanda said firmly.

"I... I don't know. Don't wanna know."

Amanda could have screamed in frustration at being so close yet so far away. "You said this guy was a friend of Lynnette's, also the reason you evicted her."

"That's right. She'd let him stay over quite often. I'm sure he was living here, though she tried to convince me otherwise."

Barry had Amanda's full attention now. "Do you know where she went after you kicked her out?"

"I don't."

"Where was she living before you took her in?" It was possible she had returned there with the shooter. He might even be holding Katherine in that location.

"I don't have any specifics. I just got the impression it was in the country around here somewhere."

Amanda made a mental note of that. It wasn't entirely helpful at first pass, but with more context it might offer a lead. "Did either of them leave anything behind?" If so, they could find some clue as to his identity.

"I do have one box of her things." He shrugged. "Did this guy kill her?"

"It's possible. Yes," Amanda said. "Where's this box?"

"It's down in the basement on the shelving near the furnace. But you both really need to get it into your heads. This guy was a dick, through and through. I'm quite sure he hit her. They did a lot of screaming, and Lynnette, an awful lot of crying. But it wasn't my place to put my nose in."

Amanda nodded to the officer to take Barry, and she and Trent started toward the front door.

Barry shrugged off the officer's hold. "Is this still necessary? I've been cooperative."

They both ignored him, and he mumbled, "Nice," behind them as they stepped into the house.

"Holden just let the guy hurt her." Trent scowled and shook his head. "Neither of them is much of a man. But the shooter buddies up to Lynnette. Did he plan to exploit her and use her to carry out his mission?"

"Barry said he's in his late forties, possibly fifties. Lynnette was twenty-nine. That would make him at least seventeen years older. It possibly made it easier to manipulate her."

"And she had a rough past that the shooter might have exploited. He could have convinced her that he was good for her and all she deserved." Trent shook his head. "It's sad that she might have fallen for it."

"Though, did she?" Amanda countered. "Maybe for a while, but it seems she broke free from his spell. We've discussed how she seemed to have left clues behind."

"And look where that got her." Trent frowned.

She stepped off the bottom step into the unfinished basement. The flooring was painted concrete.

Her phone rang, and it startled her. She came close to hitting her head on a low doorway. "Detective Steele," she answered without looking at the caller ID.

"Mandy, another late night?" It was Logan, and the question was offensive. She was putting all her energy into saving a woman's life and finding justice for two others, and he was upset because she wasn't home for dinner.

"Katherine is still missing, Logan. The man who took her has already killed at least two people."

Logan's end of the line fell silent.

Trent looked over his shoulder at her, and his widened eyes told her how sharp her tone must have been. She could have softened her response, but she was running on a few hours' sleep and could be on the verge of discovering their greatest lead yet. This wasn't the time for the conversation that Logan wanted to have.

"Zoe's at Maria's so you don't need to worry about her. Enjoy some quiet." The goal was to present a pleasing alternative and get his mind off her abrupt reaction.

"I thought we would together, starting with a nice dinner and a bottle of wine. Then we'd curl up on the couch with a movie."

His proposal for the evening was appealing, but she didn't have the luxury of tapping out because she wanted to. Katherine needed her, even more than Logan. "I'll be home when I can."

A few beats, then, "Okay, well, do what you need to do."

Was he being sincere or snide? She opened her mouth, shut it, looked up to the ceiling, cringed and retreated at the sight of a huge black spider making its way toward a fly caught in its web. The fine gauze flinching as the insect resisted its fate. "I appreciate your understanding."

"Don't mention it. See you when you get here." And he was gone.

She hugged her phone against her chest. He was already slipping away from her. Imagine his reaction when she confessed what she'd done with Trent.

"I found what we were after." Trent came over holding an overstuffed cardboard box.

"Let's take it upstairs." She led the way to the main level, which was cast in shadows. The sunlight was fading as it was already after six in the evening. She flipped the lights in the kitchen on, and Trent set the box on the counter.

A travel mug, a pillow embroidered with *Bite Me*, a bucket of pens, an alarm clock, a small table lamp, three well-worn paperbacks with a receipt in one being used as a bookmark, a

Bobblehead troll doll, a pair of cheap sunglasses, a half tub of Tic Tacs, and a few sticks of white chalk.

"A strange assortment of stuff, but not exactly telling," Trent said, standing back from the table.

"Well, she wouldn't leave behind anything of sentimental or monetary value."

"Say that again." He gestured toward the unimpressive haul.

"We could still find something to link us to the mystery guy though." She picked up the novel with the receipt and cracked the spine. "Look at this." She held the book spread open for Trent to see the stamp on the first page that read *Most Loved Bookshop, Gainesville.*

Trent picked up the others. "These too. But Gainesville? Is it a coincidence her body was found not far north of there? Maybe that's where Lynnette lived before moving in with Barry?"

"Also where she returned? Except there isn't an address in Gainesville on file for her." She flipped to the page with the receipt. It was from the East End Pirate, showing two as the number at the table, and listed several drinks. No note of debit or credit, so it must have been settled in cash. The date stamp showed it was from a month and a half ago. Amanda pointed this out to Trent.

"According to Barry, Lynnette and the shooter were a couple then," he said. "He could have been the second person at that table."

"That's what I thought." It was a shot in the dark, but sometimes shooting blind paid off.

FIFTY-EIGHT

Amanda and Trent popped by Central to drop off the box of Lynnette Johnson's things. Malone stopped them before they had the chance to leave again.

"Hold up. Where have you two been? Holden is holding." He shook his head as if disgusted by his turn of phrase. "He's in an interrogation room. What are you waiting for?"

"He's good to sit for a minute," she said. "We came across another lead we need to follow."

"Not before you talk to me, you don't." He turned, and it was implied they were to follow him.

Malone led them to his office where neither Amanda nor Trent sat down. It just showed her partner was eager to get moving too.

"All right, bring me up to speed." Malone rubbed his hands together.

"Investigators are processing Holden's place to see if they can find any trace of Katherine," she offered. Blair and Donnelly had arrived before she and Trent had left. "Though I doubt they will. Holden confirmed that Lynnette Johnson had been living with him, but he kicked her out a few weeks ago."

"This sounds like you're releasing Holden from suspicion." Malone flushed and raised his eyebrows, as if unimpressed by all the manpower that went into bringing the man in if that were the case.

She mustered the courage to say, "We have yet to connect him to Katherine, or theorize a reason he'd hold a vendetta against her. The strongest thing that implies any involvement at all are those plates put on Katherine's Mercedes."

"And Lynnette Johnson, don't forget. You should know motive doesn't always get tied up in a neat bow. What we had was strong enough to secure the warrants, why Holden is here now. You were both convinced of Holden's involvement the last time you were in my office, or am I wrong?"

So manpower and time were the basis for his foul mood, as she had guessed. "We followed the evidence we had before us. Due to that, there is something else we'd like to explore before speaking with Holden again."

Malone put his hands on his hips and angled his head. "Hit me."

"He identified the shooter as Lynnette's boyfriend." They weren't completely without water to douse the flames of his anger.

Malone slumped back in his chair and pointed at them. "You should have led with that. Where can we find him? The guy's name?"

"We don't know either. Yet," Trent added.

"Well, get the answers."

"Which is what we plan to do." She told him about the receipt and their suspicion about the second person at that table.

"I want to be supportive, but let me get this straight. You plan to go to the East End Pirate and see if they can give you the name of a male, brown-eyed, brown-haired Caucasian?" He tucked his chin to his chest and looked up at her, his brow full of wrinkles, his eyes drenched in skepticism.

"Remember the snake tattoo on his left wrist," Trent put in. "We can show them a picture of that."

Malone held up his hands. "Then that should make all the difference."

Amanda laughed.

"I'm missing what's funny about any of this," Malone said.

"Just letting off some stress, Sarge. We have to try this place. We've gotten further with less before. Let us explore this angle to see where it takes us before we talk with Holden." If the mild-mannered appeal didn't work, their long history should have sway.

"Fine." He swept a hand toward his door, and Amanda and Trent wasted no time leaving.

FIFTY-NINE

Katherine's skin was slimy and sticky with blood and sweat. Her body ached in places she hadn't known existed. Her mind betrayed her as it continued sweeping her in and out of consciousness. Every time she'd plead for an explanation, he'd just stare and remain mute. And the more she'd pushed, the shadows on his face grew dark, his expression tightened.

It had turned to night, back to day, and now it was growing dark again. It must be Wednesday evening unless she'd blacked out an entire day. With the way he was beating on her, it was possible.

Hours must have passed since he allowed her sips from a water bottle. At that time, she also had a few mouthfuls of canned beans that he'd spoon-fed her as one would a child. Before that it had just been protein bars and chips. Just the fact he had all this prepackaged food signified premeditation. When the stash ran out, did her time also? Speaking of, she hadn't seen or heard the woman for at least twenty-four hours.

"Where's your... friend?" Her voice cracked, her throat dry from thirst.

"You don't worry about her," he hissed, getting down close in front of her. Still seated on the chair on which she was strapped, she could barely feel her legs anymore and her back was seizing.

"Did you kill—?"

He punched her in the face, torquing her neck to the side. White light swam in her vision as pain flashed through. But it passed quickly. Her body must be shutting down.

Tears fell down her cheeks as thoughts of May entered in. She'd had so little time with her aunt, the years stolen from her due to a feud between sisters. *If only there was more time.*

As her eyes fluttered shut, she saw her mother's face as if she stood before her now. Her blue eyes twinkled and were full of love. Her mother stepped back, her arms open and beckoning for Katherine to come to her.

The fight started to leach from her body, but she fought against it. She refused to die without knowing what she had done to deserve this, how he figured she was responsible for his suffering. "Please, just tell me who you are."

He paced around to the front of her. "Fine. I'll play. You ask a question, I'll answer, or I'll punish you. I'll decide in the moment."

Katherine wasn't sure she could withstand more beatings, but this might be the only way to get answers. "Are you from New York?"

"Uh-huh."

She breathed easier when he didn't strike her. "You blame me for—"

He slapped her.

She spit blood to clear her mouth and reframed her question. "I am responsible for—"

Another strike.

Her body was on fire, but at the same time a warm numbness moved in, buffering her from the full extent of pain. She spit blood. "I caused your suffering."

"Yes, you did."

She was afraid to ask how. "Am I why your girlfriend is no longer here? That woman who helped you take me."

He smiled, sending chills through Katherine. "Nah, that's not on you. She was a stupid bitch, threatened to mess up everything."

The absence of denial and the use of past tense told Katherine all she needed to know. He had killed her. His statement also implied the woman had a conscience. Katherine prayed she had left a trail for the police before he took her life.

"What? Already out of questions?"

"Do you plan to kill me?"

Another wicked grin. "Oh, we'll get there. First, you deserve to suffer, just like you made me suffer for the last two years."

Her mind was foggy, her thoughts intersecting like fine webbed gauze but not binding together. "How did I...?"

"Do you know what guys do to other guys in prison? How that affects a grown man who should be able to protect himself?"

She drew back in the chair, bracing for an attack, but none came. "Why that poor teenage girl? Why kill her?"

He smiled. "To hurt you. To torment you. And I see it's working."

Tears were snaking down her cheeks.

"And I knew if I took you from a public place, I'd forever steal your sense of security. Not that you have much time left. You took my life!" He pulled his gun and flailed it in the air, paused for a few seconds, the muzzle pointed at his temple.

She held her breath. "I'm sorry for what you suffered."

"No!" he roared and put the end of the gun to her nose. "You don't get to apologize. You are a liar! You just get to suffer and die! That's the least of what you deserve!"

Katherine's heart was pounding. She'd only lied about one thing in her entire life. She took a hard look at his face and studied the contours and his eyes. There was something vaguely familiar about him.

Was it possible...?

SIXTY

Amanda's stomach growled in hungry protest, and Trent took them through the drive-thru for Petey's Patties, Zoe's favorite fast-food place. They each quickly ate a cheeseburger in the car, and then carried on to the East End Pirate.

She'd always thought it was an odd name for a bar but her best friend, Becky Tulson, had explained to her in the past why it wasn't *that* strange. "Think about it. Captain Morgan rum. There's a pirate standing right on the bottle." Becky had given her this look like Amanda had lost her mind.

Unquestionably a dive bar and living up to its name, the East End Pirate was in the east end of Woodbridge. Its clientele would be sketchy people with things to hide. She and Trent wouldn't be popular once they flashed their badges around.

Eighties rock music was thumping inside, the bass turned up to the point that it distorted the lyrics, but to a drunk person, it wouldn't matter. They were all about the beat.

The place was practically empty, and they sat on stools at the counter.

The bartender came over to them. "What can I get ya?"

She lifted her badge, just enough that the gold shield would have winked at him. The bartender groaned and braced both his hands on the counter. His muscled biceps bulged from beneath the edge of his short sleeves, no tattoos.

"So much for *anonymous* tipline."

Tingles laced down her arms. "You're the one who called in about Lynnette Johnson?"

"Ah, yeah. Isn't that why you're here?"

This was an exciting turn of events, and he could provide them the break they'd been after. "We are here about Lynnette Johnson but not because we knew you called."

"Oh. Well, is she all right? I haven't seen her since Sunday."

"Before I answer that, who are you?" she asked.

"Davis Dunlap. Owner of this fine establishment."

"How do you know Lynnette?" She suspected this might be the dive bar that Barry Holden had mentioned.

"She worked here. Are you going to tell me if she's okay?"

"I wish that I could. Lynnette was found murdered yesterday, gunshot to the back of her head." As much as Amanda stuck to the facts, a splinter of sadness ran through her at the loss of life.

Davis clenched his jaw and didn't say anything.

Despite his silence, it was clear this news upset him. "Were you and Lynnette close?"

"I've known her a long time. She used to go to Striving Minds school with my much younger half-sister. Obviously, that was years ago, but I'd often run into Lynnette and ended up offering her a job about six months ago."

Amanda nodded. This was *the* dive bar that Barry told them about.

"What can you tell us about her boyfriend? We were just told he has brown eyes, brown hair, is in his late forties, with a snake tattoo on his left wrist. That sound right to you?" Trent inserted.

"It does."

"And this tattoo?" Trent showed him a photo of the ink.

Davis barely glanced at it but growled, "Did that bastard kill her?"

She'd take that as an identification. "We believe he may have."

"You catch the son of a bitch, because if I find him, I'm going to kill him." He slammed his right fist into the palm of his left hand. "He take that sergeant lady too?"

"We suspect so," Trent replied. "Do you have any idea where we might find him? We know Lynnette moved rather recently. He might have gone along with her."

"Last I knew she was boarding with some guy in the east end. Barry, something or other."

"Do you know the boyfriend's name?" she asked.

"That I don't know. Just know he's a dick. From the second he started coming in here, he was obsessed with Lynn. He was always hanging on her like she was his property."

His character description aligned with what Barry Holden had told them. Going from being physically abusive to a killer and abductor wasn't a huge leap. "You saw Lynnette on Sunday. Was he with her?"

"Yep."

"You wouldn't happen to have security cameras here?" she countered.

"In this neighborhood? You bet." He pointed out two in the bar area alone.

"Could we watch the footage from Sunday night? No one needs to know you helped the cops," she added for good measure.

"Heck, I'm doing this for Lynnette. She had bad taste in men, a cycle on repeat." He motioned for them to follow him. Passing a server, he paused to let them know he'd be a minute.

He took Amanda and Trent to a small office in the back. There he brought up the video for Sunday night and forwarded to 8 PM, obviously recalling when Lynnette had been in. Immediately after hitting play, she walked into view, holding hands with a man.

"That's him," Davis pointed out.

Amanda's body flushed with rage at laying eyes on the man who had caused so much heartache. "Could we get a close-up of his face?"

"Let's watch and see if we get a better angle."

It wasn't a full minute later, and he paused the feed and zoomed in. "Will that work for you?"

The man was looking right in the direction of the camera. He had brown hair, brown eyes, and a cleft chin. Average, average, average, except for the snake tattoo on his left wrist. "Can you print that?"

He clicked a few buttons, and a nearby printer whirred to life.

SIXTY-ONE

Amanda, Trent, and Malone looked at Barry Holden and his lawyer in the interrogation room through the one-way mirror.

"The lawyer's been griping for hours," Malone said. "I've done my best to hold him at bay, but he's like a pacing tiger in a cage."

Amanda could see that. Alan Gaines was doing laps of the perimeter of the room. He'd be wearing a pattern in the concrete floor if it were possible. He had a cell phone to his ear.

"Well, no time like the present," she said before shooting from the room with Trent.

When she cracked open the door on the interrogation room, the lawyer flailed his arms in the air. "About time. You've had my client waiting for hours." He ended his call and pocketed his phone.

She suspected this wasn't about his client's time but his own. Though when he'd be billing out hundreds, if not thousands an hour, he shouldn't complain.

"I didn't do anything but offer shelter to a young woman," Barry said.

She and Trent sat down, not responding to the lawyer's

impatient gripe or Barry's claims of innocence. She pulled the photo they'd obtained from Davis Dunlap at the East End Pirate and pushed it across the table.

His gaze barely landed on the picture before he jabbed a fingertip to it. "That's the guy... Lynnette's boyfriend."

"And you're telling us the guy lived under your roof, and you don't know his name?"

"I swear I don't."

The lab already had a copy of the photo to run through the facial recognition databases. She crossed her fingers for a hit. "Did you know they conspired to abduct Katherine Graves, a former police sergeant with the PWCPD?"

"No."

"How familiar are you with Ms. Graves?" The question demanded honesty if it was going to be of any advantage.

Alan scoffed laughter. "This is utterly absurd. You don't even have a connection between my client and the victim, yet you have him dragged in here like a criminal."

"There is a connection, of which you know," she volleyed back.

"The plates put on her car. Sure. We've covered all that, but my client's not the one who put them there. Lynnette Johnson did."

"But how did she come into their possession? After all, your client says she was kicked out a few weeks ago." She recalled Barry's half-baked suggestion that Lynnette saw them and took them, but she wanted to open the topic as if it were fresh. Amanda kept her gaze on Barry, but he refused eye contact. There was something he was holding back. "Do you have something to say, Mr. Holden?"

The lawyer sat down, flipped out his tie, and faced Barry.

Barry shook his head, but in a stiff manner, as if he were responding to the prompting of a puppet master's strings.

"You sure?" She leaned forward across the table. "I'm

getting the impression that maybe Lynnette was around more recently." It was a jab in the dark, but based on her read of his facial and body language. The sudden denial of eye contact and his rounded, hunched shoulders suggested he wanted to deny what he said at the house.

Barry didn't respond, and the lawyer uncharacteristically remained quiet.

Amanda sat back, passed a casual side-glance at Trent and raised her eyebrows. The silence filled her with expectation.

"Fine," Barry eventually said. "She came around last week."

"Day?" she fired back.

"Wednesday."

Every second they were in here, Katherine was out there. She tamped down her impatience so as not to put Alan Gaines on the defensive. "Why was she there?"

"She begged to come back, said she wanted away from the guy."

This sounded like a cover story. She'd looked rather cozy with the man at East End Pirate Sunday night. Or had she seen the plates when she lived with Barry and concocted her own plan? Did she think taking them might help police track her down? But there was an obvious hole in Barry's story. "If Lynnette was there, why didn't you return her things to her?"

"She never asked, and I never thought of it. Not everything is a conspiracy, Detective."

Snide response, but she'd let it pass. Besides, it was in their favor that Lynnette hadn't reclaimed her things. "Going back to the plates, would she have known they were kicking around?"

Barry nodded. "I don't see why she wouldn't."

"How?"

"She'd been in my garage with me before, she'd even walked around the space, looking at the shelves."

"Why didn't you share any of this with us before today?" Trent's cheeks were flushed, and he was clearly aggravated.

"Hold up," Alan said. "My client has been cooperative with you. Save the lecture."

"Lecture?" Trent spat. "Time was wasted. Yours, ours. Meanwhile Katherine Graves remains in the hands of a madman."

Barry all but shrugged, and his probation officer's words came back to Amanda. He was out for himself, or at least most of the time. It seemed Lynnette Johnson had penetrated his armor.

Amanda softened her approach. "I am with my partner. Why didn't you tell us any of this sooner?"

"I wasn't going to point my finger at her. She's had a rough life, which I told you. I also didn't want to accept she'd be involved with all you said. I was sure you'd find some way of turning it all back on me."

She flailed her arms. "And there it is. The real reason. It was about you."

"Whatever you want to think. I don't care. Once you cops set your sights on someone, you're relentless. Look where I am. Again." Now he met her gaze, his eyes enclosing a challenge to prove him wrong.

"If a person gets our attention, there are good reasons for it." She clasped her hands on the table and leaned forward. "I was under the impression you only cared about yourself, but you cared about Lynnette, didn't you?"

"So what if I did?"

Just not enough to step in and save her from an abusive boyfriend... "And one more time for the record, you don't know her boyfriend's name or where she might have lived? Remember, we think that he killed her." Amanda didn't think she needed to remind him of the stakes but did so anyway.

"I don't know. I wish I did."

She nodded, accepting his word now, but before leaving she wanted to satisfy a curiosity that was born from watching the video at the marina. "We have reason to believe Lynnette disabled the GPS in Ms. Graves's Mercedes. How would she have that knowledge?" She suspected it was under Barry's tutelage.

"The internet?" Barry shrugged. "Young people are smart with technology."

Amanda wasn't so sure she was buying his story here, but she still stood and said, "You're free to go." No district attorney would run with charges against Barry. Simon Wheable, on the other hand, would be prosecuted regarding the plates and his illegal business dealings.

Trent joined her in the hallway. "Care to share what you're thinking with me?"

"Yep. Barry Holden's in the dark. He cares about Lynnette. If he had a name to give us for the mystery guy, he'd hand it over without hesitation."

"Unless he plans to get street justice for himself."

"We can't watch everyone twenty-four seven." A caustic attitude, but this shooter needed to be stopped one way or another. And Katherine needed to be saved.

SIXTY-TWO

Amanda went home to find Logan looking comfortable on the couch. In the rainbow of lights coming from the television, he was so handsome, it had her taking pause. He was a great father to Zoe, reliable, loyal, and a fantastic lover. Amanda had his heart. What was wrong with her that she'd put all that in jeopardy?

Logan stood and greeted her with a hug and kiss. When they parted, she caught sight of plastic totes at the side of the room. They were full of Christmas decorations. He must have hauled them out of the garage. They were among the things she'd kept from her time with Kevin and Lindsey, though she had taken out sentimental ornaments and ensured they were wrapped with care in tissue paper and tucked away in another spot.

"What's going on there?" She pointed to the haul.

"I thought I'd get things started. Christmas is only a week away, and I know of one little girl around here who is eager for some seasonal cheer." He smiled at her, and she touched a hand gently to his cheek as her heart burned.

"Zoe does love Christmas, but no decorating without her or me."

"Then you'll need to take some time off work."

She opened her mouth to respond, shut it, and turned away from him. His comment came as a jab and insulted her. It was true she was banking a lot of hours, but it wasn't sunshine and lollipops. Two women had been murdered and someone she knew was at risk of losing her life. The lack of progress with the case was painful enough, and Logan's words were a slap in her face. As if all her efforts were meaningless, and she could just *take off* without repercussions.

"I shouldn't have put it that way, but you have been working a lot lately."

White-hot fury ran through her, and her mind was spinning about what to say.

He held up his hand. "Before you lay into me, I realize this is a special situation. No luck in finding her yet?"

She shook her head. Words locked in her throat as she scanned his face. He'd never fully understand her or get everything about what made her tick. Was their love enough to bind them together or was she fooling herself?

"Do you want a glass of wine? Talk about your day?" He jacked a thumb over his shoulder toward the kitchen.

Her body longed for bed, for her pillow under her head, but they should talk. "Sure."

He brushed a hand to her shoulder before setting out to do as he'd offered. She shrugged off her shoes and hung her jacket on the coatrack by the front door. Her movements were slow and awkward like a prisoner being walked in shackles toward her execution. Her conscience was beating her mercilessly. Logan didn't deserve the betrayal or her disloyalty. It wasn't his fault he didn't know what it was like being a cop. That was her job, not his. He had done nothing wrong, everything right.

"Here you go." He smiled as he returned with two wine-glasses.

She took one. "Thank you."

"To us and Zoe." He lifted his glass in a toast gesture, and the instant she parroted his words and clicked her glass against his, tears came to her eyes.

"Oh." He wrapped an arm around her and guided her to the couch. "I can't imagine how horrible this all is for you."

She set down her glass, not even having taken a sip yet, knowing she wouldn't be able to swallow it. He sat beside her and took her hand.

"I can't do this," she blurted out. Some tears fell, and she quickly palmed her cheeks as if by swiping them away they'd never happened in the first place.

"It's okay. Let it out."

She let the tears fall, as if his permission was what she needed.

He put his glass down to pull her into a hug, but she pulled back. "What is it?" The three words were saturated with pain and suspicion as he regarded her with a face contorted in confusion.

"I need to tell you something." Her voice cracked. It was tempting to pass the crying off as relating to Katherine. He'd probably even believe her because he had faith in her. She sobbed and covered her mouth. Love shouldn't hurt this badly and neither should honesty, but she owed that much to Logan.

He didn't say a word, held the space in silence. His handsome face, his deep soulful eyes.

"I did something really stupid," she eventually managed to push out.

Logan stayed motionless, swallowed roughly, his Adam's apple jutting out. Still silent.

"It will never happen again. It didn't mean anything." She wasn't sure if he caught the underlying hypocrisy. Her words coiled in her gut as an outright lie. Her kissing Trent had meant *something*. Her feelings for him were real even if they weren't practical, no matter how much she wanted to fight against them. *Would* fight against them. They weren't meant to be a couple. She and Logan were, and they were good together.

"What did you do?" He stood, facing her, demanding a confession.

Will he understand? Will he forgive me?

"Amanda, talk to me. Right now." His firm voice had her trembling, not because she feared he'd hurt her, but the opposite. He was prepared to take a blow.

She pinched her eyes shut for a second, took a deep breath, opened them. "I kissed Trent—"

"Oh, Amanda." Logan gasped, raking a hand through his hair and turning as if he were going to leave but his feet remained planted.

"It didn't mean anything." *And there is my default fallback position...* If she repeated it enough times, maybe she'd accept her claim.

"Why did you do it? And what are we talking about here? A quick peck? Tongue? A make-out session? When did this— God, Amanda. You know what? I don't care. Don't tell me. I don't want to know." He shuffled toward the door.

She hopped up from the couch to stop him. She pulled on his arm, and he glowered at her. Fresh, hot tears spattered her cheeks.

"Please don't go. We need to talk. Zoe," she blurted out and realized her error when he leveled a cold glare at her.

"Don't bring her into this." He pushed his feet into his shoes and snatched his coat and was out the door.

As his truck rumbled in the drive, Amanda sank against the back of the door and lowered to the floor. Logan had been a gift, and she'd found a way to screw it up.

SIXTY-THREE

8:30 AM, THURSDAY

Missing for 3 days, 3 hours, 40 minutes

Amanda's head was pounding when she walked into Central the next morning. Logan hadn't returned home all night, and she ended up emptying that wine bottle. As someone who didn't typically drink much, she was paying the price.

She dropped at her desk and rummaged through her drawers in search of ibuprofen.

"Good morning," Trent said.

She winced. "Do you have to be so loud?"

"I wasn't." He raised his eyebrows at her.

"Could have fooled me." She was an idiot three times over. First, kissing Trent. Two, confessing this sin to Logan. Three, downing a bottle of wine.

"Oh."

She narrowed her eyes at him, and he disappeared into his cubicle and came back with a bottle of Aleve, which she happily accepted from him. "You're my hero. Thank you." She took one with water.

"Rough night?"

She didn't answer, just held eye contact.

"Tell me you didn't tell him."

She blinked slowly.

"Crap. And I'm to gather that he didn't take it well."

"Solid detective work, Ace. He left me."

"He what?"

There was no way she was going to repeat herself and risk breaking down like a blubbering idiot. "Forget about me. We have a job to do. Katherine was taken three days ago." Her phone rang, and the sound drilled into her skull. She rushed to answer. Anything to stop that blasted ringing. "Detective Steele."

"It's CSI Blair."

She put the crime scene investigator on speaker and motioned for Trent to stay put.

"The ballistics results are in, and the same Glock 19 was used to kill both Leah Bernard and Lynnette Johnson."

"What we figured," Amanda said. "Thanks for letting us know. Did you get any hits on the shooter's face?"

"Unfortunately not. I know that wasn't what you wanted to hear."

Facial recognition databases weren't without their limitations. "You can say that again." Amanda ended the call and shook her head. Frustrated, overwhelmed, heartbroken, hungover.

"We'll find him," Trent said.

"I don't see how." Everything was lost starting with Katherine and ending with Amanda's relationship with Logan.

"We start at the beginning."

"Which is essentially where we are."

"Not entirely true." He stiffened, obviously taking offense to her summation of events. "We just need to reassess, talk it out. If money wasn't the initial motive, I'd say we're back to revenge."

"Uh-huh. This guy likes to feel he calls the shots. Take as an example his last call to May. He said he'd be in touch within two days, which leaves May in hell."

"He must enjoy causing pain and emotional torment. It's not good enough he's hurting Katherine, he wants to inflict agony on someone she loves too."

"It sounds personal." Amanda rubbed her forehead, thankful the pain pill was helping somewhat, but she was still having a hard time focusing. "How did Katherine wrong this person?" She got up and paced, thinking through the investigation thus far and the leads they'd followed. All of them had been dead ends. *Think personal*, she nudged herself. Then an idea hit, and she dropped into her chair. She opened her email and brought up the small evidence list from the Fill N Go that Blair had emailed. She stopped on the mention of the silver locket.

The photo of an oval-faced woman with black hair that framed her cheekbones.

Amanda recalled thinking she'd looked dimly familiar. Then she snapped her fingers, and Trent flinched. She laughed, elated she might finally be on to something. "Sorry," she told him.

"No need. It's got to be good. Let's hear it."

"It might not be anything, but it is a new path to follow. The picture in Katherine's locket, I'm pretty sure that was her mother. I mean, who else would she wear around her neck?"

She brought up an internet search window and searched *Tori Hurst*, the name of Katherine's mother. The first result rewarded her with a photograph of the same woman in Katherine's locket. By this time, Trent had moved into her cubicle.

"Let me explain what I'm thinking. Could all this have something to do with her stepfather's incarceration? And, if so, what?"

"Along the lines of personal motives, someone who holds

Katherine responsible for his prison sentence? The stepfather himself? He could have reach from behind bars, or a friend or relative may be acting on their own accord?"

"Let's limit the questions to one at a time." She massaged her forehead. "But remember that Lieutenant Catherwood told us Katherine left New York in a hurry? That it wasn't long after her stepfather's trial ended?"

"That sounds like two questions."

"One. Continued." She smiled at him.

"Well, maybe Katherine brought those threats that we found in her drawer from New York, after all. But if this is about the stepfather going to prison, what was Katherine's role in that? Did she testify during the trial?"

She'd let the double question pass. "Let's see if we can find out." She clicked on some articles that came up with her current search for Tori Hurst. They covered her murder and the trial of Katherine's stepfather, Rick Stokes. At least one of them should give them the answer they were after. Another option was calling Natasha Bauer. As a close friend she'd know whether Katherine was called upon to testify or if she handed over anything incriminating to the police.

They scanned several news pieces. Katherine, cited only as the victim's daughter, had indeed testified to the stepfather's ongoing abuse of her mother. One piece credited her testimony as "sealing the deal" against a master manipulator and violent offender.

Amanda sat back, speechless for a moment. "This was sitting here all this time, and we never even saw it."

"We couldn't have known Katherine's abduction tied back to this. We still don't."

But a burning in her gut told her otherwise. She clicked on another article. This one had a photograph taken from outside the courtroom. The main focus was a man and woman in the forefront, but there was another man lingering in the background. The caption told them the ones in the front were Rick's brother and sister. The third person wasn't named, but the woman was looking over her shoulder at him.

A hunch told her there was something to that. Amanda looked closely at the unidentified man. There was something very familiar about him, and it didn't take long to figure out why.

He was of a smaller physique then, but there, on his left wrist, was a snake tattoo.

SIXTY-FOUR

"I'd say he's with Rick Stokes's brother and sister." Amanda pointed out how the woman was looking back at him.

"All right, so someone related to Stokes. Someone who held Katherine responsible for him going to prison."

"But, if so, why now, two years later?"

"They could have been imprisoned themselves. Or ill. They might not have known where to catch up with Katherine until more recently," Trent said, his voice rising in volume with each proposition.

"Once that article hit. But, still, that was a year and a half ago." She pulled backgrounds on Rick's siblings. Neither had children, but there must be some relation they were missing. She put a call in to ADA Bauer but couldn't reach her, but she got right through to Detective Fitz. He said he'd get back as soon as possible.

When her phone finally rang two hours later, she jumped. Fitz showed on the caller ID. She put the call on speaker and told him Trent was joining them. "Tell me you have his name."

"Rodney Mitchell, fifty-three. He's Rick Stokes's son, from before he got together with Kat's mother. Rodney was twelve at the time. Kat would have been six. Now Stokes isn't on record as the father, but his sister confirmed she raised him after the boy's mother took off around the same time the dad moved in with Kat's mother. Apparently, he didn't want to bring the kid into the mix."

"He must have felt rejected. As the new child, Katherine got all his father's attention," Trent reasoned. "But he's not a kid anymore. You said he's fifty-three. Why now? There has to be more to this."

"It's only where it started, and I'll get to everything in a minute."

"Just one second," Amanda inserted. "Did Katherine know about him?"

"I don't see how she would have."

"But he was at her stepfather's trial," Trent put in. "There's that picture."

"Sure, but that doesn't mean Katherine knew him. You should know this Rodney is bad news. He's been in brushes with the law all his life, but it's only more recently he got himself a criminal record. In fact, he was released from prison only six months ago, having gone away not long after his father did. I believe that's the reason Rodney went after Katherine. See, the father might not have wanted to bring his son in under his roof, but he didn't completely abandon him. Even when Rodney became an adult, Stokes did what he could to keep Rodney out of jail."

"What charges did he get put away for?" Amanda asked.

"Drug possession. After his release from prison, he had to serve time in community service for three months. Now, I popped by and had a chat with Rodney's aunt, Stokes's sister, and she wouldn't tell me where he is. In her words, 'he's a freakin' adult.' Of course, I am PG'ing that, but she said he left New York for a bit."

"When was this?" Trent asked.

"After he finished his stint with community service, which was three months ago."

Amanda turned to Trent. "We were told he started hanging around Lynnette about two months ago. It didn't take him long to find a partner in crime."

Trent nodded.

"What's that?" Fitz asked.

Amanda filled him in and said, "Please, go on."

"Going back to Stokes as a dad, he didn't completely leave Rodney out to dry. He gave him money and bailed him out whenever he got himself into trouble. As I said, even as an adult."

"But with Stokes in prison, his son was left to fend for himself," Trent surmised.

"Yep. Hence, jailtime within months. Rodney's not the smartest criminal out there."

"Guess we figured out our motive," she said to Trent.

Fitz was the one who replied. "Rodney holds Kat responsible for not only putting his father in prison, but for his own troubles."

"It makes sense why he might want a payday out of this too," Trent inserted.

Amanda had one thing running through her mind. "As long as he hasn't killed her yet."

SIXTY-FIVE

They had their shooter's name but no clue where to find him or Katherine. Another call for ransom hadn't been received yet and with every passing hour, it tightened the ball in Amanda's gut. "Okay, let's recap. Do we have anything that can help us find this son of a bitch?"

"Well, Rodney Mitchell lived in New York. Most likely he wasn't familiar with this area."

"But Lynnette was. He has been out here for a few months, according to his aunt."

Trent nodded. "During which time he met Lynnette. Barry said he started coming around a couple of months ago. Then he found out where Katherine was."

"Which brings up how he got here in the first place. He must have had gas money, but where did he get the van with the New York plates?"

"He could have borrowed it from a friend or relative."

"We'll have Fitz push the aunt on that. She could know." Amanda would call him in a minute.

"All right, now circling back. A guy from New York teams

up with a local who knows the area. She could have suggested a spot to hold Katherine."

She snapped her fingers. "We need to look closer at her. Barry told us he suspected that Lynnette lived someplace rural before moving in with him."

"Rural would fit with holding a hostage, but where to start looking?"

"Well, the Mercedes was dumped, with Lynnette's body, north of Gainesville. The paperbacks among her things were bought from a store there."

"But, as you pointed out before, there's no address on record for her there."

"Which is true. But Barry told us Lynnette had a rough life. Usually that implies abuse and possibly living below the poverty line. He took mercy on her by inviting her into his home, just as Davis Dunlap offered her a job. Did she live on the streets or squat somewhere?" She paused there, letting everything she had just said sink in. *Penniless, jobless, home-less...* "Chalk."

"I need more than that."

"Me too. It's just such an odd thing for her to have, let alone leave behind. Lynnette wasn't a teacher."

"She could have liked the smell of it? Not sure if it means anything to our case though."

"Me either. But we have theorized before Lynnette left breadcrumbs for us to follow."

"And you think the chalk may be one?"

"It's odd enough." She shrugged and assembled more of the pieces in her head. The Gainesville bookstore, the fact that Katherine's Mercedes was found north of there, Lynnette needing shelter where the rent was free... *Chalk.* "Striving Minds," she blurted out. "The owner of the East End Pirate said that his half-sister had gone to school there with Lynnette. I thought the name sounded familiar when he said it, but I just clued into why." She googled the school, and her instinct was rewarded. "I think I know where Rodney might be holding Katherine."

SIXTY-SIX

Striving Minds was once a privately owned elementary school, but it fell into receivership several years ago and had remained abandoned ever since. The closure made news, and that was why Amanda had heard of the place. It sat on a parcel of land northeast of Gainesville and about ten minutes from where the Mercedes was found. As soon as they put it together, Amanda and Trent brought Malone up to speed. An officer was sent to check out the location and confirmed a white Ford van with NY plates appeared to be parked around the back amid overgrowth and evergreens. SWAT was called into action.

The approach was going to be quiet. No sirens and all PWCPD vehicles, including the SWAT command center, would park at a distance down the road.

It was nearing three thirty by the time everyone was on site. The drive there had passed excruciatingly slowly. Amanda didn't say much and neither did Trent. Her mind was on Katherine and Logan. She hadn't heard a word from him since he'd walked out last night, and she wanted to give him space to process what she'd told him and not pressure him into any sort of decision. This was all on her. She's the one who messed up.

She also beat herself up for taking this long to find Katherine. If only she or Trent had thought of someone associated with Katherine's mother's murder before now. Amanda had expressed this to Trent, and he'd made good points in their defense. To start, nothing pointed them there. Even if they had looked into that angle prior to getting the shooter's face and the snake tattoo, they never could have linked Rodney Mitchell to this. And without learning about Lynnette Johnson's rough past and her connection to Gainesville, they never would have been led here. Sadly, they'd had to jump through all the hoops.

Trent parked behind Malone's SUV, and they approached the structure on foot. They were directed to stay at the property's edge while SWAT did their thing.

Her heart was racing as she stood there watching their forms advance on the school. There was a cluster of cedar trees that would provide concealment, and she tucked in there.

"Where do you think you're going?" Trent crept up behind her and spoke close to her ear.

"Just getting another vantage point."

"Uh-huh."

"Turn back around if you want to," she said. Just the fact that Malone or any of the other SWAT officers hadn't attempted to stop her gave her all the permission and freedom she needed to keep going.

"You know I go where you go."

She dipped into another life trajectory for a moment. How would things look if the situation was different and they weren't partners? But now wasn't the time to daydream. "If you're prepared to come with me, then stop all the whining," she teased with a smile.

"Yeah-yeah."

They walked for a bit, the chill in the air biting. The trees offered little shelter from the cold breeze.

She stopped and looked at the school. Most windows were

boarded but not all. Those that weren't refracted the sun and acted as mirrors. It was impossible to see through them.

"Preparing to go into position now." A SWAT officer spoke over the comms.

"See? They're on this," Trent said. "We don't have to play hero today." His phone rang.

She turned and hissed, "Turn that thing on silent."

Trent answered swiftly. "It's Malone. For you." He handed his phone to her.

"Kind of busy, boss."

"I don't know what you think you're doing, but turn back and leave this to SWAT."

Being this close to Katherine and needing to stand by was killing her. "I'm just checking things out for my—"

A scream tore through the afternoon air. She ended the call and tossed Trent's phone back at him and ran toward the school. As she approached, she took advantage of the boarded windows but still ducked down as she inched her way to the rear doors.

She didn't hear anything.

Was that scream Katherine's last? Had Rodney been alerted to police presence and decided to kill Katherine?

Amanda shook the crippling thoughts aside.

Katherine being alive was Rodney's strongest bargaining chip for remaining that way too. But was surviving high on his list of priorities? Amanda had to believe it was. His actions thus far indicated someone who relished having control. They were also armed with the knowledge he had a history of drug abuse. It was possible he was high and out of his mind right now. There was the real risk he was volatile and unpredictable.

Another scream.

"We don't have time to wait on SWAT." She hurried her pace, aware that Trent was right at her heels.

Her legs weren't moving as fast as she'd like and running

hunched forward wasn't exactly top form to support speed. She stopped below an unblocked window. As tempting as it was to look inside, she resisted the urge. The last thing she wanted was to pop her head up and have it blown off.

She continued, keeping a low profile, to the back of the school. Rodney could be holding Katherine anywhere inside.

The Ford van was back here, tucked between an outbuilding and more cedar trees. The scouting cop never would have seen this from the road. If he wasn't discreet, his snooping could have tipped off Rodney. Though if he had, Rodney would have moved Katherine before everyone arrived.

She made it to a set of doors and tugged on a handle. Locked.

"Tell me you're not going in," Trent said. "SWAT's already on their—"

This time it wasn't a scream but a strangled cry.

There wasn't a SWAT officer in sight. "They won't get here in time. We have no choice."

"And how do you propose we get inside?"

There was the dilemma. She didn't have a lock-picking kit in her back pocket. The glass wasn't wired, but it would be tempered and take a heavy hit to break. The butt of her gun might work, but then she spied a huge rock on the ground and figured she could throw it at the window. The sound of smashing glass could alert Rodney, though.

Another scream.

Damn it all... Amanda acted quickly, grabbing the rock and heaving it toward the door. The glass shattered, and she reached inside and turned the bolt. A jagged piece of glass tore the sleeve of her coat, and it had her taking a millisecond to think what could have happened if she hadn't been wearing one.

She shook the thought aside, and she and Trent moved in, each balancing a flashlight with their guns. The hallways were dark with light only coming through some unblocked windows.

They swept through the building, each tucking against one side of the hallway.

Trent said over the comms, "Steele and Stenson have breached the premises."

Amanda poked her head in one room, casting the beam from her light inside, and found a large sleeping bag in the middle of the floor. Clothing was stacked at one end of the room.

Trent walked up behind her, his back to hers, covering her.

"Rodney and Lynnette were squatting here," she said.

They carried on down the hall and passed a kitchen. Dirty dishes were piled on the counter with takeout containers and empty liquor and beer bottles. There were the lingering stenches of rotting food and tobacco smoke. A voice broke through the silence.

"No, don't!" It was Katherine, and she didn't sound far away.

SIXTY-SEVEN

Amanda motioned to Trent that they needed to continue forward, and they hustled along. She stopped at a doorway marked 12. There was no doubt Rodney and Katherine were inside. Katherine's sobs and Rodney's heavy steps traveled into the hallway. He sounded as if he were circling Katherine like prey. The air here hung heavy with cigarette smoke.

She pointed to the room, and Trent nodded.

Slowly, she crept ahead, ears straining to determine if she could place Rodney's location. Light was seeping into the hall. One of the windows must not be boarded.

The light winked. All it told them was Rodney had crossed in the path of the sun, not how close he was to the door. His shadow didn't cast into the hall.

"You had everything while I had nothing!" The man's yell was followed by Katherine crying out.

Amanda's heart squeezed. She couldn't just stand here doing nothing. She quickly peeked into the room.

Katherine was tied to a chair, bound by her wrists and ankles. Vibrant bruises marred her face. Cuts and burn marks scarred her arms. Rodney had a lit cigarette in hand.

"I just want you to die!" Rodney lunged forward and pressed the burning tip to Katherine's cheek.

Katherine cried out, but the sound was strangled in her throat. Her eyes widened. For a fraction of a second, her gaze locked with Amanda's.

Rodney turned. It was like time stopped as he stared at Amanda. The coldness of his gaze leached into her veins and had her frozen in place.

He raised his gun and fired.

Amanda drew back, barely escaping a date with a bullet. The round impacted a locker across from the doorway.

Heaving for breath, she called out, "Prince William County Police—"

He fired off another round, and it zinged into the hall and struck near the first one. "Stay back! Leave me alone!"

"You know we can't do that. Let Katherine go. We can talk."

"There's nothing to talk about. She deserves to die. To suffer."

Katherine screamed. He must have burned her again, but it opened a window to act. He would be distracted, and Amanda was going to take full advantage of it.

She rounded the corner, gun raised. "Put your gun down."

Rodney was about five feet from Katherine, and a shadow crossed his face. He lifted his gun on Amanda.

Time suspended. Again, she froze.

All she had to do was pull the trigger. Instead, her life flashed before her eyes bringing in thoughts of Zoe, Logan, her parents, sisters, her brother... Trent. Would she be reunited with Kevin and Lindsey? A warmth overcame her at the prospect.

The loud report of a gun being fired was followed by chaos and yelling all around her.

SIXTY-EIGHT

Amanda's head cleared. She looked down at her chest, but she wasn't the one hit. The bullet had come from Trent's gun and hit Rodney in his right shoulder. His Glock clattered to the floor with the cigarette.

Rodney was staggering, a hand over his wound and his eyes round and wide like someone who was stark-raving mad.

"No!" He lunged for his gun. It had skittered to the opposite side of the room, away from Katherine.

Trent took off toward Rodney while Amanda stomped out the cigarette and went to free Katherine. She was crying and repeating over and over, "He's my stepbrother."

"We know," Amanda said softly, "and you're safe now."

But she spoke too soon. Trent and Rodney had been scuffling but broke apart.

Rodney had ahold of his gun again and ran into the hall.

Trent followed him.

Amanda was torn whether to stay with Katherine until SWAT caught up or aid her partner against a lunatic.

"Go." Katherine was groggy, her head lolling to the side.

Amanda left, stepping cautiously into the hall. She spoke

into her comms. "Graves is in room twelve. Detective Stenson and Steele in pursuit of suspect through rear doors of the school."

Outside, small snowflakes were falling, but the sky was dark with cloud cover. There was more coming.

Drops of blood led her to the surrounding woods. She could hear their footsteps crunching twigs and Trent's calls for Rodney to stop. Amanda tucked her flashlight away and kept moving.

"Katherine Graves is secured," a man's voice came over the comms.

Then, a gunshot cracked the afternoon air.

It propelled her legs to move even faster. She kept going, edging toward them.

"She's the one! This is all her fault!" Rodney was screaming.

Amanda was coming up to a creek that fringed the school property. The snowflakes were getting larger and clinging to her eyelashes.

Then all fell silent. Eerie. Tall trees towered above her, their branches bare of leaves, while they slept until spring.

She ducked behind one of them, holding her gun up. Her lungs were heaving for a solid breath, the adrenaline infusing her system as a drug and keeping her alert.

Still, she didn't hear Rodney come up on her until it was too late.

She was pulled from behind and thrown to the ground. The wind gushed from her lungs, making it impossible to scream for help.

Rodney lowered over her, straddling her. "You bitches never leave me alone. Ever!" His hands encircled her neck.

She batted at his injured shoulder, and he howled, but the pain seemed to make him stronger. He pulled her arms down and pinned them beneath him, then wrapped his hands around her neck and squeezed.

Amanda's body convulsed, and her hearing began to fade. It was like she was in a snow globe. Such stillness, snow falling ever so gracefully. Any light that had been there retreated from her vision like a stage actor taking their final bow.

SIXTY-NINE

NEXT DAY

Katherine was all set up with cable television and a room full of blooms. May Byrd hadn't left her side since her admission to the hospital, or so the nurses told Amanda and Trent when they dropped by to see her. They brought a bouquet they'd picked up from the gift shop downstairs, but it was an insignificant offering considering what Katherine had suffered. But that wasn't all they arrived with.

"You didn't need to bring flowers." Katherine struggled to sit straighter, but Amanda and May both motioned for her to be careful. She looked like she'd been used as a human punching bag, and her cheek was bandaged where she'd been burned with the cigarette.

"Nonsense. You've been through a lot." It went without saying that Amanda wished she had gotten to her sooner.

"Well, I'm safe now." Katherine squeezed May's hand. "You don't look so great." She flicked a finger toward Trent. "That's quite the shiner you have."

"It will heal," Trent said.

"We also brought you this." Amanda held up the chain and locket.

"Oh. I thought I'd lost that."

May helped Katherine put it on, and said, "You guys just missed Hannah by about fifteen minutes. She insisted on coming home when I called about Kat."

"I can understand that," Amanda said.

A brief silence fell in the room. Trent was the one to break it.

"Did you know about Rodney?" he asked.

"No. But I did receive threats after the trial that were left for me at my precinct."

"The ones in your drawer?" Amanda asked, thinking about what they'd said.

You ruined my life. I will ruin yours.

You owe me. I'm coming to collect.

You lie. I will expose the truth and bring you to your knees.

You will hurt. I will get you alone one day.

"That's right."

"Why didn't you confide in anyone?"

"I don't know. Pride?" She smiled.

But other pieces now fit and made sense. "If you didn't know about Rodney, then he's not why you left New York?"

"Not at all. I knew May was here, and I wanted to reconnect with her. The appeal of a fresh start didn't hurt."

It would seem what appeared as Katherine isolating herself was just a woman working through her grief and adjusting to life without her mother. She probably turned dark at talk of the NYPD because of Julie Gilbert. "Tell us about your mom."

Katherine smiled. "She was beautiful with a smile that lit up a room. Her dream was to become an actress, but she never got there. First, my real dad died, making her a single mother. Then she met Rick two years after. He made himself out like he was a prince."

"They always do," Trent mumbled. "And you were just six then?"

"That's right. I lived in that hell with him and Mom until I turned eighteen."

"I'm so sorry I abandoned you," May said, tears on her cheeks.

"No, Aunt May. None of this is your fault."

May leaned over and pressed her forehead to her niece's.

"Mom used to call me her little badass ninja," Katherine volunteered.

Amanda glanced at Trent. Katherine had inadvertently answered a curiosity they had from the moment they learned the password for her home security system.

A smile was gracing her lips, as Katherine continued. "She'd say I'd never let anything stand in my way because I'd karate chop it all down." She chuckled but winced in pain. "She didn't care that ninjas and karate had nothing to do with each other."

"It's those types of memories that will always keep her with us," May said, smoothing back Katherine's hair as if she were still a little girl.

Amanda looked at Trent, and he nodded. They'd worked out a silent code before coming up here. Amanda wanted to discuss the storage unit and the Julie Gilbert case, but not with May in the room.

"Hey, Ms. Byrd," Trent said, stepping next to the older woman.

"It's May. I've told you how many times?"

"Just one more." He smiled at her. "How about we get a coffee from the cafeteria?"

"Uh-huh." She drew that out and distributed her gaze to Amanda and her niece. "If you two want to talk privately, just say so." With that, she looped her arm through Trent's. "Lead on, young man."

"You got it," Trent said.

When they cleared out, Katherine said, "I can't thank you

enough. There were times I didn't think I would survive." Katherine's chin quivered.

Amanda could relate, even though her ordeal wasn't nearly as drawn out as Katherine's had been. She'd still come close to dying. It was mere seconds before she would have lost complete consciousness that Trent had come to her rescue. He pulled Rodney from her and managed to disarm him. SWAT moved in around the same time. Rodney was lucky he got off without a hole in his head and just one in his shoulder. She and Trent expected the go-ahead to talk with him soon.

"Well, you're safe now," Amanda eventually said, while clutching at the collar of her turtleneck. She wasn't used to wearing them, but it served to hide the bruising caused by Rodney's hands. She was also struggling with why she hesitated to fire on Rodney. Not just once, but twice. Her conscience wasn't letting her dismiss it as being down to timing. She could have pulled the trigger just as easily as he had. Why she hadn't would eat away at her until she could figure it out.

"Yeah. You found the storage unit." It wasn't said as a question.

"We did."

"Then you also found my burner phone."

"And the cash, *and* your passport."

"The passport was just there for safe keeping. As for the money, it's wise to have a rainy-day fund."

Amanda smiled but having five K in cash sitting around was a lot. She wasn't one to judge, though, with a hundred grand in a bag still sitting in a locker down at Central. "Why a burner?"

"I use it sometimes when I make inquiries, to stay anonymous. You must think I'm obsessed."

Amanda teetered her hand and smiled.

"You can say it."

"I can say you don't have a fan in Thad Coffey."

"Not going to disagree there." Katherine tried to laugh, and again it was cut short by pain.

"What about the case has you so committed to seeing it through? I know she was a sweet, innocent child, but is it somehow personal?" The last bit snuck out, even taking Amanda by surprise.

"If you're interested, you could help me. Together, I'm sure we could figure out what happened to Julie Gilbert."

Amanda could see herself doing just that. Ever since seeing that storage unit, that little girl's face had haunted her. Katherine's avoidance of Amanda's question made her suspect even more that the case was personal for the former sergeant. "Who is Amy?"

Katherine's gaze popped to Amanda's, and she shook her head. "There's no reason for you to know that."

"You asked for my help, and I would be happy to. But not unless you tell me who Amy is."

"Who Amy *was*." Katherine's voice broke, and tears beaded in her eyes. "You'll want to sit for this story."

SEVENTY

Amanda and Trent received the go-ahead to talk to Rodney Mitchell while they were still at the hospital. She hadn't yet received any messages from Logan, and she was considering whether she should say something to him. As it currently stood, Amanda's sister Kristen was going to pick up Zoe from Maria's house at the end of the day. Amanda had told her Logan took off for a few days but avoided her questions of why and where. Who even knew if he was coming back, or when? And if he did, was he going to stay or simply collect his things and be on his way?

Before she and Trent went into Rodney's room, his doctors told them he was on a heavy dose of pain medication and asked them to keep things brief.

Amanda made no promises.

Rodney looked away from her and Trent. His wrists were cuffed to the bed.

The Glock 19 in his possession had already been preliminarily confirmed by the lab as the one used to kill Leah Bernard and Lynnette Johnson. Rodney could have sourced it on the streets, either in the county or back in New York. Forensic trace at the Fill N Go, the blood and saliva from the gum aisle, was sent out of the county for rapid DNA testing, and it was a match to Rodney Mitchell. There was no question as to his innocence, but Amanda wanted to hear his motive straight from him. "Why did you do it?"

"Why did I—?" Rodney faced them. "She deserved every blow. Even worse."

"Because she testified against your father? A violent and abusive man who killed his wife?" Trent asked, his voice loud.

"She would have done something to piss him off."

Trent took a step toward the bed, and Amanda held out her arm to block him from going any farther. "You going to tell us she deserved it too?"

"You said it."

Trent bunched up his face in a bitter scowl.

"A teenage girl got caught up in this vendetta of yours. You shot her twice. Killed her," Amanda put out. "Did *she* deserve that?" The question rolled off her tongue, leaving bitterness in its wake.

Rodney didn't respond.

"And what about Lynnette Johnson?" Amanda said. "Why did you kill her?"

"She was a liability. The idiot left the money, took off her mask. She was working against me."

"Even after she helped you, worked with you to orchestrate the kidnapping?" Amanda asked.

"She really went batshit after I shot that girl."

"Leah Bernard." She had to say her name, even if trying to humanize her to this man was a waste of breath. He was past compassion.

"So you shot Lynnette Johnson," Trent said. "How did you persuade her to drive the Mercedes out to where you shot her?"

"She did anything I said."

"Because you scared her," Trent barked.

Rodney bobbed his brows as if that was quite an accomplishment. He then shrugged. "I convinced her we needed to ditch the car. She was stupid enough to go along." He laughed. "Even though the car was to be her compensation."

"Just because she changed the plates, it wouldn't protect her from being found with a stolen Mercedes," Amanda said. "Eventually she would have been caught because the registration wouldn't match."

"She changed what now?"

It would seem Rodney had been left in the dark about the plates. Lynnette must have seen it as a way to lead the police to them. She wanted out even before Leah Bernard was shot. It also explained why she detoured the few minutes to Lorton and picked the marina with its surveillance. Amanda's turn to smile. "Lynnette Johnson is why we found you. She left clues." In hindsight Amanda suspected the chalk, paperbacks, and bar receipt were breadcrumbs too. After all, the plan to abduct Katherine had been in the works for months. Lynnette may have even suggested the school as a place to take her. The cigarette butt with pink lipstick was a match to Lynnette's DNA.

"Not much of a surprise. Teaches me for partnering with a bitch."

Trent stepped forward, but Amanda held out an arm to stop him, no matter how tempting it was to let him kick the shit out of the guy.

"Why not kill Katherine?" This question was at the forefront of her mind.

"Oh, I would have gotten there, but I was having fun in the meantime."

Torture was *fun* to this monster. "How did you even know where to find her?"

"Let's call it fate. As part of my community service, I had to clean out a hoarder's house. The guy had paper subscriptions from all over. I found one from *Prince Willam Times* and the headline caught my eye. I started reading, and there she was. All I had to do was get myself to Prince William County. It didn't take long to find her from there."

They had run the plates on the van, and it came back to a Rueben Christian from New York City. He was a friend of Rodney's. Rueben was interrogated in depth, and swore that he had no idea about Rodney's intentions, or he never would have let him borrow his van. Apparently, Rodney had fed him a bull-shit story about needing to get away for a few months.

"I know you think Katherine is some saint, but she's a liar and she ruined my life."

"You sent her typewritten threats," Amanda volleyed.

"I did. You can't say she wasn't warned this day was coming."

Amanda should leave it alone, not prod the words of a madman, but she did anyway. "How is she a liar?"

"She lied under oath at Dad's trial," Rodney spat out. "I know it for a fact."

One article had stated that Katherine's testimony had sealed Stokes's fate. Amanda's next breath held in her chest. "She'd have no reason. Your father beat her mother."

"She claimed to be in the room when he shot her, but she wasn't."

The back of her neck tightened. "And you would know that how?"

"I was watching her that night, when my dad supposedly murdered her mother. She was with her friend, that ADA lady, sipping wine in a window seat at some fancy restaurant in SoHo."

A batch of lies to make himself look better? But they didn't. "You were stalking her even then?"

"All my life. I wanted to know what was so special about her that Dad chose to live with her over me. He left me when I was twelve. My life would have been so different if it wasn't for her and her mother. I blame Katherine for everything wrong in my life. She is a liar," he repeated.

"I don't know why we'd believe you," she countered.

"Me either," Trent chimed in.

"She. Didn't. See. It. Happen." Rodney was screaming and thrashing, and the machines attached to him started beeping and sputtering.

Nurses rushed into the room and told Amanda and Trent to leave.

In the parking lot, Amanda stopped under the overhang.

"Amanda?" Trent prompted.

"Katherine lied under oath."

"Only if you take the word of a man who killed two people in three days and beat Katherine to within an inch of her life."

She scanned his face, balancing how his personal life colored his viewpoint. "You're right. Look what he's done. What he's capable of."

"Exactly." Trent started to walk toward the car.

She eventually followed. So what if Katherine lied about being there? It didn't change the fact her stepfather had shot her mother. Or did it?

EPILOGUE

SATURDAY

Amanda hadn't heard much from Logan. Just a single text on Thursday to say he was staying with a friend. Also that he was fine but processing things. He'd added, *in case you were worried.*

She almost responded on instinct with, *Of course I've been worried...* But she backspaced the message. Instead, she told him to take all the time he needed.

Zoe had asked after him several times, and Amanda hated holding this secret from her. She continued to tell her that Logan was away for a few days. Zoe didn't understand why he'd take off so close to Christmas. Meanwhile, he could be out there finding a place to rent.

Amanda had removed the cash bag from the locker at Central and redeposited it in the bank earlier that morning, but she dropped Zoe at Libby and Penny's so she could attend Leah Bernard's funeral.

She accepted a memorial card from an usher at the entrance of the church. On the front was a grinning photo of Leah Bernard. Such an immense loss.

Amanda found a seat at the back of the church, not altogether comfortable in "the house of God." The Bernards were in the front row. The girl's mother was crying loudly, and a white-haired woman was rubbing her back. She was presumably the great-grandma, one hundred years old as of yesterday.

Amanda let her own tears fall, slowly, gracefully. Her grief was empathy for Leah's family and friends but also for losing Logan. Because she was quite sure she had. Part of her pain was also in empathy for Katherine. She'd lived with a secret for the last sixteen years, until revealing it to Amanda at the hospital.

When Katherine was thirty-one and an officer with the NYPD, she was raped and became pregnant as a result. She took leave from work, had the baby, and gave it away for adoption. Her mother never even knew she'd had a granddaughter. Katherine hadn't wanted to be reminded of her rapist every time she looked at the girl. But forward six years, and Katherine's a detective in Homicide and assigned the Julie Gilbert case.

During the investigation, Katherine watched hours of video of the girl. She saw herself in her brown hair, long limbs, and a smile just like her mother's. At that point, she knew in her heart the girl was hers. DNA tests that Katherine had done off the books confirmed it. As for the name Amy, Katherine said if she'd felt able to keep her, that's what she would have named her.

It was tough dwelling on what Katherine must have suffered losing her child twice. First, when she gave her up for adoption and then again when she found out she'd been murdered. But all this had Amanda reflecting on her personal situation, how she'd lost her unborn son. He'd been snatched from her in the same accident that claimed the lives of Kevin and Lindsey. He was the child she never had the chance to meet, only bury. He was laid to rest beneath a tombstone with his name, Nathan James, after her father and Amanda's married name.

Amanda's gut twisted in grief as she let the undercurrents sweep her away. The accident had stolen so much, including leaving her unable to conceive. This was a loss she'd pushed aside while grieving her husband and six-year-old daughter, but today seemed a day for reflection.

She finally figured out why she hadn't fired at Rodney and landed on it being due to seeing someone she knew suffering like that. Katherine had been there tied to a chair, bloody, and bruised. It must have been too much for Amanda's mind to process.

Someone slid into the pew next to her and handed her a tissue, cutting through her thoughts.

She looked over, and it was Trent. She took his offering but was arrested by his eyes, his kindness, his understanding, and she wanted nothing more than to sink into his arms. Instead she sniffled, thanked him, and turned to the front as the service started.

It turned out to be a mournful celebration of the teenager's life, full of colorful hymns that stood in contrast to the day.

Before leaving, she offered words of intended comfort to the Bernards, a goodbye to Trent, and headed home.

Amanda entered her house and was suffocated by the silence, the stillness, the emptiness. She was here to change before going to pick up Zoe. The separation would also allow her to shake some sorrow from the funeral. Zoe had a way of picking up on Amanda's emotions, and she didn't want to bring her down.

She'd just finished getting changed into a pair of jeans and a sweater when she heard the front door open.

It could only be one person. That realization was enough to render her motionless. She was in their bedroom, facing the mirror on top of her dresser, when Logan stepped into the doorway.

She mentally prepared herself and turned to face him.

"I drove by that funeral. The lot and streets around the church were packed," he said.

"It was a full house." Her heart fluttered as she feared he'd seen her sitting in the church beside Trent.

Logan rubbed his temple. "I just had to get away. Put some separation between us and what you told me." He paused there, and she wasn't sure if she was to step in or wait. She opted for the latter. "I've concluded one thing. Life's too short to waste time."

"I agree." Her chest was aching. Was he going to forgive her or cut and run?

They were standing several feet apart, neither of them making a move to bridge the distance.

"Is the other day the only time that you kissed Trent?" He flinched upon saying Trent's name as if it alone were a dagger to his chest. "Be honest with me. I need to know."

"It's not."

"Oh, Mandy."

"Please, listen. It happened before you and I got together. A long time ago. Back around the time of your wife's murder." She was rushing all of this out as a torrent, afraid she'd lose his attention, that he'd shut her out.

"Have you guys ever...?" He drew a finger between them, the implication clearly to imply sex.

"No. Never."

"And that was the only other time you kissed him? Not another time since you and I got together?"

"No. I swear to you."

He drew back as if her words stung.

"You need to decide whether you can believe me, trust me."

"I don't know at the moment."

His honesty had tears springing to her eyes. "I understand. It's up to you what happens moving forward to us, to..." She snapped her mouth shut, not about to bring up Zoe. As he'd said before, it was unfair to bring her into this. The girl wasn't some bargaining chip for leveraging their relationship.

"Do you love him?"

"He's my partner, Logan. A dear friend. I can't lie to you and say he means nothing to me."

"Do. You. *Love*. Him?"

A few tears splashed onto her cheeks, which she let be. "I do, but *not* like I love *you*." She left it there, not about to claim she loved Trent like a brother. That would have been a lie. "I don't know what else to say. This is your decision, but as I said, I love you and I want you to stay." Her voice cracked at that last admission and had his gaze seeking hers.

After what stretched out as agonizing hours, but was only seconds in reality, he said, "Okay."

"Okay...?"

"I'll stay, but please don't make me regret this. If you ever do something like this again, I'm out. Life's too short, and I'm too..." He stopped talking, and she sensed a part of him had broken.

There was a tension in the air that told her to hold her space, let him keep his.

"You tell me there's nothing there, you'll never do this again. Then we'll be all right, but it won't be right away. You can understand that?"

"I can." Her stomach and chest were clenched in agony. It was taking all her willpower not to hug him and somehow make everything okay between them instantly.

"Let's move forward then, but I do have another question for you. Where is Zoe?"

"Libby's, while I attended the funeral."

"How about we go pick her up, get back here, and put up that freaking tree?" His attempt at being upbeat came out shallow, but it would take time to rebuild what they'd had. "What do you say?" He opened his arms to her, and she found herself running into them.

He was rigid and distant at first, but in seconds, his tough exterior melted. While a wall might still surround his heart, he clearly wanted to move past this. He hugged her tightly and tapped a kiss to her forehead.

Amanda put her head against his chest and listened to his heartbeat. They just might be okay, after all.

A LETTER FROM CAROLYN

Dear reader,

I want to say a huge thank you for choosing to read *Missing Before Daylight*. If you enjoyed it and would like to hear about new releases in the Amanda Steele series, just sign up at the following link. Your email address will never be shared, and you can unsubscribe at any time.

www.bookouture.com/carolyn-arnold

If you loved *Missing Before Daylight*, I would be incredibly grateful if you would write a brief, honest review. Also, if you'd like to continue investigating murder, you'll be happy to know there will be more Detective Amanda Steele books. I also offer several other international bestselling series for you to savor— everything from crime fiction, to cozy mysteries, to thrillers and action adventures. One of these series features Detective Madison Knight, another kick-ass female detective, who will risk her life, her badge—whatever it takes—to find justice for murder victims.

Also, if you enjoyed being in the Prince William County, Virginia, area, you might want to return in my Brandon Fisher FBI series. Brandon is Becky Tulson's boyfriend and was mentioned in this book, but you'll be able to be there when they meet in *Silent Graves* (book two in my FBI series). These books are perfect for readers who love heart-pounding thrillers and are fascinated with the psychology of serial killers. Each installment is a new case with a fresh bloody trail to follow. Hunt with the FBI's Behavioral Analysis Unit and profile some of the most devious and darkest minds on the planet.

And if you're familiar with the Prince William County, Virginia area, or have done some internet sleuthing, you'll realize some differences between reality and my book. Two examples are the marina and the jurisdiction that I assigned to the PWCPD in this book. That's me taking creative liberties.

Last but certainly not least, I love hearing from my readers! You can get in touch with me on social media or through my website. This is also a good way to stay notified of my new releases. You can also reach out to me via email at Carolyn@CarolynArnold.net.

Wishing you a thrill a word!

Carolyn Arnold

www.carolynarnold.net

 facebook.com/AuthorCarolynArnold

 x.com/Carolyn_Arnold

 goodreads.com/carolyn_arnold

PUBLISHING TEAM

Turning a manuscript into a book requires the efforts of many people. The publishing team at Bookouture would like to acknowledge everyone who contributed to this publication.

Audio
Alba Proko
Sinead O'Connor
Melissa Tran

Commercial
Lauren Morrissette
Jil Thielen
Imogen Allport

Cover design
Head Design Ltd

Data and analysis
Mark Alder
Mohamed Bussuri

Editorial
Claire Simmonds
Jen Shannon

Copyeditor
Fraser Crichton

Proofreader
Becca Allen

Marketing
Alex Crow
Melanie Price
Occy Carr
Cíara Rosney

Operations and distribution
Marina Valles
Stephanie Straub

Production
Hannah Snetsinger
Mandy Kullar

Publicity
Kim Nash
Noelle Holten
Myrto Kalavrezou
Jess Readett
Sarah Hardy

Rights and contracts
Peta Nightingale
Richard King
Saidah Graham

Printed in Great Britain
by Amazon

43896132R00199